Ann walked to the top of the terrace steps and lazily stretched her arms above her head. What a gorgeous day!

She drew a deep breath, then suddenly dropped her arms and stared while her heart seemed to stop beating. Could that be Myles Langdon who stood in the opening of the box hedge at the end of the garden? She was dreaming! She brushed a hand across her eyes—she *was* awake, and it was no mirage. It *was* Myles. He was coming into the garden, walking toward her!

Ann took the steps in one flying leap, met him as he reached the path, threw her arms about his neck and kissed him wildly.

"Myles!" she sobbed, "Myles darling! Welcome home!"

Bantam Books by Emilie Loring
Ask your bookseller for the books you have missed

How Can the Heart Forget

by
Emilie Loring

BANTAM BOOKS · TORONTO · NEW YORK · LONDON

*This low-priced Bantam Book
has been completely reset in a type face
designed for easy reading, and was printed
from new plates. It contains the complete
text of the original hard-cover edition.*
NOT ONE WORD HAS BEEN OMITTED.

HOW CAN THE HEART FORGET

*A Bantam Book | published by arrangement with
Little, Brown and Company, Inc.*

PRINTING HISTORY

*Little, Brown edition published June 1960
2nd printing .... November 1960*

Grosset & Dunlap edition published August 1961

Bantam edition | October 1962

2nd printing .... *March 1963*	8th printing . *November 1965*
3rd printing .... *May 1964*	9th printing .. *December 1966*
4th printing .... *June 1964*	10th printing .... *May 1967*
5th printing .... *August 1964*	11th printing .. *February 1968*
6th printing .... *February 1965*	12th printing .... *June 1968*
7th printing .... *May 1965*	13th printing .. *February 1969*

14th printing .... October 1969
New Bantam edition | March 1974
2nd printing .. September 1975   3rd printing .. September 1976
4th printing .... January 1979

ISBN 0-553-12409-9

Published simultaneously in the United States and Canada

*Bantam Books are published by Bantam Books, Inc. Its trade-
mark, consisting of the words "Bantam Books" and the por-
trayal of a bantam, is Registered in U.S. Patent and Trademark
Office and in other countries. Marca Registrada. Bantam
Books, Inc., 666 Fifth Avenue, New York, New York 10019.*

I

Ann Jerome walked slowly along the grassy path, admiring the cool sheen of moonlight on the silent garden and the brick end of her house with its delicate pattern of shadows cast by the feathery trees beyond the wall. Her flame-colored evening dress was muted to a purple monochrome, the black and white springer spaniel to a ghost of dark and lighter gray at her side.

House and garden sank into darkness when a cloud slipped across the moon. Its soft glow was replaced by glaring headlights which swung from the road, flickered between the gateposts and swept over the broad lawn. The car slowed, crawled to a stop at the front steps. Its doors banged shut and two figures mounted the steps. Under the revealing glare of the porch light they merged into one.

For a shocked instant Ann stared, then resolutely turned her back, but shook her head in silent disparagement. Snapping her fingers at the dog, she led him swiftly across the terrace to the side door.

She waited for her younger sister in the upstairs sitting room they shared—waited tensely, hands clenched at her sides, eyes misted with tears. When Sonia came in Ann whirled from the window, lips curled in distaste and the deep blue of her eyes dark with resentment.

"Before you let that Joe Snell kiss you, Sonia," she reproved bitterly, "you might wait till you know Myles has your letter breaking your engagement to him!"

Sonia slumped into the big high-backed chair and rumpled her red-gold curls against the gay cretonne.

"Myles must know by this time," she complained. "I

wrote him weeks ago and airmail to South America takes only days. No letter yet; isn't it maddening!"

She sighed and closed her eyes. Monty, the springer, who had been dozing on the couch, padded softly across the room and jumped into her lap. He licked a tear from her flushed cheek and then curled into a ball on her green dress. For once she failed to reprove him for mussing her skirt.

The utter weariness of the pose, the sadness in the lovely face and a second tear forming under the dark fringe of the long lashes made Ann's throat contract. Sonia looked so very pretty—and so young! Perhaps she had been too harsh, but—

"How did you know that Joe kissed me?" Sonia demanded abruptly. "It's the first time he ever did, in case you care."

"I saw you when you left the car. I—I wasn't snooping, Sunny—cross my heart! I was in the garden, walking Monty; couldn't help seeing you."

"And couldn't help bawling me out!"

The younger girl leaned forward with fire in her blue eyes. They were lighter than Ann's, but they were the Jerome eyes and they could blaze.

Ann forced her voice to gentleness.

"Myles Langdon is doing his job, working down there in that awful hellhole, away from all his—his friends— from all of us. You're still engaged to him until he agrees to release you."

"And how long must I wait?" Sonia came out of the chair with an angry rush that plunged Monty to the floor. She ignored his whimper of protest and faced Ann with icy scorn. "It's all right for you to talk, you care nothing for men. But I do! And my man"—her laugh was bitter —"*my man* is a thousand miles away and has been for months and months! What am I supposed to do, sit at home and—and knit? Don't think I haven't spent hours trying to decide what's the best thing to do! You wouldn't tell me, and with Father in Washington so much—and looking like a thundercloud when he *is* home—I didn't feel like consulting him!"

"You're not a child now, Sunny," Ann reminded quietly. "At twenty-three you should be able to make decisions for yourself. I know we've always tried to smooth life's road for you, but this is different."

"You wouldn't help me write to Myles!"

"How could I?" Ann protested. "How would I know what you should say? I'll admit that writing a brush-off letter to a man in far-off places is a major problem. If you don't believe it, read those 'Are You Worried?—Ask Me' columns in the papers. But it was your problem, something you had to work out for yourself."

"Well, I did it, didn't I? I finally wrote Myles—and a lot of good it did. No answer! This intolerable situation remains exactly the same!" Sonia flounced over to the window and turned back impatiently. "You know something, Ann? While I puzzled over how to tell him I was through, I kept trying to visualize him. But I couldn't! Just a shadowy face, like a face in a dream."

"Myles Langdon's face shadowy?" Ann gasped. "He's been away for a year, but I can see him as clearly as if he were standing here now. Tall and lean, brown hair with a kink in it, brown eyes shot with tiny sparks of gold when he laughs and an indomitable mouth when he's mad—"

She caught her sister's curious expression and stopped. With an effort she smothered the eager warmth in her voice to add in a more matter-of-fact tone, "A smile, as they used to say, to warm the cockles of your heart, and the nicest manners, too."

Sonia sat down in the chair again, absently patting her knee invitingly until Monty scrambled back to his place on her lap. Lost in thought, she ran her fingers along his silky ears.

"I didn't say I'd forgotten Myles," she murmured, "only that I couldn't picture him. That proves something, I guess. Just because we grew up here side by side, our families with adjoining places, we did what everyone expected of us and got engaged before he went off engineering. What's that old French expression—something *oblige?*"

"*Noblesse oblige,*" Ann prompted, without turning from where she was straightening the pillows on the couch.

"Yes. Only this was the modern version—family *oblige.* So we got engaged," she muttered, shaking her head. "I should have realized that my feeling for him wasn't that kind of love. Was his for me?"

"That I wouldn't know."

Sonia curled her feet under her and shifted the spaniel to a more comfortable position.

"You backed me up when I finally decided to write him that our engagement was a mistake and I was in love with somebody else. Remember?"

"I remember," Ann admitted grimly. "And you don't know how often I get the jitters, wondering if I did right. I've lain awake for hours going over the question and I still feel that it was the only fair thing to do."

Sonia pounded the chair arm impatiently.

"Myles is so sweet, and it seemed like such a heartless letter to send when you think of all he has to contend with down there on his job. I—I hope it won't make him desperate! I can't sleep either, worrying about the crazy things he may do because I've failed him."

"You should have thought of that before you started running around with Snell." Ann lifted a silencing hand when her sister started to protest. "You needn't explain, I know the whole scenario! Joe is manager of the foundry and as his secretary you're constantly with him. Work after hours, supper together—naturally." Sarcasm edged every word. "You're lonely without Myles, who has been our—your beau since dancing-school days. Suddenly—you are shocked, and so is Joe—you find that you are *that way* about each other!"

"You needn't act so darned superior!" Sonia broke in at last. "You don't know what you're talking about. Look at you! Dark and tall and beautiful, with dash and sparkle, voted the most popular girl in your class at college! Gay, lots of fun, *but*—" and she leveled an accusing finger, "you're twenty-five and have never fallen *hard* for any-one—as far as I know—so you know absolutely nothing about love!"

"We were discussing *you*, Sunny—"

"I'm discussing you—and I'm not through! Men would go for you, but you won't give them a chance to get senti-mental. Why, Joe says the way your outsized blue eyes take a man's measure the first time you meet him freezes him for good!"

Ann gave a most unladylike snort. "Nice of your boy friend to take such an interest in my love life! He'd better concentrate on his own!"

"You'd better concentrate on yours," Sunny retorted with equal heat, "or you'll never get anywhere! You never will, anyway, cooped up in a teller's cage at that old bank." She arched her brows in sudden seriousness. "Honestly, do you like that sort of thing?"

"Not the cage, but the rest of my job is interesting, and I'm only a temporary teller until the regular man gets over an auto accident. Then I go back as confidential secretary, and I have something on the ball in customer relations, if I do say so who shouldn't."

Sunny sniffed. "With a college degree it seems as though you could do better than that!"

"You should talk, a stenographer with a B.A. after her name! And look what you landed—" Ann bit her lip to halt the gibe. "Sorry, child! But I just can't believe that you're really in love with that flashy manager!"

"Joe Snell is *not* flashy!" Sonia sat bolt upright and words came in a furious tide. "He's a coming young executive with plenty of zip and dash, and I *am* in love with him, and don't you try—" The declaration ended in a smothered gasp as the half-open door swung wide and her father stepped into the room.

"Hello, Dad," Sonia tried for an airy casualness, but it wilted under the level glare of the Jerome eyes which had cowed more than one witness in the courtroom. "I guess you heard me," she muttered.

"I did." Robert Jerome tightened the cord of his dressing gown and folded his arms. In ominous silence he studied his younger daughter.

Ann perched on a chair arm and fastened her gaze on one aimlessly swinging foot. What now? Fireworks? Her father's thick gray hair—no Jerome ever became bald—stood up in tousled disorder, but his granite face gave no clue to his thoughts. Yet he must be deeply shocked. Darling Sonia infatuated with Joe Snell, the town's tough guy when they were growing up! And she did mean *tough!*

The silence was too much for Sunny.

"You want a playback of the record, Dad?" she asked defiantly. "All right, I'm in love with Joe Snell. What have *you* got against him?"

Ann could have shaken her for her ill-timed flippancy. It had no apparent effect on Mr. Jerome.

"Joe Snell? Joe is all right," he said gravely. "He had no advantages as a boy and deserves a lot of credit for working his way through that—that trade school and making good at the foundry. But you've had plenty of opportunity to know him well, Sonia, as his secretary there. I—I wouldn't have supposed you two had anything in common."

"We have plenty! And I'm going to marry him!"

Again the silence became unbearable while Ann searched desperately for a soothing remark. But Sonia spoke first.

"Well, for heaven's sake, Dad, why don't you say something? You look as if you're getting ready to declare in the best melodramatic tradition that if I marry Joe I must never darken your door again!"

Mr. Jerome's face paled, but he shook his head gently.

"You've been watching too many old films on television, Sunny. Let us stick to facts. When did you break your engagement to Myles?"

"I wrote him weeks ago—airmail!"

"And he consented?"

Sonia flushed under the questioning.

"He—he hasn't deigned to reply."

Her father seemed lost in thought.

"Hmm, of course Snell knew you were engaged," he mused, his blue eyes watching her face. "Have you ever suspected that he might be trying to cut in from spite rather than love?"

"What are you talking about?"

"I suggest," he said in his courtroom tone, "that it would be natural for Snell to be jealous of Myles Langdon, who grew up in the same town but with many more advantages."

"There's nothing in that. Joe *loves* me all right!"

Her father nodded. "Far be it from me to try to read a woman's mind, but your tone carries conviction." He looked at Ann, who still sat wordlessly praying for peace. "You knew about this?"

"I knew Sunny wanted to break with—with Myles, but not about her intention to marry Joe. Not until tonight."

"But neither of you told me." When there was no answer he sighed. "Well, I've had no part in this up to now, so it's rather late to take a hand. I don't approve, Sunny, but—I won't oppose you. Bring Joe here whenever you like and we'll try to make him feel welcome. I only ask that you have the decency not to marry until three months after your break with Myles is accepted by him."

"But Joe wants to be married next month!" Sonia wailed.

"No doubt, but I want your promise that you will meet my deadline." With a tired smile he suggested, "The least you can do is give us time to get used to the idea."

"Well, okay—I promise," she murmured without meeting his eyes. She pushed Monty off her lap, stood up and hesitated. Then she crossed to her bedroom, went in and closed the door with a restrained but obvious slam.

Mr. Jerome let his breath go in a weary sigh and dropped his hands into the pockets of the black and gold dressing gown. To Ann, watching him with aching sympathy, he seemed to grow older, new lines showing on his face.

"How have I failed her, Ann?" he asked despairingly. "With your Mother gone, I tried— But I failed if Sonia could fall in love with—with—"

"A roughneck like Snell!" she supplied promptly. "You're not to blame, Dad, no one is but Sunny. She's so young."

Jerome's glance held a trace of amusement.

"Two years younger than you! You may be right, though. I suppose Snell's vital, masterful manner might appeal to an inexperienced girl who had never associated with his type."

"For vital and masterful substitute cocky, wise-cracking and obnoxious, and I'll agree with you," she suggested bitterly.

"To pass up Myles Langdon for that!" he muttered.

"Sunny was never in love with Myles, Dad, just carried away with romance—the handsome young engineer going off into the wilds to build a bridge. She admitted tonight that she couldn't remember how he looks!"

"Well, after all, it's been almost a year. She might forget."

"How can the heart forget?" The impulsive words were out before she could halt them, and she saw her father glance at her in surprise. Breathlessly she switched the subject.

"I suspected Sunny wasn't in love with Myles months ago, when that magazine article came with pictures of him and the frightful river he's trying to span. She read the story, from a sense of duty I suppose, but it meant nothing to her. Just a man building a bridge. The primitive country he's in, the danger from wild animals, natives, accidents, sickness, seemed to make no impression on her. Maybe even then she was in love with Joe Snell; maybe that explains her indifference to what might be happening to him."

"Quite possible." Mr. Jerome gave his elder daughter a further probing look and then shrugged. "Well, we must wait and see how this turns out."

He paused on his way to the door, walked to the end table by the couch and meticulously straightened the magazines piled on it.

"Ann, I overheard the conversation just before Sonia made her dramatic announcement," he said slowly. "You *are* happy in your work at Leslie's bank, aren't you?"

"Perfectly! Don't let Sunny worry you about that. She's been crazy about typing and shorthand ever since I can remember, but my tastes are different. I like the atmosphere of system and efficiency that pervades banking. Besides, there's the feeling of accomplishment; our bank is important to the people in this small city and it must function smoothly. With the growing power of women in finance, it needs the feminine touch. I've been lucky enough to make a few suggestions along that line, see them adopted and later see them work. That's really satisfying.

"Then we've lost a number of the younger employees —to better paying jobs or the draft—which leaves some of the departments short-handed and requiring more supervision. That part I like, too. My occasional tours of duty in the teller's cage aren't very stimulating, but then—" Ann smiled apologetically. "Do I sound as though I ran the whole bank?"

"You sound like a particularly valuable employee," her father assured gravely. "Giving the job the best in you, even though you don't enjoy all of it, is simply being honest. I've never worried about you, Ann, but Sunny—" He shook his head. "I didn't dare oppose her just now, for fear of rousing resentment which might end in an elopement. You understand that?"

"Of course." She smiled and patted his hand. "Don't worry, Dad, I didn't get the impression that you were giving your blessing to the proposed union—and I'm sure Sunny didn't, either."

"No, that was quite evident from her actions." He nodded toward the clock on the bookcase. "Don't you young people ever need sleep? I am leaving for Washington bright and early, so I do. Pleasant dreams, my dear."

"Good night, Dad."

When he had gone she switched off the lights and went into her bedroom. In the dark she walked to the window and stood there, removing her crystal earrings and unclasping the rhinestone bracelet from her arm. Moonlight and the black shadow of the house divided the terrace below and a corner of the formal garden beyond. How familiar and peaceful seemed the portion she could see; the other half was shrouded in mystery. The present and the future?

Pleasant dreams had been her father's parting wish. Perhaps. If only Myles would write, accepting Sonia's break—or rejecting it. The uncertainty seemed worse than anything which could happen. August had slipped into September with no word. Why hadn't he answered?

II

It was barely seven-thirty when Ann drove toward town along the road bordered by maples just beginning to turn to autumn flame, their glowing colors tempered by dark hemlocks and cedars. The lawns were still as green as her dress, every garden a luxurious tapestry of scarlet, crimson, purple, orange and vibrant lemon yellow. In the morning sunlight the spire of a white church shone like a golden finger pointing to heaven. The whole countryside seemed a haven of peace at this early hour.

She drew a deep breath. The air smelled of burning leaves and morning mist. That poet, she thought, who wrote "What is so rare as a day in June?" must have forgotten the perfection which New England can pour out with lavish hand in autumn.

At the railroad crossing a slow freight held her up for minutes. Idly she played the childhood game of counting the cars as they lumbered noisily past; sixty-five before she was allowed to proceed and turn down the street to the bank. She left her convertible in the almost empty parking lot behind the building and walked to the back door, which opened as if by magic as she approached.

"Morning, Miss Jerome!" The night watchman swung the door wide with a flourish. "Always count on you being first in, except the boss, of course," he qualified with a grin.

It pleased her to see that the authorities had adopted another of her suggestions. During the night, as though by magic, long draperies of cocoa brown and old gold plaid had been hung beside the big front windows of the banking room. Their warmth made a world of difference in the formerly chill marble walls.

Before a small mirror in the teller's cage she settled

the flat necklace of gold leaves around her throat and wrinkled her nose at her reflection.

"Not too bad, if you do 'freeze 'em for good,' " she reassured the looking-glass girl.

She picked up pencil and notebook, snapped the lock on the cage door, and crossed the railed-off area of the junior officers' desks at the rear of the room. There a short hall led to the private offices. She knocked at the half-open door which announced in bold black letters:

JOHN LESLIE
President

"Come in, come in! Good morning, Ann." The short slender man removed a sheaf of bonds from the safe and paused, peering at her.

The anxiety in the pale gray eyes behind the shell-framed glasses tightened Ann's throat; that worried look had grown more evident with every passing week. The president of the bank might be a respected authority in the economic field, but at the moment he was a pathetic, lonely figure.

"Anyone at your house heard from my nephew, Ann?" he asked hopefully.

"Still nothing since July, Mr. Leslie." Ann never slipped into informality with the president in the bank, although he was a next-door neighbor whom for years she had called Uncle John, just as his wife was beloved Aunt Pamela. Rather than watch his unhappiness, she swung the typewriter from its cavern in her mahogany desk and laid out letterheads and carbon paper in neat piles. The walnut-paneled room was so silent that she looked up.

He stood in deep thought, his eyes fixed on the framed hunting print above the safe, although Ann felt certain that he saw a heat-stricken jungle instead of the cool autumn fields in the picture.

"Nothing for us, either." He fingered the bonds absently. "His Aunt Pamela is getting more anxious every day, though she won't admit it. Good Lord, Ann! Tomorrow is his birthday! Myles Langdon thirty years old—and it seems only yesterday that he stood in this office, a boy of fifteen, the loneliness in his eyes tearing my heart out.

" 'Now that my mother and father are gone, I understand that you are my guardian, Uncle John,' he said."

Mr. Leslie sat down heavily and leaned his elbows on his desk, still staring at the picture.

"I had to match his bravery; at least I tried. Made some joke about being his mother's only brother, so it looked as if Aunt Pamela and I would have to take on the job of whipping him into shape for the battle of life."

When he was silent a moment Ann said gently, "You two did a wonderful job of it."

"We never had a boy of our own, so we loved it. Even more when Jean married; the house would have been terribly empty without Myles. But it wasn't difficult; he had the right stuff in him from the start." The banker stared earnestly at Ann over his glasses.

"Why, that first day I told him his father had left me a letter about him, and that we'd go over it together when he felt he could take it. And like a shot he said, 'I can take it now, Uncle John. Go to it.' "

Mr. Leslie shook his head and smiled in admiration. "Myles has been like that ever since; prep school, engineering school, working in here summers, although he never liked it. His father was a director, and I always hoped he'd come in with us. But no, Myles was set on an engineering career from the first and nothing could sway him. Don't know why I worry so about him when he's always met every crisis in life with a sort of gay courage which masked an iron determination."

For a moment Ann's attention wandered. Would Myles Langdon meet Sunny's letter breaking their engagement with that courage?

"I do worry, though," the banker sighed. "I hope and pray he'll come back, marry your sister, and settle near us. But—suppose he's fallen for some—some gold digger he's met down in South America! What then?"

Ann felt a sinking sensation in the pit of her stomach. Even in her most fevered dreams that explanation of Myles's silence had never occurred to her. She thrust the thought into the back of her mind, ashamed of such disloyalty.

"I don't believe that could happen to Myles," she defended hotly.

"Anything can happen in a world gone mad like this one," John Leslie insisted. "Everything is speed and change now. Off with the old, on with the new—*anything* that's new, no matter how outlandish. That's what seems to attract the younger generation. Hasty marriages are among the greatest tragedies."

"Myles would never be satisfied with second best."

Mr. Leslie seemed not to hear her; he was lost in unpleasant thoughts.

"Real marriage," he continued, "is something a man and woman make out of dreams and disappointments, success and failure, the struggles and sacrifices experienced together. *We* know that. But Myles is sunk in a rough country, surrounded by strangers whose ideas and ideals are far different from those he was brought up by. Who knows what that may have done to his character, to him?"

"I don't care where he is, or what kind of people he lives with, nothing could ever change Myles!" Ann stated with conviction.

Mr. Leslie blinked, bent his head to eye her over his glasses and nodded.

"Of course you're right, my dear, and I deserve the reprimand. 'O, ye of little faith—' as the Good Book says. I apologize to my nephew, abjectly. And now to work. Take a letter to the Board of Investments regarding these securities."

For an hour and later in the teller's cage she was too busy to think of personal problems. She cashed checks, accepted deposits, and listened to happy reports of prospective jobs or tearful admissions of failure and hardship. I'm rapidly becoming the town confidante, she thought; if only I could help more.

"Hi, Ann! How about lunch with me?"

She looked up in surprise, that emotion quickly changing to annoyance when she found Joe Snell at her window. His almost handsome face with its crown of smooth blond hair was pressed against the glass, a determined grin on his lips but anxiety in his eyes.

"Lunch—with—*you?*" she stammered.

He leaned an elbow on the counter, then pushed his hat to the back of his head.

"Come on, take a chance." The bravado was assumed, for he hastily amended, "Please, Ann! I've got to talk to you."

Of course he wanted to discuss the situation between Sonia and himself. Equally of course, Ann realized with resignation, she would have to listen, no matter how much she disliked him. She consulted her wrist watch.

"Okay, Joe. Where? I get out at twelve."

"I'll reserve a booth at the Chop House—if that's all right with you," he offered. "It's kind of rough, I guess, but the food is tops." Relief widened his grin as he set the sage-green Homburg more firmly on his head, then fingered his hand-painted tie whose gaudiness literally turned Ann's stomach.

With an audacious wink he warned, "I intend to ply you with the very best to get you in a sympathetic mood."

"Sympathetic mood! *Ha!*" She threw all the scorn of which she was capable into a sarcastic laugh. "You and who else?"

Joe shrugged it off as she knew he would. Sarcasm was wasted on him, she thought, while she watched his swaggering departure toward the door. Brimming with self-assurance, vital, dominant; maybe he was the type to sweep a youngster like Sunny off her feet.

If one believed his boasting Joe could run the foundry with one hand while the other settled the country's problems. A diamond in the rough, according to one school of thought in the town. A blowhard and a severe pain in the neck as far as she was concerned. And she was concerned in this triangle, worse luck! Why—and how—could Sonia love Joe Snell instead of Myles? Incredible! But doubtless biology would have a word for it.

Near the door a girl in smartly tailored gray gabardine spoke to Joe. He stopped but did not remove the rakish hat until she said something which snapped his hand up to the offending headgear. Ann could see his face darken with resentment at the obvious lesson in manners. He shook his head, slapped the green hat back in place and went out through the revolving door.

The girl turned then, and Ann saw that it was Cecile Parker, whose father owned the foundry. She made straight for Ann's cage and slid a check across the counter.

Her pretty but thin face was set in suspicious lines as she demanded, "Why was Joe in such a hurry, Ann? What's he up to—has he been dating you?"

With cold efficiency Ann held up the check.

"Fifty dollars. How do you want it?"

"I don't care—tens. I asked you a question!"

"You asked me three questions." Ann took a handful of bills from the drawer, counted off the required number and then counted again as she snapped them down one by one before the girl.

Inwardly she smoldered; it was none of Cecile's business whom Joe Snell dated. Or was it? Either way, if Ann told her off in the harsh words trembling on her tongue it might boomerang and hurt Sonia. And Sunny, whether or not she deserved it, was already being hurt, perhaps with worse to come. But she must say something; she couldn't stand fiddling with the money forever.

Cecile Parker saved her from having to make a decision. She put her orange-red lips close to the opening in the window while she picked up the bills.

"You lay off Joe, Ann Jerome! I saw him first—he's mine if I want him!" The green eyes glaring through the glass were narrowed in fury. "I can scratch—and how!"

Ann replaced the sheaf of tens in the drawer while her thoughts raced wildly. Apparently Cecile had no idea that Sonia was Snell's current heart-interest. "He's mine if I want him." What a lucky break if she did take him out of circulation—and out of the picture. Aside from that happy prospect, Ann resented the implication that she herself could be in pursuit of the diamond in the rough.

"My word, you're not engaged to that male menace, are you?" she inquired with a flippancy she was far from feeling. "If you are, you won't have to *scratch,* Miss Parker! Married men and fiancés are definitely off my wave length."

To put an end to the interview she looked past Cecile's petulant face and smiled warmly at the elderly man who had been registering impatience. "May I help you, Mr. Sarley?"

It was a relief to have Cecile scowl, thrust the money into her shoulder bag and stalk away.

A little after twelve Ann faced Joe Snell across a small table adorned with a not too clean red and white checked cloth. A jukebox at one end of the room filled the smoky Chop House with the incessant jarring beat of a popular tune.

"Charming spot; such atmosphere," she remarked coolly.

"A cocktail would help," Joe growled, "but I know you don't drink—and I don't until after business hours. But I could sure use one *now*."

"What's gone wrong now in this vale of tears that you crave alcohol as well as sympathy?"

"I've ordered steak, French fries and a green salad. Nothing wrong with *that*, is there?" Joe growled. "I mean, is that okay for Your Highness?"

"A steak? Double okay, since I had only time for coffee and a roll at breakfast. I thank you kindly, sir." She smiled in a vain effort to get the chip off her shoulder and was relieved when Joe responded with a grin.

"That's better," he said. "No need to start throwing punches till the bell rings. Here comes our food now. Hi, Marge!" he greeted the waitress who slapped their plates on the table with practiced nonchalance.

The steaks were up to Chop House standards and Joe proved to have a gift for reviving their conversation whenever it threatened to languish. That might be part of the reason for his success in business, Ann decided; he probably kept a stubborn customer in good humor until he carried his point.

They chatted about the latest May-December romance which had the town by the ears; expressed identical views on the jerry-built ranch houses flooding the new West End development and wondered how the city fathers permitted what seemed a flagrant violation of the zoning laws. That led to agreement on the importance of women as well as men keeping posted and critical of government processes, and a discussion of the progress of our diplomats abroad. It was the last subject which reminded Ann of Myles

Langdon, somewhere in the tropic jungle, and caused her to plunge abruptly into the purpose of their meeting.

She waved away the waitress, who was offering a second pot of coffee, and leaned forward to fix Snell with steady blue eyes.

"You didn't ask me to lunch to confer on foreign and domestic problems, Joe. I'd better talk first because what I have to say could make any further conversation unnecessary. Have you given Cecile Parker reason to believe that you're in love with her?"

Snell dropped his cigarette and fumbled to recover it. When he looked up his face matched the red checks of the tablecloth.

"That's *my* business," he muttered.

"It certainly is," she agreed sharply, "but I'm making it mine, too. I've been drawn into this mix-up between you, Sunny and the man to whom she is still engaged. And right now we three have landed on a beachhead that may be mined with complications. If I let my sister throw over the best man in the world for a cheap chaser—"

"Hold everything!" Snell snapped, now pale with indignation. "There's nothing between Cecile and me—nothing much, anyway."

"Nothing much!" Ann mocked.

"Now look. Be reasonable, will you? She's my boss's daughter. When he gave me a chance to prove I could hold down the job of general manager at the foundry the whole family was darned nice to me. You know, had me to dinner, took me to the Country Club—stuff like that. Darned nice! So I tried to—to reciprocate, I guess you call it—by taking her out.

"But long before I ever noticed Sunny I was getting fed up with Cecile, believe me!" His fist pounded the table for emphasis. "She's the possessive type, always wanted to know where I was every minute, always correcting my manners, watching me. And if I didn't say anything for a while she'd want to know what I was thinking. Damn it, no man wants somebody forever riding herd on him!"

In spite of her dislike Ann rather admired him for that. Certainly any man would object to such surveillance, and for Snell's domineering self-sufficient type it must be unbearably irritating. It had never occurred to her that his mental make-up might be more sensitive than his crude outer shell. A pity that there wasn't some sort of spiritual radar with which to probe the workings of the human heart. Or was it a pity? The thought shook her. She'd hate to have a detector applied to hers.

"Your eyes have lost that freezing look," Joe said, puzzled. "What are you thinking?"

She knew that the coldness returned while she studied the man who had upset her sister's romance, but before she could speak he slapped the table.

"Forget that question!" he commanded with a sheepish smile. "There I go, putting on Cecile's inquisition act that makes me see red!"

"I'll answer your question just the same," Ann said slowly. "I was wondering—among other things—what kind of a person you are to steal the fiancée of a man who isn't here to protect his rights."

"Whew!" Snell pushed back and raised a protesting hand. "You sure fire straight from the shoulder! You wouldn't want to put that a little nicer, would you?"

"I don't know any other words for it."

"Maybe you don't." Scowling, Joe ground out his cigarette and then leaned toward her, his folded arms on the table. "Maybe you don't know what this is all about, either. Ann, have you ever been in love?"

"I didn't come here to talk about myself."

"Don't stall. Have you?"

She took refuge in contempt. "Not as you mean it, I'm sure."

"*I* mean it?" He shook his head. "You're the one who doesn't know what it means! You don't know what it's like to see a face that sends the blood pounding through your veins, your heart racing its motor; to meet eyes that plunge into your soul—and stay there, glowing!"

Unable to meet the challenge, Ann resorted to humor. "Frankly, it sounds horribly—uncomfortable."

"You're darn tootin' it is—until the other person reciprocates. Then—then you've really got something!" For a long moment his hot eyes held hers, then they dropped and he gave a self-conscious laugh. "I'm talking like a damn book!"

Ann sat nonplused at the unsuspected depth of feeling in his outburst. It was so out of character that she wondered if it was genuine or carefully rehearsed for her benefit.

"You might have waited until Myles Langdon came back," she rebuked.

"How long do I have to wait?" Unknowingly he echoed Sunny's plea. "When your sister took a job at the plant I knew she was engaged, but she acted lonely, so I give the little girl a break, take her out a few times. Pretty soon I'm interested in her, and before I know it—Bang! I'm hooked."

"Why didn't you leave her alone, before it was too late? She adored Myles."

"Myles! Myles!" Joe banged the table again. "All you think of is his side of it! But I'm thinking of me—me and Sunny—and you're too cold-blooded to get it. Finished your coffee? Then let's go; I've had all I can take of this!"

III

Myles Langdon crossed the austere lobby of San Diego's Angel of Mercy Hospital and with a sigh of relief rested the weight of a bulging paper bag on the information desk. Flexing cramped fingers, he lifted his arm until his left hand, protruding from a sling, could massage the aching muscles. The deeply tanned girl at the switchboard looked inquiringly from the parked bag to its bearer.

"Calling on Mr. Michael Fallon," Myles said.

"Visiting hours are—"

"This is an emergency," he interrupted. "I've come from Los Angeles and must go right back." He fumbled a card from his shirt pocket and presented it. "Langdon, Carrington Construction Company; Red Fallon worked with me. In fact," he offered with a smile, "we were blown up together—with a bridge."

"Oh, you mean that *redhead* on the third!" The girl snorted. "Gee, he's had the whole floor in a turmoil ever since he came in. Taking him out?" she asked hopefully.

"I'd like to, but this is just a visit."

"Too bad—but go ahead and see him." She waved his card toward the ceiling before she returned it. "Third floor, 308; the elevator is at the end of the hall. And Mr. Langdon—if he *should* talk you into lugging him out of here it will be very okay with *all* of us!"

Myles laughed. "I imagine Red isn't a model patient, but maybe what I've brought will keep him quiet a while."

"Chloroform, I hope!"

"Not quite that, but still very relaxing."

He carried his package to the self-service elevator and ran it to the third floor. Walking down the hall, reading the numbered doors, he tried to ignore the penetrating hospital odors; he'd had more than enough of those in the last weeks.

In 308 he lowered himself with a weary grunt into the wicker armchair beside the bed and nodded to the gaunt man propped up by wrinkled pillows. It was a different Mike Fallon from the beefy works manager who had been his right hand in the Loma jungle. The drawn cheeks retained only faint traces of the once heavy tropical tan, and thick bandages showed on chest and neck. Only the crew-cut hair, red as rusty iron, looked like the old Mike.

Myles made no comment on the change, knowing that sympathy would be certain to arouse profane impatience.

"How's it going, Red?" he asked with a smile.

"Good, boss—except for this." Fallon slapped the cast on the leg, which was hoisted on a complicated machine of gears and pulleys. "Gave me hell for a while, but it comes off the derrick tomorrow—I hope. I'm so tickled to be here—all in one piece—anything's *good!* What you got in that bag, huh?"

Myles upended the paper bag and dumped a stream of paperbacks on the bed.

"Your homework, pal. You don't look too beat up to appreciate your favorite classics of crime."

The older man pawed through the books and his eyes glistened.

"Gee, thanks!" He fingered an unusually lurid cover and chuckled. "Lookit! With an ice pick! That's real *murder* and ought to be good. Thanks, boss."

He lay back against the pillows and frowned at his caller.

"I heard you had quite a session in the hospital at Los Angeles. You look good now, though."

"Who are you kidding, Red? When I get this sling off my arm I'll look better, and I guess I'll live. Too bad they were full up in L.A. and had to dump you here; that's why I haven't been in to see you sooner."

"Did you come way down here just to see *me?* Well, I sure appreciate that, boss—"

"Quit calling me 'boss'—you're not working for me now. I'd be pretty ungrateful if I didn't look you up to thank you for saving my life."

"Nuts!" Fallon hid his embarrassment by shuffling through the books in his lap. "When our bridge went up in that blast I was knocked so silly I didn't know what I was doing."

"Well, I know. In spite of a smashed leg you were hauling me out of the river and—"

"Skip it, will you!" Red growled. "Okay, so you thank me; so you're welcome! Now let's talk about something interesting. Have you heard how bad the bridge is, and do they know who did it?"

"The rebels set off the dynamite," Myles explained, "as part of their campaign of terror against the government. They made good propaganda of it, too; claimed our bridge and the railroad were being put in so the dictator could overrun the back country and loot it just like he's done in the coastal towns."

"They might have something there," Fallon muttered. "I didn't like the looks of that Medina—the few times I saw him dictating all over the place. An oily scup in his trick general's uniform."

Myles grinned. "You didn't like *any* of the natives, dictators or not, did you? Believe me, Red," he continued seriously, "swapping him for the rebel leaders would be no bargain for the poor people. Those liberators, as they call themselves, are simply trying to get control of the country to feather their own nests. The outs are trying to get in, and they'll stop at nothing to do it. We found that out."

"The hard way! What I can't figure, though, is where those ragged peons hiding in the jungle could collect enough dynamite to make a blast like that. It sounded like the end of the world. It wasn't stolen from our job, you bet!"

"No, it wasn't ours. Nobody knows where they're getting all the stuff they seem to have; perhaps from a neighboring country or even from farther away. It's a cinch they have powerful friends *somewhere,* including financial backing, or they couldn't keep on operating."

"They didn't look like they had a nickel," Red snorted. "All I saw were a pretty scraggy lot."

"So would you be, if you hid out in that kind of country for long. They looked like scarecrows that had missed a lot of square meals, but you didn't notice any shortage of rifles, Tommy guns and ammunition. Those are coming in from an outside source, and keeping them coming in is a number one priority job, I'll bet. The rebel leaders won't let anything interfere with their shipments if they can help it.

"But you wanted to hear about the damage to the bridge." Myles scowled at the thought. "It seems that the entire span at the west end is in the river. Piers shattered, piles wrecked, cofferdam wiped out, five men smashed up and one man missing. The whole works"—he waved a hand—"blooey!"

"So it means starting all over again at that end?"

Myles rubbed his chin thoughtfully.

"Even that is questionable as things stand now. There'll be a long wrangle over responsibility, because you can bet the local government will try to void the contract or make the company pay for a new span, claiming *we* were careless."

He grinned in sympathy with Fallon's heartfelt oath.

"Moreover, I gather that our company isn't so keen about getting mixed up with that type of government a second time. They may pull out of there entirely and take their loss. Even if they start construction again, Red, they'll do it without me. I may be yellow, but I'm not going back."

"What d'ya mean *yellow!* It's common sense. Me, I wouldn't go down to Loma again for anything. That was a haywire layout from the start, with God knows how many guys callin' themselves 'government inspectors' and nosing around the works looking for a bribe! Most of 'em didn't know a welder from a blowtorch, you could see that in a minute. Besides, when anybody starts planting dynamite behind my back, I've had it! Somebody's liable to get killed in a deal like that, boss. As far as South America goes, I'm through."

There was silence in the room while the two men, each in his own manner, appraised the situation.

To Mike Fallon it meant that his hours, days, of heartbreaking work with that assorted crew of experienced and green laborers had been wasted.

Myles Langdon fell it more deeply. His whole life had been dedicated to a career, and now it was ended. There would be no place in engineering for a physically handicapped man. Disappointment dragged at his spirits intolerably. He pushed himself out of the chair and went to stand at the window to stare over the city toward the ocean.

Fallon sensed his discouragement and attempted to divert his thoughts.

"You said that a guy is missing. I hadn't heard that."

"The company's still checking," Myles answered in a tone which offered little hope, "but I guess he's gone for sure. Walter Bruce must have been blown to pieces."

"*Bruce?* The clerk?" Red Fallon sat up with a jerk, swore at the pain and lay back rubbing gently at his chest. "Somebody's got their wires crossed, boy, because Bruce came into your shack *after* the blast and he sure looked okay."

Myles wheeled from the window and stared at the other man.

"He was in my office?"

"Yup! He come in after the doc had patched you up and stashed you in a corner to wait for the jeep. I was laid out on the big drawing table and the doc was starting to murder my leg. Bruce came in wide-eyed—and who could blame him—talked to the doc and then went over to look at you."

"What did he talk to the doctor about?"

Fallon spread his hands and shook his head.

"Don't know. I was still pretty deaf from the blast, couldn't hear a word, but I saw their lips moving. Anyway, Bruce sat at your desk and wrote a while, biting his pencil and scratching his head. I watched him, see, to keep my mind off my leg. I figured he was writing a report on the blow-up."

"It wasn't up to him to do that and no report came in from him."

Myles paced thoughtfully around the bed and sat in the chair.

"What happened next?"

"A couple of natives came in— No, that was later on," Fallon corrected, wrinkling his forehead in thought. "Bruce picked up the stuff on your desk, papers and books, and some of your equipment that was laying around, and packed it in one of them shipping boxes."

"So that's who did it; I wondered. The box came north with us, I guess, because it's waiting for me at the main office."

"Then these two guys show up," Fallon went on, "both carrying guns and one of 'em juggling a grenade."

"Rebels?" Myles asked doubtfully. "Or local police?"

"Boss, I was too groggy to care. And the feller playing jacks with the grenade worried me plenty. He says something to Bruce like 'The *señor* will come with us, or not? Decide quick.' I could hear pretty good by then and I remember that much."

"He spoke English?"

Fallon looked surprised and nodded.

"He must have, because I wouldn't have understood that much otherwise. Never thought of that before. Gee, I must have been off my rocker to imagine I heard a peon speaking English."

"Not at all," Myles reassured him. "A few of the top policemen as well as some of the rebel leaders are educated men who wouldn't seem out of place in an embassy or here in the United States, either. Perfectly possible he spoke good English. What then?"

Red pursed his lips and thought for a moment.

"I saw Bruce go out with them. Then I must have passed out; didn't come to until we were flying back here in the company plane."

Myles got up and paced the floor, rubbing his jaw in puzzled consideration.

"If those men were police they would have told the company what became of Walter Bruce, wouldn't they?"

"Don't bet on those people down there to do anything —unless it'll pay 'em," Red advised bitterly.

"You might have something there. Anyway, I'll report what you saw to the office. It will be up to them to take it from here, because I've severed my connection with Carrington Construction. And with engineering, too."

"Come off it!" Fallon jeered. "You'll get over this and be back on another job before you know it. When you do land something, let me know, will you? I'd like to be with you again—anywhere but South America. No more of that revolution stuff for me!"

A large motherly-looking nurse sailed into the room and planted a covered tray on the bedside table.

"Well, Mr. Fallon!" she gurgled with theatrical cheer. "How are we today? Time to change your bandages, you know."

"Oh, my—*gosh!*" The big man writhed lower under the sheets and gave Myles an anguished glare. "This is murder, boss, but it won't take long. Wait outside, will ya, huh?"

"Afraid I can't, Red. I want to drop in at our L.A. office before it closes, to pass along what you've told me about Bruce. Then I'm flying home. You behave yourself here and get well soon."

He gripped the older man's hand warmly.

"Lucky guy!" Fallon grinned. "I bet the whole family'll be lined up at the airport with a brass band, huh?"

Myles stepped back and shook his head.

"I haven't told anyone I'm coming."

"You *haven't?* Going to surprise 'em? Yeah, but honest, I think you'd ought to let 'em know."

"I don't—too many things to explain." He thought grimly how very much there would be to explain and how difficult it was going to be. "I need time to straighten out my thinking," he added soberly.

Myles waved a hand in farewell to the man in the bed. *"Adios, mi amigo,"* he said softly. "I won't forget what you did for me—"

"Forget it, I tell ya!" Fallon yelled. "Beat it, before this old butcher goes to work on me!"

"Now, now, Mr. Fallon!" the nurse reproved grimly. "That's no way to talk!"

"Here, Red." Myles took a book from the heap on the bed and pushed it into Fallon's hand. "Look at the beautiful girl waiting to be murdered in the ritzy nightclub! Feast your eyes on that breath-taking cover and forget your troubles."

"You're a big help!" Fallon growled, but he gripped the book obediently. "Get out before I start yelling!"

Myles left him staring with furrowed brow and clenched teeth at the doomed victim of *Murder in the Swan Club*.

IV

This Sunday morning began in the Jerome household like any other Sunday when the weather permitted, with breakfast buffet style on the terrace behind the house. In spite of their father's prolonged absence in Washington neither Ann nor Sonia thought of breaking the routine, all the more because even to suggest such a thing would also have broken the heart of faithful old Sarah.

Their maid had been a fixture at Sunnyfield almost since they could remember, and breakfast on the terrace was her chief delight. She made a field day of it, hurrying out through the open French door to fuss with the electric coffee-maker on the long trestle table, scurrying in again

to bring out hot popovers or a tray of jams and marma-
lade, and always seizing any excuse to join in the conversation.

It had rained in the night. Every plant and shrub in
the garden below the terrace sparkled as though powdered
with diamond dust. Fluffy clouds of boltonia, marigolds
running the whole scale of yellow, monkshoods purple and
violet, zinnias crimson, and the delicate pink of cosmos
made an enchanted carpet all the way to the border hedge.
The air was fragrant with the scent of the flowers and
drenched earth.

Ann drank her second cup of coffee at ease on the green
and white cushioned glider near the edge of the terrace.
The glass of the picture window reflected her white sports
suit and the American Beauty hue of her cardigan, with
a companion view of Sonia huddled on a bronze plastic
chaise longue while she leafed through the Sunday paper
with noticeable boredom.

Ann studied her sister covertly. The turquoise pullover
which matched her slacks and sandals and the lustrous
white silk shirt accentuated the gold of her hair and her
faintly flushed cheeks. There were hollows in those
cheeks, and shadows under the wistful eyes, signs of unhappiness which had not been there a few weeks ago. Ann
pursed her lips in helpless sympathy and shifted her gaze
to the garden.

A breeze was stirring the vines so that they ticked and
rustled on the wall; it swayed the cascades of nasturtiums
along the steps. A bronzed grackle performed his morning
ablutions in the bird bath, flinging showers of water from
iridescent wings. From the highway in front of the house
drifted the faint hum of passing cars; more distant still
a church bell called the faithful to early prayer.

Gray-haired Sarah stalked out onto the terrace.

"You're wanted on the telephone, Miss Sonia," she announced with the ominous gravity of a hanging judge.

Gone in a flash was the girl's lassitude. She bounded
from the chaise and dashed for the doorway, barely avoiding a collision with the advancing maid.

Sarah frowned after the departing girl, straightened her
rumpled apron and pushed up the glasses which had a
way of slipping down her pointed nose.

"I don't understand an engaged woman being so all-fired anxious to talk to a fella that ain't her intended!" she complained.

When Ann refrained from comment, Sarah sniffed and commenced to clear the breakfast table.

"It was that *manager* of hers calling," she explained as though Ann had begged for enlightenment. " 'Hello, friend Sarah,' " she mimicked with syrupy sweetness. "Pouring on the old oil with both hands—but it don't fool me! He's still a baboon!" She clattered the dishes onto a tray with impatient resentment.

"Mr. Snell has been very kind and helpful to Sonia in her work," Ann defended halfheartedly.

"And why shouldn't he be? The manager of a foundry's supposed to keep everybody up to snuff, isn't he? Say! Miss Sunny hasn't been like the same person lately." The elderly maid paused, hands on hips, to scowl. "You think maybe that job's getting her down?"

"No, no, Sarah. She loves the work."

"Maybe, but she goes at it so! Same as you do at that bank. You Jerome girls don't ever do things by halves," the woman grumbled with a mixture of disapproval and pride. "If you're in something, you're in head over heels." She reverted to her original complaint. "Just the same, I bet that Snell is a real slave-driver!" Muttering further disparagement, she carried the loaded tray into the house.

Ann walked to the top of the terrace steps and lazily stretched her arms above her head. What a gorgeous day! The sky was dazzling ultramarine, its clouds mountainous islands of purest alabaster. The sun had banished the September chill of the early morning air but had left it fresh and tingling with life.

She drew a deep breath, then suddenly dropped her arms and stared while her heart seemed to stop beating. Could that be Myles Langdon who stood in the opening of the box hedge at the end of the garden? She was dreaming! She brushed a hand across her eyes—she *was* awake, and it was no mirage. It *was* Myles, wearing the blue slacks outfit which had been his favorite before he went away. He was coming into the garden, walking toward her!

Ann took the steps in one flying leap, met him as he

reached the path, threw her arms about his neck and kissed him wildly.

"Myles!" she sobbed, "Myles darling! We hadn't heard —I was so afraid!"

A comforting arm hugged her as she pressed her face against his chest and fought for control, and the remembered voice soothed, "Take it easy, Ann." It was Myles Langdon's voice, but an undertone of tension chilled her.

She conquered her burst of emotion and stepped back from the encircling arm, and only then realized how he had changed. There was a touch of white now in the brown hair at his temples; a newly healed scar across his right cheek emphasized the pallor of his face, and deep crow's-feet marked the corners of his tired eyes. Most frightening of all to her, his left hand was thrust into the pocket of the blue flannel jacket and that arm had a strangely useless look.

Somehow Ann smothered her panic while her mind repeated wildly, "You mustn't show that you're shocked! You mustn't!" With an unsteady smile she managed to stammer, "Welcome—welcome home, Myles! It's—it's wonderful to see you."

To her relief she saw the shadows in his brown eyes driven out by golden sparks as he returned her smile.

"Thanks, pal—and *you* look good enough to eat." Myles tucked his right hand under her arm and turned her toward the house. "How about my fiancée? Is Sunny at home?"

Ann's heart performed an uncomfortable somersault and began to pound. He asked for her sister as though everything remained the same between them. Was he going to ignore her break-off letter, confident that his love would win her back again? Or was he only pretending, meeting this disappointment with the calm courage which he always showed?

And where *was* Sonia now? That phone call from Joe Snell might have been a date; they might have arranged to take off in his car for the whole day. It was becoming a Sunday habit, and if she had already left the house, Ann's road would be rough. In that case what could she tell Myles about her sister—what *should* she tell? To postpone the possible crisis, she halted at the terrace steps.

"Isn't our garden beautiful, Myles!" she exclaimed. "But perhaps you've enjoyed such exotic tropical patios that this seems commonplace."

"Ha!" he snorted. "Don't get the idea that we lolled in the gardens of Loma's high society down there. After that slimy jungle this is paradise. Does your father still spend his spare time puttering here, as he used to?"

"Very little now. He seems to spend *all* his time, spare or not, in Washington, one court case after another."

"Don't tell me that you keep this garden up! You and Sunny?"

Sunny again! Where was she? Ann switched away from that tack.

"We supervise—isn't that what you engineers call it?—but Old Charley still does the work. You remember Charley Duval, don't you?"

"I haven't been away for Rip Winkle's twenty years," Myles reminded with a grin. "Sure, I remember him—'the hero of World War One,' as we boys called him, but not to his face."

As they went up the steps from the garden, he asked, "Anything wrong with Sonia, Ann? I couldn't get a word about her from Aunt Pam. Of course, my arriving unannounced at dawn threw her into near hysterics and a sort of coma, but when she came out of it she was evasive."

Ann shivered. He hadn't received the letter—couldn't have, to remain so calm. But it wasn't up to her to tell him! Evasive as his aunt, she demanded:

"Why did you arrive at the unearthly hour of daylight?"

"I flew in from California, the plane was delayed. Rather than hang around the deserted airport at this end I beat it for home. By the way, someone blew up the bridge we were working on, blew me up with it, sort of," he said lightly. "That's how I got these souvenirs."

He touched the scar and flexed his left arm. Ann saw him wince at even that slight motion.

"There's Sunny now!" he exclaimed.

She stood in the open doorway as still as a statue. A lovely statue, Ann thought, a vision for a man just returned from exile. Why did Myles remain staring instead of rushing to her, seizing her and kissing her until she forgot her madness with Joe Snell?

Sonia's immobility, though, she could forgive—the suddenness of Myles's appearance had frozen her. Ann knew that paralysis; when he had come through the hedge toward her it was like seeing the dead return. But *Myles!* Would he never move? In another second her own overwrought emotion would burst out in a scream.

"You idiot!" she told herself fiercely, "if ever there was a cue for a third party's prompt exit, this is it!"

She ran down the steps and along the garden path to the hedge, her anguished mind seeing only Myles, his scarred face and helpless arm. Why did he keep that hand hidden so—was it maimed or—or *gone?* She must know. Aunt Pam would tell her. Fighting back tears of dread, she hurried toward the Leslies' rambling stone house.

Myles Langdon took his eyes off Sonia long enough to watch Ann disappear through the hedge. Then he turned back, squared his shoulders and marched across the terrace to Sunny.

She retreated a step, her blue eyes enormous, hands clasped against the white shirt, every inch of her suggesting a frightened bird poised for flight.

"Myles—*Myles!* What's happened to you?" she whispered, and then realized the cruelty of the question. Color flooded her waxen face and she hastily transferred the blame to him. "You stare at me as though you'd never seen me before!" she gasped.

"It's been a long time, Sunny." He held out his hand.

Her flushed face paled again as she stepped forward and laid her hand in his, and Myles had the sensation of being slowly, inexorably frozen until he dropped it.

"A long time?" Sonia echoed indignantly. "I'll say so! It's months since I heard a word from you!" Nervousness made her voice tremble; she brushed a hand across her eyes while she slipped past him and sat on the glider. "Why didn't you write—at least let us or your family know you were coming?"

Myles leaned against the table, keeping his eyes steadily on hers.

"Perhaps I should have," he admitted. "As to not writing, I apologize but plead extenuating circumstances. Most of August I was laid up, off and on, with a very unpleasant variety of fever they have down there. Whenever I could stay on my feet I tried to keep the job going and promptly came down with a relapse. Poor judgment, I admit, but I had that bridge on my mind even in fits of delirium. And it was time wasted, as things turned out, because eventually a bunch of rebels blew the whole end of it into the river."

Sonia's exclamation of horror was coupled with a darting glance at his cheek and left arm, but she looked away instantly.

Myles nodded. "Yes, you notice I carry souvenirs of the adventure. Some of the other men weren't as lucky as I, though, so I should have no complaints. The company flew me back to a hospital in L.A. where I got wonderful care until I recovered. I still didn't write home. No sense in scaring you people to death; better to wait until I could show up under my own power."

While he talked he wondered if he saw her expression soften in sympathy with his hardships, or if he only imagined it. For after that one glance she had kept her eyes on the garden and he could read nothing in them. What he had come to say needed encouragement, and he was receiving none. Was she disappointed because his greeting had been anything but impassioned? He couldn't help it; he had decided on the casual line and he'd stick to it.

Myles swung a chair away from the table and lowered himself into it with a muffled sigh.

"So here I am," he said, trying for a cheerful tone, "the prodigal returned, no longer an engineer but a budding banker. Uncle John seems delighted at the prospect of another Langdon for an eventual partner."

"You're giving up your career?" At last Sonia was startled out of her silence.

Myles nodded. "Such as it was, yes. A man with only one good arm doesn't fit the picture of the sturdy builder of bridges, does he?"

"Then—then you aren't going away again?"

"No. Settling down as—I hope—a respected citizen and taxpayer. I'll go on living with Uncle John and Aunt

Pamela, for a while anyway. And that brings me to another matter which you may not understand at first."

She looked at him curiously then and his courage almost failed, but he met her eyes without flinching.

"I guess the best way is to come right out with it. Our engagement is off, Sonia." He paused at the sudden light in her eyes, the quick glow of her cheeks, and studied her with a puzzled frown. Then the light faded and her pretty chin set with determination, which confused him even more. But he plowed doggedly on.

"I had a lot of time to think down there, Sunny, and even more time in the hospital. Months ago I began to suspect that our engagement was a mistake, that we were never meant for each other and were courting unhappiness if we married."

She spoke then, sharply. "What are you trying to say?"

"To put it in plain English, Sunny, I'm throwing you over."

"That's what I thought!" There was color in her cheeks now, the red flags of anger. "What a lovely speech that was!" she jeered. "Really impressive. But it was too long and too neatly phrased to be convincing, my friend."

"Believe me, Sunny, I meant it. Every word!"

"Do you know what I think?" She was on her feet, trembling with anger. "I suspect that you've rehearsed it over and over until you were letter-perfect in the part. And all the while you were wallowing in self-pity—and deciding to save me from myself!"

Myles stood up to confront her.

"Sunny, you don't understand!" he protested.

"Oh, but I do! A year ago you were in perfect health when you proposed to me and I accepted you, and we've been engaged ever since. But now, because you've come back more or less shopworn and feeling sorry for yourself, you think it would be noble to release me. Well, evidently it will surprise you, but I'm not interested in your good deed for the day! I hold you to our engagement and you can—can just make the best of it!" she finished in a breathless, sobbing rush.

If her stark reference to his condition hurt Myles Langdon, the only sign he gave was an involuntary whitening of knuckles on the hand which gripped the chair. His mind was too intent on his purpose to be swayed from it. He felt as though he and the girl stood on opposite sides of a yawning chasm, neither able to cross it except with bitter words.

"Listen to me!" he commanded, his voice taut with strain. "We will break our engagement here and now without any more of this foolishness! I—"

"You listen to *me*, Myles Langdon—"

"Let me finish, Sonia!" He spaced his words with all the emphasis he could bring to them. "I—don't—want—to—marry—you! Get it?"

"We won't break off!" She pounded his chest with a little fist clenched in fury. "You're only thinking of yourself—not of me at all!"

"Sunny!" he pleaded, grasping her hand and holding it tightly. "I'm thinking only of you."

"You can't be! We've been engaged for months—everyone knows about it. What do you suppose people will say—they'll say *I* broke it off—discarded you because of your condition! That's what they'll say—and you know it! If you thought *anything* of me, Myles Langdon, you couldn't possibly let me in for something as ghastly as that!"

V

Ann found Pamela Leslie in her garden. The small plump woman was on her knees beside a freshly dug border, ignoring the damage to her purple jersey dress while she dropped a bulb into its hole and patted the earth firmly over it. She tipped back the broad-brimmed hat to look up with reddened eyes when Ann stopped beside her.

"Myles is home!" she said, adding apologetically, "I had to work off my excitement this way." The glove with which she wiped away a tear left a smooch of dirt from gray eyes to chin.

Ann dropped onto the small green wheelbarrow in the path and tried desperately to control her shaking body.

"I—I know, Aunt Pam." Even her teeth were chattering. "I saw—saw him—just now!" She gripped her hands tight in her lap and dared to take the plunge. "Has—has he lost a hand?"

"Great heavens *no,* child! He keeps it in his pocket that way because his arm is partially paralyzed and it takes the strain off it, that's all. And you noticed that vicious scar on his cheek?" When Ann could only nod and gulp at the lump in her throat, Mrs. Leslie added hastily, "I'm sure it will fade in time, be hardly noticeable."

She eyed the girl sharply.

"For goodness' sake, let yourself go! Cry, cry hard, dear! Tears will stop those shakes quicker than anything."

"It was see-seeing him come in through the h-hedge so suddenly, Aunt Pam, when—when we hadn't heard for so long!" Tears did help, Ann found.

Mrs. Leslie was considerate enough to turn away and plant another bulb. She did it with fierce stabs of the trowel.

"Men are so stupid, sometimes!" she complained. "I told Myles not to go barging over to your house without warning, but I don't believe he even heard me. Most of the time he sat staring at his feet, or apologizing for coming home such a wreck! The idiot! To hear him talk one would wonder that he dared to come home at all!"

"What do you mean, Aunt Pam?"

"Why, he seemed to be afraid his friends would be embarrassingly sympathetic about his looks and what he calls his 'useless arm.' Baby him—insist on helping him, you know."

The flow of tears shut off as Ann stiffened with indignation.

"Myles Langdon would never let a thing like *that* keep him away! Even if he'd lost an arm he'd face anyone and everything!"

"Of course he would, honey! I was just explaining how he acted with me—his Aunt Pam. And about that arm," she announced, standing up to face Ann and brandishing the trowel. "I understand the doctors say that the nerves are damaged—*traumatic neurosis* is their word for it—damage from an injury. A good bit of the trouble is mental, they claim. That means it *could* recover—and it isn't going to *stay* useless if I can help! If the Lord lets me live I'll get action into it somehow, so help me!"

She was her cheerful brisk self again and lifted Ann's spirits along with hers. Aunt Pamela had a remedy for almost every ache and pain in the world, to hear her tell it, and quite often one of her prescriptions did work wonders. Now she had her beloved Myles to concentrate on —and could she concentrate!

She went back to her planting with a will, talking over her shoulder between thrusts of the trowel.

"Did Myles see Sonia? Was she there?"

"Yes."

"How did she take his unexpected return? Surprised?"

Ann rubbed the tears from her cheeks with the back of her hand and laughed hollowly.

"A terrific understatement, Aunt Pam. She was as bowled over as I. Really *snowed,* if you get the vernacular. I met Myles in the garden and"—she caught herself back from any description of their greeting and hurried on—"then Sunny came to the door, and I left them staring at each other. It was no place for a third party, so I ran over to see you."

The older woman dug a neat hole in the soft black loam, scooped sand from a tin pail, poured a layer of it in and followed that with a bulb. As she covered it with earth she asked casually:

"Hasn't Sonia been seeing a lot of that Snell fellow at the foundry? I've been hearing things about them which upset me."

"They have been—dating at times," Ann admitted cautiously. "I hope you didn't tell Myles what you've heard."

Mrs. Leslie shook her head violently and buried another bulb.

"Of course I didn't! My friends may call me 'Prescription Pam,' and laugh at my remedies, but I draw the line at trying to doctor heart trouble, physical or emotional.

If there's anything to find out, Myles will do it fast enough by himself."

She stood up, shooed Ann from her perch, and packed trowel and pail in the wheelbarrow.

"Why don't you and Sonia come to supper tonight?" she suggested. "We'll have a grand get-together to celebrate our boy's return."

At any other time Ann would have accepted with enthusiasm but not today. Not until she knew the outcome of the meeting between the engaged couple from which she had fled in panic. Fortunately she could make her excuse with almost complete honesty.

"I'd love to, Aunt Pam," she sighed, "but your nephew's unheralded appearance catches me with another date. Betty Wilder, who works at the bank, asked me to a cook-out this evening. She's new in town, still a blushing bride, and *very young.*"

Ann smiled at the memory. "When she invited me she behaved as though it took all her courage to ask an old settler like a *Jerome* to share the Wilder barbecue—even though we work side by side every day."

That had been perfectly true, Ann insisted mentally, as she walked back to her own garden. Betty Wilder had been obviously nervous; if Ann begged off now from the party she would be crushed. And Betty was too nice and too friendly to be hurt unnecessarily.

Ann took the long way around the garden to stay as far as possible from the house. She'd get her car from the garage and *continue* to stay as far as possible— She halted with a gasp. The thick privet hedge beside her swayed and crackled and a stooping man pushed through and stood upright, rubbing his back. To her relief it was their part-time gardener.

"Charley!" she protested. "Must you come bursting out of the bushes like that? You scared me half to death!"

"Aw, go on!" Duval chuckled, his lined face wrinkling in an affectionate grin. "What's making you so jumpy, Ann? Swell day, ain't it!"

"Perfect—but it's Sunday. What are you doing here?"

"I've got me a new part-time job for weekdays so I

figured I'd better put in some work here Sundays. Just look at this garden!"

With a familiarity born of years spent working for the Jeromes Charley caught her shoulder and swung her to follow his sweeping arm.

"Look at what's got to be done, will ya!" he ordered. "The place is going haywire, and you know what store your Pa sets by it! Ain't he ever coming back from Washington, D.C., to give me some overseeing?"

Ann smiled at the deep concern in his voice but reassured him gravely. "You're a dear to worry so, Charley, but you shouldn't. Everything looks thriving—never more beautiful, in fact. Goodness, you've worked here since I was a little girl, so I guess nobody can tell you anything about gardening!"

"Well, that's about right, of course," he admitted, standing straighter and squaring his shoulders. "I do see things most folks would miss. Look at that witch grass cropping up in the path, now—got to get at that before it spreads. And the dead branch on the side of that azalea —have to lop that off. I see lots of work here to keep it prettied-up to suit your Pa."

He shook his white-thatched head.

"Hope I ain't making a mistake, taking on another job. But I see by the papers, one of them doctor's advice columns, how it's dangerous for a man to retire and do nothing. He'd ought to keep busy or he'll rust out quick; senile dementia, they call it—whatever that is."

"You're far from rusting out," Ann encouraged. "What is the new job, Charley?"

"Security officer at Mr. Leslie's bank—your bank," he stated importantly. "Seems Fred Tomkins got himself some leg trouble and the doc won't let him stand all day. So he's keeping the P.M. shift, and I take over the mornings. Thirty smackers a week, and they give me a gun, too. A .45, and it's a beaut!"

"*You—a bank guard!*" An incredulous giggle rippled through the words as she took in the gangling figure with oversize ears and a perpetual look of helplessness. She could not imagine anyone less fitted for the role of stalwart defender—but he was such a dear! She turned the laughter into a squeal of excitement and thrust out her hand.

"Congratulations, *Mr.* Duval! I think you'll be *super!*"

The aged gardener wiped his fingers on a trouser leg before he pumped her slender hand vigorously. Clearing his throat importantly, he announced:

"I got qualifications, you know. Seems they like ex-soldiers for that kind of job."

"Oh? That's right, you fought in World War One, didn't you!"

Charley Duval hesitated, scuffing a scarred boot toe in the grass. Then he slanted a look at Ann.

"Well, yes. I was an MP in Brest, France, and that wasn't no Sunday School outing sometimes. I guess the bankers figure even an army has-been might have more nerve than some of these young squirts around town if there's trouble—like a hold-up, for instance."

Ann couldn't help laughing.

"A *hold-up!* You're dreaming if you figure to be a hero that way. Who ever heard of a bank being robbed around here?" She saw the chagrined flush on his wrinkled cheeks and instantly regretted the taunt.

"Just the same," she admitted kindly, "I'll feel a lot safer in my cage now, knowing you and your trusty gun are on hand, even if nothing should happen."

"I ain't kidding you," he persisted grimly. "Just because there's never *been* a stick-up, according to the percentages the first one's coming nearer all the time."

"Calamity howler!"

"No, I ain't! You people sit around here in your nice houses and think everything's lovely; you don't know what's going on in the world. Talk to the cops, like I do, and you'll get a different slant on our city."

"I don't know what you mean." Ann frowned.

" 'Course you don't, that's what I'm saying. Did you know that right now the cops are on their toes—if them lamebrains ever can be—watching out for some slick crooks who make a specialty of robbing country houses? There's a pair of 'em; a guy that's called 'the Duke' on account of he looks and acts like one, and he's teamed up with a girl called 'Tiger Cat'—'cause *she* acts like one. Can she claw! The cops say she scratched up one guy who tried to bring her in so bad he's in the hospital. And she got clean away."

"Charley Duval, what a story! Your head's been turned by TV!"

He shook the maligned member stubbornly.

"No, sir—ma'am! I got it straight from the police about this pair. They specialize in big houses, like I said, and they're after jewelry—nothing else."

Instinctively Ann's hand went to the circle of pearls at her throat—her mother's bequest, Sunny had received the rings—and she laughed sheepishly.

"No self-respecting jewel thief would waste his time around here, Charley. There isn't enough to be worth-while."

"Maybe—but do they know it?"

The old man shook a finger at her.

"I'm plenty worried, if you ain't. These burglars are supposed to rent a house in a neighborhood; gives 'em a chance to look it over, size it up. I wish to goodness your Pa would come back from Washington—and stay. Somebody'd ought to keep an eye on you girls."

"The Jerome girls," Ann jeered, "who run wild while the parent is away." Saying it in fun made her remember the far from amusing jam her sister was in and sobered her at once. "Calamity howler Duval!" she accused again and left him to his work.

She slipped into the garage and drove away quietly in her car. A whole day to kill before she would dare to return to the house, dress quickly and be off to Betty Wilder's. By then, surely, Myles and Sonia would have settled everything, settled it in one way or another.

Resolutely she closed her mind against consideration of the possible conclusion and centered her attention on driving—driving anywhere as long as it was away from Sunnyfield.

It was almost six when she returned and went through the quiet house to the upstairs living room. Only a few hours since she'd left it, but they seemed endless years. She closed her eyes, pressed fingers against her temples and rubbed hard before she looked again at the familiar surroundings. In spite of the turmoil of the day nothing had changed.

The Wedgwood blue walls, the stark white hangings at the windows, the rose pattern slipcover of the couch, seemed to enfold her with loving arms. In a shining brass basket beside the fireplace gleamed the silvery birch logs which they had brought back from Maine at no small trouble. The automatic record changer and portable TV, bought with the sisters' own earnings, beckoned invitingly as though saying, "We're right here as always, waiting for you. Use us! Have fun!"

A surge of anger, rebellion, shook her. How could these lovely things be so indifferent to the anxiety seething in her heart. She crossed the room quickly to a window, rested her forehead against the cool glass and stared out at the garden lying silent in the gathering dusk.

Beyond the hedge and bordering trees a chimney sent faint threads of smoke into the still air. The Leslies—Aunt Pam and Uncle John—and Myles Langdon. With an uncontrollable shiver she turned and opened her bedroom door, stopped on the threshold when she saw the lights were on.

"I'll say you've given your happy home the brush-off today, sister dear," Sonia reproached from the depths of the boudoir chair. Its sea-green covering made a charming background for her Titian hair, but her face above the aqua housecoat was colorless, her eyes enormous.

Monty scrambled from her lap with a joyful yelp and raced for Ann.

"I didn't think I was needed around here today," Ann defended resentfully. "Why are you lying in wait here? I'm going out for supper, you know. Monty!" she snapped. "Stop dancing around—you make me dizzy. Go over in the corner and park!"

With her reflection watching from the full-length mirror on the closet door, she stripped off the rose cardigan and stowed it in a drawer of her antique applewood dresser, killing time by a most meticulous arrangement of the other garments there.

"Where have you been, anyway?" Sonia probed.

Ann opened the closet door and made a show of deciding on a dress for the party.

"Oh, driving around here and there," she answered airily. "Down to the shore, tramped along the beach, lunch at a divine diner—if there could be such a thing. Then home. Pleasant, unexciting—but that's the story of 'My Day.'"

When Sonia made no comment, merely settled deeper into the chair, Ann realized that it was useless to attempt side-stepping the inevitable. She lay down on the bed and clasped her hands under her head.

"How about you, Sunny? Let's have it! That's what you waited here for, isn't it?"

"Yes." It was the faintest murmur.

Sonia sat up and leaned forward. The springer, as though scenting an emotional crisis, jumped to her knees, licked her cheek and settled down in her lap with a gusty sigh.

"Myles never received my letter!" she announced in a dramatic still, small voice.

"For Peter's sake, don't whisper!" her sister protested irritably. "It gives me the merry-pranks! How do you know he didn't, Sunny? Did he say so—or did you ask him?"

"He didn't, and I didn't. I—I just couldn't! He would have spoken of it if he *had* received it, wouldn't he?"

Ann found a more comfortable position and nodded.

"I should think so." She tried for lightness when she added, "Seems to me a letter from his girl giving a man the old heave-ho would be the first topic of conversation when they met. Did you tell him about you and Snell?"

"No."

"Oh, you're chicken!" Ann groaned. "Then he still believes that you love him? Jeepers! Couldn't he *feel* the truth when he—he kissed you?"

"He didn't kiss me."

"*What?*" Ann sat up with a jerk. No kiss? She drew down the corners of her mouth at the memory of the greeting with which *she* had welcomed Myles. Arms hugging her knees, she demanded:

"You mean to sit there and tell me that he didn't kiss you when he saw you for the first time in *a year?*" She quelled the rising note of hysteria in her voice, "Long time no see. What's the catch?"

"There isn't any catch." Two tears like outsized diamonds rolled slowly down Sunny's cheeks. "He—he hardly touched me. And he insisted that we break our engagement!"

"Well—" Ann stared, at a loss for a suitable epithet. "Well, *jeepers!* That's what you want, isn't it? Why tears instead of cheers?"

"Don't be like that, Ann," Sonia implored. "I don't want it ended because of his—his injuries, and I'm sure that was the reason for his trying to step out. I know you think I'm out of my head to have fallen for Joe—and that he's a heel for trying to cut Myles out, but—"

Ann lay back on the bed with a disgusted sigh.

"Sorry, but that's the way I do feel, Sunny," she acknowledged. "But never mind that now; don't keep me in suspense. How did you handle it when Myles sprang his proposition on you?"

Sonia shot a nervous glance at her sister, then bent over the dog in her lap, gently rubbing his silky ears until his eyes rolled up in ecstasy.

"There was only one thing I *could.* do," she murmured. "I flatly refused to break the engagement."

VI

Ann sat up again to stare in bewilderment at her sister.

"*You* refused to break the engagement?" she exclaimed while her heart sank. "What in the world for? Maybe I'm dumb but I simply can't follow you! For weeks you've moped around here, looking more and more like a ghost, bewailing the fact that Myles never accepted the brush-off in your last letter. Then he comes home, announces that the engagement is off and you—you *refuse!*"

She threw herself back on the bed and stared wildly at the ceiling as though she hoped to find an explanation there.

"And may I inquire," she went on scathingly, "what our friend from the wilds of South America said to that?"

"Well, I didn't give him a chance to say anything. I kept talking fast for fear I'd lose my courage and agree to what he wanted."

"Oh, my aching head!" Ann groaned. "What *he* wanted! You mean, my lovely addle-pate, what *you* wanted. This is the most involved explanation I ever tried to understand."

"You must understand," Sunny pleaded. "I knew he was doing it because of—of his condition and I couldn't take it! I told him that the scar on his face and the bad arm wouldn't make the slightest difference to a girl who loved him. That's perfectly true—I think. But"—her voice sank to a whisper of regret—"I didn't tell him that I wasn't that girl."

She waited hopefully for some comment from Ann, who lay silent. Getting no help there, she continued slowly.

"Then I told him, 'Myles, if you insist on breaking our engagement you know what will happen. Our friends will think that *I* threw you over because of your injuries and they'll never have any use for me.'"

"I'll bet that did it!" Ann muttered.

"Well, it did. He agreed to let the engagement stand for my sake. But he assured me that he would claim none of the privileges of a fiancé."

There was no mirth in Ann's choking laugh.

"That's pretty tough on him but a break for you, feeling as you do about Joe Snell. Perhaps though, Myles won't stay here long, with things as they are—"

"Yes, he will." Sonia was relieved to shift to a less disturbing discussion. "He's going into Uncle John's bank and, as he says, learn to be a vice-president."

"Give up engineering?" Indignation shocked Ann bolt upright. "Myles can't do that—abandon the one thing he's wanted to do all his life! It wouldn't be worth living then!"

"Well, I asked him if it wasn't going to be hard to settle down in a town like this after all the excitement and danger in South America. And he gave me a queer look and said, 'Life isn't always as smooth as a trotting park, even here, Sunny.' "

"How right he was," Ann murmured.

Sonia rested her head against the chair back and closed her eyes.

"Myles left then and Joe came over and I fought it out with him." She sighed. "It's been a perfectly horrible day. Sometimes I think there is more pain than joy in being in love."

Silently Ann agreed but avoided that subject. "I take it that Joe didn't approve of your arrangement with Myles."

"He's furious, even though I explained that I couldn't hurt Myles, now that he's returned disabled."

"At least that sounds better than your other reason, 'What would people say?' " Ann shook her head. "But it was neither kind nor accurate. Lucky you didn't use it on Myles; he would have knocked your lovely auburn-haired block off—figuratively speaking—if he suspected you were holding him out of pity.

"And he is not *disabled!*" she said sharply, pink with indignation. "What's a stiff arm, that will be normal again any time? As for the scar, plenty of girls will consider it romantic and go all out for him!"

Unconsciously her fingers stroked her cheek while she spoke. When she realized it she dropped her hand abruptly.

"Returning to the triangle, what does Snell intend to do about this complicated deal you and Myles have so neatly cooked up?"

"He swore—and I mean *swore*—that he won't recognize the engagement; that he'll keep on seeing me even if it means trouble with Myles. He really was mad—and nasty about it."

"He could be," Ann agreed soberly.

Sunny put her hands to her eyes and sobbed.

"Joe says if I don't break off at once—he—he'll find another girl. And—and he means it!"

"Of course he means it. He's a tough egg," was Ann's discouraging comment. On the screen of her memory flashed a hard and hostile face glaring through the glass of the teller's window at the bank. "As a matter of fact,

I'll bet that a certain Cecile Parker will be standing by in the most prominent position when he goes looking for that other girl."

"That slinky blonde with the green eyes?" Sunny shrilled contemptuously. "Joe wouldn't look at *her!*"

"You've got a lot to learn, sister. It's the way she looks at him that will count. But, judging Joe on past performance, he'll do his Don Juan act out of your sight, so why worry?" Ann suggested callously. " 'What the eye doth not see, the heart doth not grieve over.' Old stuff, but it still holds good."

She swung her feet to the floor, rested her elbows on her knees, her chin in her hands.

"I know Myles," she stated levelly, "and he'll end your engagement, regardless of everything, as soon as he finds that you don't love him. It won't take him long to discover that—if he doesn't suspect it already. Your expression of stark horror, or whatever it was, as you stood in the doorway this morning, would open even eyes blinded with love."

"I—I was too stunned to move," Sunny confessed.

"You certainly looked it. The surprise didn't affect *me* that way." Ann clamped her lips shut to prevent further revelations and stood up. "This meeting is hereby adjourned—indefinitely. I have to dress for an outdoor banquet, so clear out and take your snoring lapdog with you."

Alone in her room Ann sank onto the bed, arms limp at her sides. In spite of her encouraging words to Sunny about the ending of the engagement her heart ached, for now everything would be as it had been. Myles would see to that; once he got over this quixotic idea of freeing Sonia for her own good he'd be back on the beam. Then his determination—and his charm—would just as surely swing Sunny to her true course and fade Joe Snell into a dimly remembered ghost of the past until he was eventually forgotten.

And where did that leave Ann Jerome? Right where Ann belonged, she brooded, as Myles's long-time friend. So better shut her eyes at once to pictures of their meeting and her impassioned kisses, wipe them forever from her mind.

It wouldn't be easy.

"You know absolutely nothing about love," Sunny had accused, and Joe Snell had growled, "You don't know what it's like to see a face that sends the blood pounding through your veins—"

She knew now; had known from the moment when she raced down the garden path and flung herself into Myles Langdon's arms. With just that intensity she loved him— and he was in love with her sister! So what? she thought bitterly. So she must get over it. The answer was as simple as that. Myles must never suspect, nor Sunny either, and she could expect no help. It was squarely up to Ann Jcrome to fill her mind so full of other thoughts that no room remained for Myles or any vain regrets.

An opportunity to embark on that courageous program came sooner than she expected, and at the Wilder cook-out. The young couple had bought one of the new houses only a few streets away, so Ann walked over through the deepening September twilight.

Betty Wilder greeted her with flattering warmth and led the way along a redwood-paneled hall to the back of the house. Ann caught a passing glimpse of the living room, one wall a sheet of glass, a black iron fireplace of contemporary design and a broad rug of black and white lightning flashes which made her think of a zebra. Evidently the young people's taste was strictly modern. Then they were out on a patio whose rose-colored bricks glowed in the flickering light from candles set in wrought-iron stands at each corner.

Here Betty introduced Sam Wilder, who raised a face glowing like the bricks from his labors at the elaborate charcoal grill, waved and went back to work. And then, with thinly veiled eagerness, she presented her cousin from Montana, Henry Little. "Free, rich and twenty-five," was her whispered aside to Ann.

"*Little?*" Ann gasped, having to look up at least ten inches to meet his eyes.

"Yes, ma'am!" The drawl was incredibly slow, as amazing as the breadth of his shoulders and his craggy handsomeness. "Back on the ranch they call me 'Little Henry'; I'm the runt of our herd. Kin I rope you a super highball, ma'am?"

"No, thanks. I don't—"

"Never tetch the pizen? Mighty smart gal!" Henry nodded sober approval and launched on a rambling tale about Uncle "Cactus" Little who fell prey to "the curse of drink."

Mrs. Wilder overheard from her preparation of the picnic table and descended on her cousin wrathfully.

"You stop it, Hank!" she ordered. "Behave yourself! You're not fooling anybody!"

The huge Little grinned down at Ann.

"Didn't I fool *you?*" he pleaded without a trace of drawl.

"I was *beginning* to suspect," she laughed. "So you're not a rancher, after all! How disappointing, when I was visualizing your miles of unfenced range and expecting you to swing me up to your saddle and ride off into the sunset."

"That's a mighty attractive proposition. The blue dress and the matching what-cha-call-it ribbon on your hair are a masterpiece of harmony—almost as blue as your eyes! My favorite color."

"Most men like blue. A handy thing for a girl to know."

"Sort of a hunting costume, is it?" He laughed softly at her indignant denial. "All right, but I did hope you wore it just to enchant me."

He spoke with so much sincerity that Ann felt a tingle of satisfaction. Evidently the freezing quality of her eyes, which annoyed Sunny and Joe Snell, was off duty tonight —or this husky gentleman from Montana was impervious to it.

"Sorry to wreck your dreams," Henry continued, seating her in a low-slung canvas chair and dragging one of the benches over so that he could face her and concentrate on her beauty. "I did some ranch work when I was a kid, but since then I've turned tenderfoot. College and medical school, and right now putting in my hitch in the Army. But never mind *me;* I want to hear all about *you!*"

Ann was saved from answering by a clarion call from Sam Wilder, "Come and get it, or I'll throw it away!" He was transferring smoking steaks from the grill to paper plates. "Pull up to the table and let's go!"

Not in a long time did Ann remember so satisfactory

a meal, but she could not decide whether this was due to the perfectly cooked meat, creamy escalloped potatoes and luscious hot cornbread, or to the company.

Betty she had liked from their first meeting and Sam Wilder, a rather serious young man employed in the design room at the foundry, proved equally pleasant. His only fault to her mind was his enthusiasm for Joe Snell's ability.

But it was Henry Little who dominated the party from the time they sat down until the last of the tomato aspic salad had disappeared and nothing was left except coffee and tiny frosted cakes in all the colors of the rainbow. He told story after story about his varied life in the West, at college and in the Army, all spiced with humor and unintentionally revealing bits of his own philosophy of life.

He spoke to them all but his eyes rested most frequently on Ann. When he paused to protest that somebody else should do some talking, she found herself joining Betty and Sam in urging him for more.

The sky was sprinkled with stars and a ruddy moon had slid above the distant hill when Henry at last looked at his watch and pushed back from the table.

"The monologue is over!" he announced with a wry smile. "Never chattered so much in my life." With a meaning glance for Ann he added, "Never had such inspiration. You brought it on yourself!"

"I loved every minute!" she protested. "Why stop now?"

"Because duty calls. Have to drive back to camp tonight; my hospital unit sails tomorrow for overseas service. In fact," he consulted his watch again, "carried away by my own eloquence I'm late getting started. So no extended leave-taking; you folks stay comfortably here and I'll take off unassisted.

"Oh!" he appeared to have a sudden inspiration. "Perhaps Ann would like to come and see my car; it's kind of snappy," he explained with a smile for her.

"Go ahead, Ann—it's terrific!" Betty urged with suspicious promptness. "Sam and I will start clearing up here."

Henry linked an arm in Ann's, then faced his hostess.

"Bett, rather than try to thank you now I'll need a ten-page letter to tell you what this evening has meant to me. So long all," he grinned and led Ann away.

His car, glistening in the floodlighted driveway in front of the garage, more than lived up to its advance publicity. Ann, who adored sports cars, saluted it with an admiring whistle. It was as low, lean and racy as any she had ever seen; she wondered how it could possibly accommodate his mammoth figure.

"Like it?" Henry asked. "It's a nice blue, I think. As you said, 'Most men like blue.' Say, wouldn't you in your snappy outfit look swell in it! How about keeping it for me while I'm away? I can find someone to drive it up here after I leave."

"Are you serious?" she gasped. "Thanks, but I'd be a nervous wreck every time I went out for fear something would happen to it. I have rather bad luck with cars. No, thank you!"

"Sure?" he insisted. When she nodded firmly he shrugged. "Okay, but I'd like to leave you something to remember me by. This has been a big evening for me, and it would come just when I have to take off, with no chance to make a good impression."

"You've made an unforgettable impression."

He glanced out of the corner of his eyes. "Maybe. But I'd sort of like to make sure. Here I am, leaving for months—perhaps forever," he amended with sudden gloom. "Who knows what may happen overseas. So in case I never see you again—"

Before she guessed his intention he gathered her in his arms and kissed her with unmistakable enthusiasm.

Ann made no resistance; perhaps this was the way to begin to forget Myles Langdon. Only a beginning, certainly; so far there was no repetition of her feelings when she kissed Myles. None at all!

Then Henry was in the car, whirling it down the drive and away along the street with an ear-shattering roar of power. Soberly she watched the twin taillights dwindle to ruby sparks and disappear.

Ann turned to re-enter the house and for the first time noticed a shadowy figure at the corner of the street. A man, standing motionless. Watching her? It was too dark and he was too distant to be sure of it.

For an instant she thought of Old Charley's grim report of thieves—the Duke and his Tiger Cat. Then, realizing that her recent fond farewell with Henry Little as played on this spotlighted stage might easily attract attention, she laughed softly.

"This is the wrong neighborhood for open-air embraces," she murmured, remembering how she had watched Sunny and Joe Snell kiss on the front porch the other evening. "I never realized before the truth of the poem, 'The night has a thousand eyes!'"

She laughed again and hurried into the house to help the Wilders put things to rights.

On the corner Myles Langdon turned away and headed for home, wondering why even this short walk had made him feel tired and old. And wondering, too, who the big fellow might be from whom Ann had parted so tenderly.

He'd better be top flight, he thought. Ann deserves the best. Who was he, anyway? Someone with the full use of both arms, all right, from the way he hugged her.

Myles kicked savagely at a stone in his path. A lot seemed to have happened since he went away; it was going to take time to catch up. And evidently it wasn't going to be all pleasant.

VII

Myles Langdon was among the early arrivals at the bank on Monday morning, but Ann was already behind her window and ready for work. He detoured that way to inquire with mock anxiety, "Is this costume suitable for a budding banker?"

How easy it was to fall into the old, friendly relationship of so many years! Hands on hips, she surveyed his beautifully tailored suit, dark blue with the faintest of stripes, the very model of conservatism. Her throat tightened when she noticed the left hand still in his pocket and she lifted her eyes quickly to his face. He looked rested, more relaxed than yesterday; she thought hopefully that the scar was a little less noticeable.

Myles caught her tremor, guessed the reason for it and fervently wished that he could stand naturally before her. But that arm needed support, so he forced a grin, twirled a nonexistent mustache and demanded, "Well, how about it? Do I pass inspection?"

"You sure do, mister!" Ann took a deep breath to slow her pulse and control her too enthusiastic voice. "What a drawing card for our bank—the handsome, romantic hero with jungles, revolutions, and I don't know what else for a background. Wait till the girls of our quiet town learn that you're here—they'll come flocking in to open accounts by the dozens! You—"

"Okay—skip the rest of the build-up!" he protested. "You've convinced *me;* now I'm going in to see if I qualify with Uncle John, which is much more to the point. If he starts me in as a teller I hope you'll show me the ropes."

"Oh, no!"

She had a momentary panic at the prospect of standing beside him in the confines of the cage, having to sustain the glance of those brown eyes at close range.

"Mrs. Greenwood always trains the new tellers," she explained demurely and indicated the elderly woman at the first window.

Myles studied the teacher's generous proportions and pursed his lips.

"Will there be room for me there?" he whispered. "However—if I don't report to the boss pretty quick he'll probably start me filling inkwells and cleaning pens."

He raised crossed fingers at Ann and headed solemnly for the president's office.

Mr. Leslie beamed with pleasure and pride when Myles walked in.

"It's going to be great to have you with us, boy!" he welcomed. "You're just in time for a trial flight, too—got something for you to do." He gestured at the man sitting by his desk. "You remember Joe Snell, of course."

"I certainly do. Hello, Joe!" Myles said with a friendly

smile, envying the blond young man's healthy tan. His own face, after weeks in the hospital, must look horribly pasty in contrast.

When Snell only gave him a silent nod Myles was annoyed. The guy had always had a chip on his shoulder and lacked manners. He walked over and held out his hand.

"It's been a long time. How've you been?"

"Fine—*fine!*" Flushing, Snell scrambled to his feet and shook hands. "Sorry, Langdon, I—I was so surprised to see you I guess I froze to the chair." To cover his embarrassment he blurted, "You look as if you'd been through the wringer!"

"They play rough down in South America sometimes," Myles said quietly, and let it go at that.

Mr. Leslie broke the awkward pause. "Joe is here representing Mr. Parker in regard to a loan for the foundry, Myles. He's general manager there, you know."

"No, I didn't know that, Uncle John. Nice going, Joe! It's queer Sonia never mentioned it in her letters; she said she was secretary to the manager, and pretty set up about it, but I had no idea it was you."

Snell hitched in his chair and scowled uneasily.

"Sunny—she probably didn't think you'd be interested."

"Of course I'd be interested in the man my girl works for," Myles laughed. "How's she doing—give you any trouble?"

"Uh—no—she's all right, doing fine!" Joe assured hastily and turned to Mr. Leslie. "If you'll tell me who to see, sir, I'll get going. I know *you* don't handle loans, but you said for me to come to your office—"

"Wanted you to meet Myles," the banker explained. "He's starting in here today and wants to learn the ropes and he'll begin with your loan."

"Him?" Snell growled. "I'd rather somebody else handled it!" He was flushed, ill at ease. "I mean—somebody that knows something about it!"

"No hard feelings," Myles grinned. "I don't blame you for wanting someone else."

Banker Leslie, who was not accustomed to having his decisions questioned, blandly ignored the objection.

"Myles, you take Joe in to Mr. Connelly and the three of you work it out," he ordered. "There's nothing to worry about, Joe, we know all about your company and will be happy to finance the new addition. I merely wish Myles to sit in on the transaction; begin to get the feel of banking. Go along now, boy, and see whether it's anything like engineering."

While Myles led the way to another office he attempted to break the ice of Snell's dissatisfaction with conversation.

"Adding to the plant, are you?" he inquired. "You must be going great guns."

"Biggest year we ever had, and still three months to go!" Joe boasted.

"Good! I'll have to catch up on what's been happening around here since I left. How about showing me over the foundry some day?"

"All right. That is," Snell revised the offer hastily, "I can have someone take you through—I might be tied up."

He darted a scowling glance at Myles.

"You mean—before you approve the loan, huh?" he sneered. "Getting to be a big shot already!"

"I *didn't* mean that!" Myles halted to face him. "What's eating you, anyway? You were always looking for a fight when we were kids. Haven't you grown up yet? You heard my uncle say that we're glad to make the loan, so come in here and tell Mr. Connelly your story. I'm just an observer this time."

When the business was finished and Snell had gone, Myles walked slowly around the main banking room, where he watched the varied transactions which were taking place. But his thoughts still centered on Joe Snell.

It was true that as a boy he had been bad-tempered, envious of those who seemed in any way superior, and wild as an untamed colt. Understandable enough, but why hadn't success softened his disposition? Meeting Myles now, for the first time in years, he acted as though he hated the sight of the battered ex-engineer. Because he was an incurable sour puss, or was there some personal reason? Myles dismissed the puzzle as another of life's mysteries, and forgot it when Charley Duval appeared in full regalia as bank guard.

The old man had belted on his pistol over the uniform coat and kept a hand on the holstered gun as though poised for instant action. He greeted Myles warmly and lost no time in alerting him to the dangers which, in Charley's opinion, threatened the bank and the city as well.

Myles was too fond of the veteran to laugh at his forebodings. He listened with grave attention, congratulated him on his job, but mildly suggested that he wear the ominous-looking .45 *under* his coat to avoid alarming the customers. When Charley grudgingly complied, Myles moved on to Ann's window, but he had no chance to speak to her.

"Myles Langdon! Well, welcome home, stranger!" It was Cecile Parker's voice with all its usual acidity replaced by honey-dripping tones. "You'll never know how we've all missed you!" she murmured, clutching his arm—fortunately the sound one—and fixing starry eyes on his face.

"Hello, Cecile," was all he had time to say before she engulfed him with another syrupy flood.

"Aren't you the picture of the returning hero! Was it truly dreadful down there, Myles? I'm dying to hear about your adventures in that hideous jungle, so you stand right here."

She tapped his chest with a dainty finger.

"I was cashing a check over there when I saw you and rushed over—wait till I get my money and then we'll go somewhere for coffee and the story of your life!"

He smiled amiably and shook his head.

"Some other time, Cecile. I'm a working man; can't leave the job even for you."

"I love that 'even for you'—if you meant it!" She gave him her most dazzling smile. "Where are you working? I'll walk back with you."

"Right here," Myles informed her, "although it's my first day, so I can't claim to be invaluable yet. But I think I should stand by in case of emergency, don't you?"

"You always were so darn conscientious! Well, all right, Myles, but I'll call you." Plainly annoyed at his evasion, Cecile's voice lost some of its honey. "Would you come to dinner some night—or does your intended keep the hobbles on you?"

Without chancing a rebuke, she hurried away to collect her waiting money.

Ann, who had heard it all, did not look up from the deposit slip she was checking, but her comment was perfectly audible.

"Ah, there, Mr. Langdon! Did I call the shot with my prophecy that the line would form on the right to adore our conquering hero?"

Disdaining to answer, Myles moved close to her window and made a face as he often had when they were children and she teased him. Then he winked and walked away, steering clear of the window where Cecile seemed to be having an altercation with that teller.

He left Ann badly shaken with the memories aroused by his boyish grimace, memories of their carefree years together before romance intruded. If his every action affected her like this, how long could she bear to see him day after day? It was like blindly groping through a fog with no hope that the heavenly blue of his response would ever show through. She should have too much pride, she advised herself fiercely, to long for a man who loved another girl. Perfectly true—only she didn't! Where's your will power? she continued the mental struggle unhappily. Get interested in something else. Or *someone* else, if there were anyone who could replace Myles in her heart.

That possibility recurred to her a day or two later when she came home after work and Sarah met her in the hall. The woman's wrinkled face was beaming, her thin arms cradled a long florist's box.

"This just came!" she chuckled, thrusting it on Ann. "Someone's sending you flowers!"

"Hooray for them! I'm all for the good old American custom of saying it with posies." She laid the box on the table while she put away hat and coat.

"Hurry up and open it—see who they're from," Sarah rubbed her hands in anticipation.

"Hold your horses." Ann snapped the string, lifted the cover and parted the green tissue paper. "Roses—the lovely things! Goodness, though—six, twelve—why, there must be two dozen of them! Who in the world—?"

Impatient, Sarah plucked the card from among them and came within a hairsbreadth of snatching it from its envelope. With superhuman control she refrained and handed it to Ann.

"Why, it's from Henry Little! How nice!"

"Who's he?"

"A man I met at the Wilders'—Betty's cousin." She read the card for the maid's benefit. " 'Sailing postponed a day but no chance to call you. Thanks a million for a big evening and a wonderful send-off. Hank.' "

Sarah pushed up her glasses to peer at the card.

"He underlined 'wonderful send-off.' What's that mean?"

"Oh—nothing. He's full of pep—very—er—energetic." Ann omitted further details and changed the subject quickly. "What can we put these in?"

"There's too many for a single vase." Sarah caressed the brilliant petals. "Real pretty, aren't they! Never seen so many in one bouquet; your Pa'd have a fit if somebody picked that many out of *his* garden. Real pretty, though. What's this Henry Little like?"

"Just a rather huge and very pleasant young man who has sailed abroad by now, so relax. Let's put half a dozen in the tall silver vase, and some in the green glass one, and I'll take a dozen over to Aunt Pam."

Ann found the Leslies' front door open and went in to be greeted by five booming notes from the grandfather's clock in the hall. She paused to hear them out. As long as she could remember, the deep tones had thrilled her and now they brought back a hundred crowding memories of childhood when she had run in and out of this house as though it were her own.

From the hall she could see into the living room with its wide fireplace at one end, the long couch facing it and the time-dulled portrait above the mantel. Always she had loved the restfulness of the neutral grasscloth walls, the gold brocade hangings at the windows, the absence of cluttered detail.

A copper bowl of sensational dried grasses glowed on the piano; a happy-go-lucky arrangement of cattails rose from the mammoth green urn in a shadowy corner. Aunt Pam had evidently been piecing out the dwindling blooms in her garden with the product of the fields which she appreciated just as much.

Some whisper of sound, a gasp or a sigh, startled her.

Immersed as she was in memories her eyes darted first to the tall Chinese screen of red lacquer at the side of the room. Always that bit of vivid splendor had awed her because it seemed to exude an aura of sinister mystery, daring a hesitant child to look behind it—and be terrified!

But the sound had not come from that direction. Ann threw off the momentary twinge of alarm and lifted her voice in the usual neighborly notice of a caller.

"Yoo-hoo!"

There was an explosive yelp from the sofa and a small head with tousled black bangs reared up above its back. Eyes popping in consternation glared at the equally dumbfounded Ann.

"Golly!" the child yelped. "You scared me!"

"We're even, then," Ann smiled. "You gave me goose bumps for a second. What are you doing here?"

"Reading."

"I meant, what are you doing in this house?"

"I live here—now. Mother and Daddy had to go to Iran, so they parked me with Grandma. That's in the Near East," she explained politely, propping her elbows on the sofa back. "Iran, I mean."

Enlightenment flooded Ann. Now she remembered Aunt Pamela's reference to overseas duty for Jean's husband, the major, and her anticipation of caring for their ten-year-old daughter if the place to which he was assigned should prove unsuitable for children.

"Of course, you're Kathy Flood!" she exclaimed, advancing to the couch and extending a welcoming hand. "I'm Ann Jerome, and very glad to meet you."

"Hi!" The solemn handshake was as brief as the greeting. "I know—Grandma says you live next door and have the loveliest garden in town. When can I see it?"

"Any time," Ann assured her. "Is Aunt—Grandma here?"

"No, she went to the store." Kathy's sober face crinkled in an elfin grin. "Mother forgot to pack my pajamas and Grandma had to go buy some. She was quite disgusted with Mother," she confided while absently leaning forward to sniff Ann's armful of roses. "M-m-m!" she sighed, rolling up her eyes.

"Here, have a flower, all to yourself." Ann detached

one of the long-stemmed beauties and presented it. "Is Mabel here?"

"Who's she?"

"The maid. If you don't know her I guess she's out or you'd have met her by now. I'll find a vase for these myself."

"I'll go with you!" The little girl slid from the couch, revealing a wrinkled wool shirt of dashing plaid and even more wrinkled dungarees. In bare feet she padded beside Ann to the hall. There inspiration struck her and she caught Ann's hand.

"Uncle Myles is here!" she exclaimed. "He probably knows where there's a vase. I'll call him." She copied Ann's previous hail in a screech which would have waked the dead. "Yoo-hoo, *Uncle Myles!*"

It brought Myles Langdon out of his room and to the head of the stairs in a frantic rush, dreading to see what catastrophe had befallen his niece. Instead he found her completely comfortable and calm, but holding by the hand such a vision of beauty that his anxious scowl cleared to a flashing smile with much the spectacular effect of the sun breaking through a cloud.

He felt every nerve tingle as he stared at Ann, spotlighted by a shaft of light from the hall window, her cheeks dimpled with laughter, eyes sparkling, parted lips more red than the roses in her arms. A soft hat of deeper shade than the striking blue of her suit perched at a rakish angle on gleaming black hair.

He drew in a long breath and braced his hands on the stair rail.

Ann laughed again. "Hello, there! You came out like a jack-in-the-box, mad enough to bite!"

"Not mad at all—petrified," he corrected with a sheepish grin and shook a finger at Kathy. "You tone down that yell or you'll have me a nervous wreck, *gatita!*"

The child giggled. "That means 'kitten' in South American," she whispered to Ann before she saluted Myles with a careful, *"Si, señor!* He's teaching me Spanish, but that's all I know so far," she confided.

"Plenty of time," Myles encouraged and shifted his eyes to Ann. "Well, fellow banker, I see that you've shed your somber business uniform for a gayer ensemble. What can

I do for you now that you've sprung me from my lair?"

"Where can I find a vase for these?" She held up the flowers. "A friend sent them—showered me with roses, in fact, to the tune of a double dozen. I thought Aunt Pam would like some of them."

Myles surprised himself by the sharpness of his demand, "Who sent them?"

"A friend, as I said. If you insist on more details, he's a cousin of Betty Wilder. She works at the bank, in case you don't remember? He was at her barbecue Sunday night. Enough identification?"

"So that's who—I mean, where you were," Myles growled. "Almost next door! Funny, I went over to your house, neither of you girls were there, and Sarah claimed she didn't know where you took off to."

"Maybe I forgot to tell her," Ann suggested in as offhand a manner as possible. Of course Sarah would be mum if Sonia was out with Joe Snell, but why should she extend that protection to Ann? It was not a subject to discuss with Myles, though, so she waved the roses and reminded, "How about a vase?"

"Hmm, both Aunt Pam and Mabel are out, aren't they." He scratched his chin with the sheaf of papers in his hand. "I haven't any idea where they keep such things. Tell you what! Bring them up and we'll stick them in one of my tennis trophies until Aunt Pam gets home. The Country Club Singles cup is a tall, skinny thing—just right."

VIII

"Excuse the mess," Myles said when they entered his room. He took a high silver cup from the bookcase and dispatched Kathy to fill it with water. Then, with a wave at the battered wooden packing case surrounded by a litter of crumpled papers and blueprints, he explained, "You caught me in the midst of house cleaning."

"Obviously!" Ann laughed. "What *is* all that?"

"My engineering stuff's in the box; they sent it up from the job when I was—when we had to quit. Those papers were on top; out-of-date estimates, notes, a lot of junk. Don't know why they put them in, unless for padding—or maybe someone was in a hurry and just swept my desk clean. Haven't even got down through it to check my things. Don't know that I will," he muttered. "I won't be needing them again."

Ann noticed with a throb of sympathy that he kept his left thumb in his belt to support his arm. She longed to offer him some encouragement but could think of nothing which would not sound artificial, and so remained silent until Kathy returned with the cup.

Ann arranged the roses as well as she could in the slender container and asked, "Kathy, can you take this downstairs without spilling?"

"Sure!"

The little girl disappeared and was back in a few moments staring wide-eyed at the packing case, tiptoeing toward it cautiously.

"Is that a treasure chest from South America, Uncle Myles?" she whispered.

He laughed. "That's where it's from, but no treasure."

"It looks very int'resting anyway." She poked a tentative finger among the papers on top and suddenly drew back. "Any spiders—or snakes in it?"

"Good Lord, no! Nothing but what you see and some instruments underneath. Go ahead and rummage, *gatita.*"

He glanced at the papers which he still held, crumpled them and tossed them into the wastebasket beside his desk.

"Ooh, binoculars!" Kathy exclaimed. "Can I look through them, Uncles Myles? I know how; Daddy has some, too." She took permission for granted and skipped over to the window.

"One thing I enjoyed in the wilds," Myles told Ann while they watched the child adjust the glasses, open the

window and lean out. "With those you could pick out all
kinds of exotic insects and animals, even when they were
in the tree-tops."

"Ann, is that your house with the brick end?" Kathy
asked from the window. "It must be; I never saw such
a garden! Someone's just come out on the bank in back."

"*Terrace*, please," Ann laughed. "You must have supper out there with us soon, Kathy, before it gets too cold.
What's the 'someone' look like? A tall, gray-haired woman
or a small one with *very* lovely golden hair?"

"It's the golden one, and she's laughing."

"A very good description of my sister Sonia, isn't it,
Myles?" She arched an eyebrow at him. "The golden
one!"

"There's a man with her," Kathy announced, "and he's
got yellow hair, too. Who's he?"

It was no help to find Myles questioning her with a
look. Ann's heart plunged into her shoes. She fought down
sudden panic and spoke quietly.

"That's probably Sonia's boss at the foundry; he sometimes drives her home—if they've worked late or something like that."

"Joe Snell?" Myles nodded. "I met him at the bank
—same old Joe," he said noncommittally. "Drives Sunny
home, does he?"

"S-sometimes, yes." Ann tried to make it careless and
unimportant. "Kathy, you'd better come in—it would be
dreadful if you dropped those binoculars."

"I won't—I'm awful careful." But the little girl was
eager to explore the box further and gave the glasses to
Myles without objection.

"One souvenir of my Loma misadventure that I'll keep
with pleasure," he admitted, studying them with a reminiscent smile.

"Wowie!" Kathy whooped. "Is this a sheath knife, like
pirates wear?" She tugged a narrow tan leather case from
the big box and held it up.

"Sorry to crush romance," Myles admitted with mock
sadness. "It's only a plebeian slide rule, the engineer's best
friend. It wouldn't interest you, chuck it back."

"No, wait!" Ann protested. "Could I borrow it, Myles?
I've been urging Sunny to try using one for her figuring

at the foundry, because she constantly has to check reports and estimates, and it takes her hours. I'm sure it would help her a lot."

"Yes, she'll save a lot of time if she can use it." Myles took the rule from Kathy and handed it to Ann.

"I'll show her how to use it; I learned at college." Ann sat down, pulled open the flap at one end and drew the rule partway out. "If she's interested I might give her one for Christmas. Not like this, I'm afraid—it's too elegant, and complicated." Replacing the rule she closed the case. "Your initials in gold on the side, too! Aren't you the sport! Must have been terribly expensive."

"Well, that's one of the fanciest, but I didn't buy it. The Los Angeles office force gave it to me, sort of a going-away present when I left for South America."

"Then I wouldn't think of borrowing it!"

"Go ahead." Myles waved her away when she offered to return it. "I'll let you in on a secret; I didn't use it much. A fellow gets accustomed to the feel of a rule, and a different one seems awkward. So I kept this on my desk, where any of the gang could see it, and went on figuring on my old one. I have that at the bank now."

"A slide rule at the bank, with all the electric adding machines and computers we have?" Ann laughingly protested. "Isn't that carrying coals to Newcastle?"

"I suppose it is, but—" He ended his hesitation with a resigned shrug and muttered, "I guess the truth is that figuring on the old rule is sort of an opiate; for a minute I forget that I'm stuck in an office job. Sometimes I can almost hear Red Fallon yelling at a crew, and the slamming of drills on ledge in the Loma River."

Myles shook his head soberly, walked to the window and stared out at the sunset sky.

Ann's eyes stung with tears at his revelation of what she had suspected; Myles Langdon was resigned to abandoning what he wanted most to do, but the longing would always be there. She swallowed the lump in her throat and spoke gaily.

"I'll bet anything you'll be back engineering before too long," she challenged.

"I've heard for years about 'a one-armed paper-hanger' but never a one-armed engineer."

"Your arm isn't *permanently* disabled, is it?" At last she came out with the question which had been on the tip of her tongue ever since his return. "If it's only damage to the nerves—a neurosis or something, Aunt Pam says —it will right itself in time. At least she thinks so—and so do I!"

"Aunt Pam is an incurable optimist," Myles growled. "Wish I had some of her courage—along with my neurosis or whatever."

"What did the doctors say? Didn't they tell you that your arm would cure itself in time?"

"Doctors aren't in the habit of going on record with prophecies like that."

Myles had spent too many sleepless nights tortured by these same questions to endure them again. Why risk bitter disappointment by kidding himself that some miracle might restore the strength to his arm. He shrugged and turned to Kathy, who was still burrowing in the packing case.

"Now what have you dug up, *gatita?*"

"A dirty old book with a pome in it. Listen—" She squinted at a crumpled piece of paper and read:

> "The Spanish call love something grand,
>   But I don't know there lingo.
> Manuel, Julio, Don Jose do—
>   And there the tops, by jingo!"

"What in the world is that?" Ann demanded. "Myles, don't tell me you took to poetry down there!"

"Never! That isn't mine."

"Oh, no? Circumstantial evidence says differently!"

"Wait a minute now." He took the book and paper from his niece. "I thought so," he laughed, "the minute I heard that 'pome.' This is my daybook—I guess *you* would call it a diary—in which I kept a day-to-day account of what happened on the job."

"And what happened," Ann jeered, "to cause that outpouring of deathless verse?"

"Not guilty! You see, from the notes in this book my clerk, Walter Bruce, would type up reports to the home office."

Myles sat down and leafed through a few pages, thinking of the man who had disappeared after the explosion.

"Nice, inoffensive young fellow, Walter was—but
slightly crazy," he continued. "Wrote poetry to a girl back
here—name of Alice and she lived in New York, I believe. Every so often Bruce would be smitten with an inspiration and dash off a world-shaking lyric to his distant
lady love."

"In your diary—daybook, I mean?"

"Oh, no! Usually on the back of our copy of a report
or any handy scrap of paper." He turned over the piece
he held. "This looks like part of the list of a shipment
from the coastal office to our camp. Just the thing for a
rough draft, to be carefully copied later."

He handed her the slip of paper and smiled.

"As you can see, this is *extremely* rough."

"What a dreadful scrawl! And what awful spelling!"

"Poetic license, I guess. After all, the 'pome' is the
thing, or at least, so I've heard."

There was an interruption when Mrs. Leslie called from
the lower hall.

"Kathy! I'm home, and wait till you see the pajamas
I picked out for you!"

"Coming!"

The girl dashed for the stairs, then the patter of her
bare feet ceased, to be followed by a swishing sound, a
thud and a triumphant whoop.

"Down the banister!" Ann sighed. "I envy her; it's a
wonderful rail to slide on, as I know from experience."

When Myles made no comment she realized that he was
far away, frowning at the book open on his knee while
he fingered his scarred cheek. She laid the poem on the
book.

"I suppose your struggling poet was in love and therefore unaccountable," she said soberly.

He nodded, crumpled the paper and threw it into the
wastebasket.

"Yup! How the men kidded him! Called him 'the Jukebox Troubador' and worse. His scribbling was a nuisance
sometimes, but otherwise he was plenty smart—and a
good clerk is hard to find down there. In fact it's hard
to find anything *good* in Loma!"

Ann reached for the stained leather volume which he had tossed on the desk.

"This is really a report of what you did down there?" The thought that this slim book held the tale of all he had accomplished in those long months away made her voice tremble when she said, "I'd love to read it, may I?"

"If you want to, but you'll find it pretty dull." He rose and began to replace the scattered papers in the box. "Don't expect any adventure story. That whole deal was one headache after another from the start and the book doesn't do much more than list them."

"It will be interesting to me," Ann assured him. "Why are you putting things back in there? I thought you were *un*packing."

"What's the use? It's nothing but junk now. I'll nail down the lid of this coffin and forget it!"

"Oh." She recognized the bitterness of defeat in his voice and yearned to cheer him somehow, but she could think of nothing worth saying. She tucked slide rule and daybook under her arm and went to the door.

"Thanks for everything, Myles—I'll be seeing you."

"Sure." He did not look up from the box.

Ann went down the stairs inwardly berating her complete failure as a comforting angel. There must be some way to encourage a disappointed man without sounding like Pollyana!

In thc lower hall she was engulfed in a maelstrom of excitement by Mrs. Leslie, breathless with thanks for the roses, and Kathy, who clamored for immediate approval of her new candy-striped pajamas. When the girl departed to lay them out on her bed, Mrs. Leslie beckoned Ann to the living room.

"You and Sunny are coming for dinner, aren't you?" she reminded unnecessarily—and loudly. Then, in case her granddaughter might be lingering on the stairs, she lowered her voice to a conspiratorial whisper.

"How does Myles seem? You've been talking to him, haven't you? What do you think?"

"Calm down and stop worrying about him," Ann advised. "He'll come through with flying colors, Aunt Pam. Just give him time to adjust."

"I hope you're right—I'm sure you are. But it wrings my heart to wait. He isn't the easygoing, cheerful boy he was when he went away."

"Did you expect," Ann asked indignantly, "that being in that terrible place and what happened to him wouldn't change him?"

Mrs. Leslie sighed and shook her head.

"I guess I—I just didn't think. Of course, what he has been through must have brought every nerve in his body to the surface and rubbed it raw."

Absently she drew off her gloves, folded them and tucked them in a pocket.

"I do hope that's it, because—" She hesitated, went to the piano and changed the position of some of the grasses in the copper bowl. "Has Sonia talked about any plans for their marriage?"

"No, not yet." A discussion of that subject was the last thing Ann wanted; she moved toward the front door.

"Is she"—Pamela Leslie took a quick breath and rushed at the question which tormented her—"is she stalling because of his injuries? That scar on his cheek is still horrid!"

"I think it has faded noticeably," Ann differed with conviction, "even in the few days he's been home. I scarcely notice it any more."

"Really—I'm glad!" Her aunt accompanied her to the door and there eyed her soberly. "Then you don't believe *that* is what bothers Sonia?"

"No, I don't." Remembering her sister's account of the lovers' meeting, she blurted, "It isn't Sunny who's holding back, Aunt Pam—it's Myles." And instantly regretted the impulsive disclosure. In her automatic defense of Sonia had she betrayed a confidence?

"So that's it!" Mrs. Leslie nodded with satisfaction. "I shouldn't wonder if something, somewhere in that awful country, finally reawakened his sense of values and jarred his emotions back into their true place."

"You sound like a medical treatise," Ann derided, "and I haven't the faintest idea what you're talking about, but if Myles got anything beneficial out of his ordeal I'm glad —and very surprised."

Aunt Pamela smiled. "It does seem unbelievable, but

I've discovered in my fairly long and observant life that good sometimes comes from evil."

Following this cryptic utterance she retired into the house, where Ann heard her humming gaily.

Ann turned the puzzling observation this way and that in her mind as she walked home but could make nothing of it, except to class it as one more of Aunt Pam's proverbs, her family's label for that lady's occasional bursts of wide-eyed wisdom.

IX

Ordinarily Pamela Leslie was a model of patience, but her brief conversation with Ann suggested such possibilities that she lost no time in making further investigation. While they awaited the arrival of dinner guests she sat on the couch beside Myles, plying her knitting needles on a red and gray sock, and covertly checked up on the other occupants of the living room.

Dungarees replaced by a brown jumper, Kathy sprawled inelegantly on the love seat in a far corner, apparently immersed in a book. John Leslie was equally comfortable, although more formal, in his favorite armchair, with the discarded *Wall Street Journal* across his knees and his nose buried in a detective story. Pamela knew that once he took up the chase of a criminal nothing less than a stroke of lightning could distract his attention.

She glanced at Myles, who was leaning forward, elbow on knee, watching new flames lick around the log just added to the fire. He, like his uncle, had dressed for dinner at her urging; this first general reunion of the two families, she'd insisted, deserved special recognition, and she'd done her part by christening a new ecru lace sheath.

She held up the sock, audibly counted stitches, and then lowered her voice to ask:

"Myles, have you and Sonia set a date yet?"

He shook his head without taking his eyes from the fire.

"Haven't discussed it, Aunt Pam. Give her time to recover from the shock of seeing the wreck who came back to her."

"Don't talk that way! Don't even think it!" His aunt recovered her poise and spoke quietly. "I should think she wouldn't even have noticed, would have rushed blindly into your arms on sight!"

"Hardly." He slanted a look at her, wondering if she suspected that a certain girl had done just that. "You're too romantic, dear Aunt, but Sunny isn't, thank goodness! Deliver me from a wife blinded by love, expecting a perpetual honeymoon!"

"What sort of a wife *do* you want?"

Myles rubbed the scar on his cheek, leaned back, and stared at the dancing flames.

"One like you, Aunt Pam," he said unexpectedly. "A woman who knows the going may be rough now and then, but is willing to make adjustments—and expects the party of the second part to reciprocate—knows that there may be difficulties to overcome, but knows, too, that the rewards will more than repay the sacrifices."

"You are describing a real, till-death-do-us-part relationship. For one so young, you have evidently given it a lot of thought."

"Had plenty of time for that during these last months," he muttered. He took up the poker and jabbed a shower of sparks from the burning logs. "After all, when I build a bridge I put in all the knowledge and experience I've acquired to make it stand up against any strain. Isn't that the way to build a successful marriage?"

"It is." Mrs. Leslie's fingers lay quiet on her work. "But it needs two of the same mind to make it succeed."

"Sure." Myles divined her thought and answered it with a shrug and the advice, "Sunny is still young—give her a chance to get her growth."

At the murmur of voices from the porch he stood up.

"And here, on a well-timed cue," he laughed, "enter the Sisters Jerome!"

The dinner was as festive as Mrs. Leslie had hoped.

Never did her ivory lace tablecloth glow more richly or the crystal goblets and silver shine with greater luster.

This was Kathy's introduction to formal dining, because her father's tours of duty had been at obscure foreign outposts as far back as she could remember, and she reveled in it. Her black bangs were slicked down like patent leather, a fresh red ribbon held the pony-tail, and her wide and sparkling eyes added a touch of enchantment to the scene.

She was particularly bewitched by the Jerome sisters, who, as they sometimes enjoyed doing, wore identically styled dresses, but in contrasting colors. And her eyes really bugged out at Ann's gorgeous pearls and Sonia's flashing rings.

They all watched with amusement while Mr. Leslie carved the imposing roast of beef and blandly ignored the advice breathed on his neck by stout, beaming Mabel from her post behind "the master's" chair. Twenty years ago Mrs. Leslie had given up hope of properly training the young girl from Dublin and settled for loyal service in place of finesse.

Once the party got under way there was no pause in the gaiety except for one period during which they listened eagerly to Myles Langdon. That was when, in answer to a question from Uncle John, he began to describe the South American wilds, Loma, and his life there.

He intended to give only a brief picture, but one bit of local color reminded him of another until he became absorbed in memories. Leaning back with half-shut eyes, his fingers twirling the glass at his place, he talked steadily, and by degrees the comfortable Leslie dining room became a boiling, rushing brown river between towering trees, thickly garlanded with vines and gigantic flowering plants with musical foreign names.

Innumerable monkeys shrilled and chattered in the trees, birds like jewels and flame and gold flashed among the branches, unseen animals scuttled softly through the undergrowth, and deadly snakes, large and small, striped, mottled or ominous gleaming black, slithered across the clearing to slip from sight in the jungle beyond.

From that he drifted into telling of his work on the bridge, the satisfaction of seeing it creep out across the river day after day, his pride in the men who drove it forward under the broiling tropic sun and through stunning, blinding rain. Then slowly realizing that his voice had grown wistful, betraying his regret at the loss of that more active life, he switched quickly to a lighter note. His imitation of Red Fallon bullying the natives to greater effort with broken English and bad Spanish convulsed every listener.

In that happier vein the dinner progressed to the end.

All of them talked at will, Kathy's gurgles of laughter capping every joke, whether she understood them or not. And in the background Mabel, flushed with excitement, kept up a running fire of impudent comment while she served and indulged in a series of hummed Irish ballads which swelled or died away as she waddled back and forth between table and kitchen.

Afterward they gathered around the fire in the living room for coffee and mints and more laughter. At eight-thirty Kathy retired, by her aunt's decree rather than her own inclination, only to reappear shortly, modeling the new pajamas. She was blushingly responding to the applause when the doorbell rang.

In a moment Mabel ducked her head into the room, startling them with the brief and unenlightening announcement, "You got company!" and disappeared. In her place stood Cecile Parker, a camel's-hair coat draped over her white angora sweater and cocoa gabardine slacks. Behind her loomed Joe Snell in equally informal sports attire.

The immediate silence was stunning. Mr. Leslie and Myles rose from their chairs automatically, but made no move or greeting, and Mrs. Leslie was too surprised to speak. Ann caught her breath in disappointment and concern. All evening she had thanked her stars because everything proceeded so smoothly, with no suggestion of strain between Sunny and Myles. Their delight in the family reunion seemed to have submerged any personal feelings.

But what might happen now, with her sister's anxious eyes fixed on Snell? Cecile, too, was as obviously thrown off stride as everyone else. Ann felt sure that she had engineered this call to begin her campaign on Myles Langdon without delay; the presence of the others must be most disconcerting.

Even so, Cecile recovered first.

"A family party, isn't it!" she cried. "Sorry to bust in; Joe and I are going bowling at the Club." She waved the special shoes in her hand. "We thought Myles might like to come along, a chance to meet some of the old crowd."

"And Sonia, too, of course!" Snell added with a grin.

"Sure," Cecile agreed after a slight but noticeable hesitation. "Ann, too, for that matter. Make a party of it."

Myles came over to them, hands in pockets.

"Nice of you to think of me, but I'm afraid this isn't the night for it. First time we've all got together and—"

"Yeah. We see it's a family party, but so what?" Joe slouched against the door frame. "You used to be tops on the alleys, Langdon. Ought to get back in the swing. As a matter of fact, it was me suggested picking you up." His grin was mocking. "Figured bowling would be *one* thing you could do, even with a bum arm."

"Shut up, Joe!" Cecile's angry whisper drew a scowl from him and mental applause from Ann.

"Very thoughtful of you, Snell." Although Myles smiled, his voice grated. "But I can do quite a few things, even with one arm. You'd be surprised."

Snell straightened and stepped back a pace.

"Glad to hear it—that's fine! I just meant you ought to get back to bowling because Sonia spends so many evenings at it." His narrowed eyes glinted as he turned to the girl. "She just *loves* to bowl, don't you, Sunny?"

"Yes—yes, I do." She flushed and stammered, "I—I took it up while you were away, Myles."

"Kept her from being lonesome," Snell explained wryly.

"A lot has happened while I've been away," Myles said. "Got to catch up on everything, and this would be a good way to begin." He turned to his aunt and uncle. "You won't mind if we break up this party, will you?"

Aunt Pam gasped, "You're going to try *bowling?*"

"Why not?" he demanded. "Have to start living sometime. Who knows"—and he glanced at Snell—"I might prove that I'm still tops—at *something*. Sunny, skip over home and hop into your bowling togs. I'll change and be right with you. Want to come along, Ann?"

"No, thank you. Four is perfect for a match, I'd be a fifth wheel." She tried to sound disinterested for fear that he might insist. With those four people together, Cecile predatory, Sunny desperate, Joe Snell resentful and Myles in a dangerous mood, anything might happen. If there was to be an explosion she preferred to be far away.

"Run along, kids," she ordered gaily, "while I take on the aunt and uncle at gin rummy. I have a feeling this is my lucky night."

Her luck did not extend to cards, not even to the hands which she dealt her opponents, and before long Uncle John could barely conceal his yawns. By mutual consent the game broke up early.

Ann was glad to be home by ten-thirty, in a house so quiet that it was balm for her wracked emotions, storm-tossed by so many conflicting currents. Tonight had begun in blessed calm and ended in an agonizing mixture of rage at Sunny, contempt for Snell and apprehension for Myles. And Cecile? Cecile Parker might be the spark which set off heaven knew what disaster.

Resolutely she pushed her fears back into the depths of her mind and determined to forget what she couldn't help. It would be pleasant to relax alone for an hour or two. Sarah had gone to the movies, the delight of her days off, and even Monty, the springer, must have found the deserted house too boring and departed to seek excitement elsewhere. Unlike her active pet, Ann blessed the silence.

She felt a cool draft of air when she entered the living room, saw the roses on the center table stir gently. Someone had left the French door to the terrace open; she snuggled down in a wing chair near the fireplace. In a moment she would switch on the reading lamp beside her and browse through the diary—daybook—which she'd borrowed from Myles, but there was no hurry about that.

Dreamily she glanced around the dusky room lighted only by a drift of silvery moonlight across the Persian rug. The roses in the silver vase beside her recalled Henry Little and he in turn reminded her of the Wilders and their ultra-modern house. A charming couple, undoubtedly with excellent taste, but somehow she preferred furniture not quite so starkly functional—if that was the right word. How lucky that she had been born to parents who loved antiques!

The moonlight reached almost to the carved feet of the

tall Sheraton secretary, a masterwork of Charlestown's Revolutionary Major Frothingham. Behind its leaded glass doors gleamed great-great-grandmother's pink luster tea set. At this desk a very small Ann had practiced her first writing exercises; at the graceful Hepplewhite card table she had learned to play hearts. Before that Georgian mirror she had balanced on a Chippendale chair to admire the huge yellow bow on her dark hair before she fared forth on the breath-snatching adventure of her first party with Myles Langdon.

To right and left of the broad fireplace rose tier upon tier of books, most of them old and treasured friends. Dickens, the *Arabian Nights,* O. Henry. Even in the darkness she could have laid her hand directly on the elaborately bound volumes of Sir Walter Scott. How she once reveled in his stately romances. Every lovely lady in distress became Ann Jerome, and every valiant knight was Myles Langdon galloping to her rescue.

What was that? She straightened in the chair, holding her breath. A bush crackling somewhere in the garden? With a shaky laugh she relaxed; thinking of Scott's endless stream of adventures and brave knights in hazardous battle must have stirred her own imagination. Or was it *imagination?*

She held her breath to listen. That noise again; it did seem to come from the garden! But what of that? There were always sounds out there, the whisper of leaves under a gust of wind, the scuffle of Monty or a neighbor's dog inspecting the premises for furred or feathered intruders. She often sat here and heard them, evenings without number, and never thought them menacing, yet tonight she shivered, nervous as a four-year-old hearing her first ghost story.

It came to her then in a flash of amused resentment why she was jittery. *Charley Duval!* He had begun his new job at the bank, his attention divided between trying to hitch the regular guard's uniform coat to a better fit on his small frame and proudly fingering the end of the holster which showed below it. Whenever he passed her window he threw her a reassuring grin and wink as if to remind her that he was ever on the alert.

Darn that bloodthirsty old soldier with his gossip about

jewel thieves—the elegant Duke and his dangerous, clawing Tiger Cat partner. But how absurd to admit that she was zany enough to let it worry her!

Just the same she'd better lock that door, she advised herself impatiently. Stop huddling here like a dumbbell and *do* something. She jumped from the chair and hurried across the room.

As she reached the glass door her heart went into a nose dive and then pounded in panic. A dark figure was flitting through the garden toward the house; it ducked down and dived behind a clump of bushes.

A man! Had he seen her and taken cover? Quickly she closed and locked the door, backed away, stumbled over a footstool and regained her balance. One hand went to her throat and felt the string of pearls there; at their touch a grain of sense penetrated her fright.

The pearls were the only really valuable jewelry in the house because Sonia had worn her rings. With shaking fingers Ann undid the clasp and pushed the necklace deep behind the cushion in the wing chair. With them out of sight she would feel less uneasy—maybe.

Even that brief comfort vanished at the sudden ghostly tapping of fingers on the glass door, although she told herself shakily that it must be the wind whipping a vine on the trellis which covered the house wall up to the bedroom windows.

Why was she allowing imaginary dangers to drive her toward hysteria? There could be nothing to fear as long as the telephone stood ready to summon aid. Myles Langdon, next door, could be here in thirty seconds—No! He had gone out with Sunny! The Crandalls then, on the other side—but they had moved south months ago and their house was for rent!

As she discarded one hope after another Ann abruptly realized the course which she should have thought of first of all—the police! That's what they were for, wasn't it? To protect lone and terrified females. Suppose they came, found nothing and laughed at her. The dimly seen intruder, real or imaginary, might have disappeared by now.

She tiptoed to the door, peered out. Moonlight, starshine, silvery shrubs and purple shadows—Her heart gave another sickening plunge more violent than before. The man was still there, stooped over—skulking! And he was moving directly toward the terrace steps and the house!

X

The sight was enough—and more than enough—to send Ann racing across the dark room. In the hall she switched on the light over the telephone table and snatched up the handset. Thank heaven that her meticulous father had carefully printed police, fire and other emergency numbers on the cover of the directory.

Her fingers trembled so on the dial that she fumbled the first attempt. Gritting her teeth to restrain a sob of frustration, she tried again. Success—and the phlegmatic official voice which answered promptly was wonderfully soothing. To her surprise she was able to speak with deceptively cool restraint.

"This is Ann Jerome at Sunnyfield—32 Camden Road."

"Why, hello, Annie!" The sedate voice warmed with pleasure. "This is Ben Snowden. How are you? Is your Pa there?"

"No!" She hesitated. What a bother to have that garrulous old patrolman take her call. Still, as a lifelong friend of her father he deserved humoring. "Listen, Ben—Dad isn't here and I'm alone in the house—"

"That ain't a good idea, Annie! These days you can't tell what'll happen nights." He chuckled happily. "That's a good one, ain't it?"

"Will you stop laughing and listen!" Ann snapped, angered by a mental picture of the fat cop lolling in his chair and enjoying his own wit.

"Don't you get sassy, Annie! Just because I've known you since you was born—"

"Please, Ben! Pay attention! I tell you I'm alone here

and there's a man sneaking through the garden, coming toward the house!"

"Yeah?" The speed with which Snowden abandoned familiarity for duty was comforting. "In the garden, eh? That's back of your house, ain't it? Sure, I know the place. We'll have a car right out there, Ann—Miss Jerome, soon as I contact one! Hold on a second!"

She heard the murmur of excited voices through the phone. Ben's was closest, so his "Hell, yes! It could be the Duke!" came clearly. Then a jumble of more talk until he spoke to her.

"We think it may be a guy we're looking for, Miss Jerome, a housebreaker they call the Duke—"

"I know about him," she interrupted impatiently. "Please hurry!"

"On the way! We're coming out from here. You keep out of sight and leave the front door unlatched so we can get in quietly."

Ann licked dry lips and gripped the phone hard.

"But—suppose *he* slips in there!"

"It'll be the Duke's last slip—if it's him. Inside the house is just where we want him—catch him red-handed, see?"

"Well, *I* don't want him in here!"

"Don't worry, Annie. Lock yourself in your room and don't come out till the party's over. Get that? Don't come out! Gosh, a woman could mess up a job like this—"

"Oh, stop talking!" she cut in. "Get busy!"

Slapping down the phone, she squared her shoulders, fear swallowed up in indignation. Old Snowden always did ramble on endlessly; no wonder he was still only a patrolman. So she was to lock herself in her room? Not a chance! She would certainly be among those present when the Duke met his Waterloo.

Icily cool now, she unlatched the front door and tiptoed to the living room for another reconnaissance. One step inside the doorway she froze; all her former fright seemed nothing to this. Were those *eyes* glaring at her from the terrace? The light behind her was reflected in two shining sparks halfway up the French door.

As she bit her lip to steady it the eyes vanished. A shadow blacked out the moonlight on the rug and the trellis creaked, and then splintered—the door crashed open with a shower of glass. A man's body sagged against the casing and settled slowly down across the threshold.

Ann looked back from the hallway where her flying feet had taken her of their own volition. When the intruder remained perfectly motionless, she edged into the room. Had the thief actually knocked himself out? Her fear departed to be replaced by a rush of bravado; suppose she captured him before the police arrived! How she would love to make Ben Snowden eat his words, by proving that here was one woman who wouldn't mess up a job.

In spite of her unexpected courage she held her breath as she crept to the fireplace, seized the brass-handled poker and cautiously advanced. The man lay crumpled on his side, so evidently unconscious that the last of her jitters left her. She set her weapon within easy reach before she grasped his arm and with much tugging and panting dragged the unresisting body into the room. When he lay clear of the door and face down on the rumpled rug, she retrieved the poker and switched on the lights.

Their comforting glow on the pine-paneled walls dispelled the sense of nightmare; once more the tall secretary, the tables and chairs stood revealed as sturdy, dependable friends. A clump of bronze chrysanthemums in the silver bowl on the end of the mantel shed a leaf which spiraled slowly to the hearth, landing with a tiny click as though to assure her of its reality.

A convulsive movement by the man on the floor startled her. He pushed up on hands and knees, caught a chair and with its support staggered upright. Then he sank into it and sat with drooping head while he panted for breath. There was blood trickling down his cheek, and more on one hand. At the sound Ann made when she moved toward him he looked up with heavy eyes and twisted his lips in an ironic grin.

"Greetings!" he said in a husky whisper, grasped the arms of the chair and tried to stand. The effort contorted his face in a grimace of pain and he shut his eyes.

"Stay where you are!" Ann commanded, brandishing the poker.

"Might as well," he muttered thickly. "The Cat's made her getaway now, no use looking for her. Boy, how my head spins!" The last words dragged, his head fell forward on his chest.

Ann stood transfixed, a prey to powerful—but sadly mixed—emotions. The Cat! Her getaway! So she had actually caught the notorious Duke, even though his dreaded accomplice, the Tiger Cat, had escaped! How she could laugh at Ben Snowden and his fellow minions of the law! Only she had never felt less like laughing in her life; the one short look she'd had of this man's face took all the pleasure out of the capture.

It was a pale face, streaked with blood, but attractive in spite of that—certainly handsome enough for any man who was not a screen hero. There was character in it, she thought, character further attested by the automatic attempt he'd made to rise when he saw her. The Duke's hands, which had gone limp on the arms of the chair, were slender but gave an impression of strength; his fair hair had an engaging suggestion of wave in the rumpled locks. His suit of a brown heather mixture and the lighter tan sweater became him well, and the cordovan loafers—

The shoes were a slight damper on her enthusiasm; they had thick crepe-rubber soles, most suitable for a housebreaker and jewel thief. That's what he was, and she had sent for the police to arrest him. But her heart was no longer in it. Officer Snowden's opinion of women still rankled. And just *where*, by the way, she asked herself with withering sarcasm, were the redoubtable Ben and his helpers? If they expected her to hold a dangerous second-story worker at bay until they finished their pinochle game—!

She would do no such thing. The Duke had come to steal *her* property, therefore it was entirely up to her what became of him. Let the police catch their own lawbreakers. She refused to hand over this attractive man who seemed so injured and dazed that he would be helpless to defend himself.

At any moment the squad car might roar into the drive. Where could she hide the Duke so that they wouldn't find him? Snowden's advice suggested the place; instead of herself she could lock her captive in her room. Ben Snowden wouldn't look there.

Ann hurried to the front door, snapped the catch, tried the outside knob to make sure the lock was on and closed it firmly. Strange that all her fears had evaporated now, when the skulking man of the moonlit garden was here in the house.

Calmly, as she returned to the living room, she considered how to get him up the stairs. First of all she must rouse him from his faint. She crossed to the fireplace, removed the mums from their silver bowl, and carried it carefully over to him.

"Wake up!" she ordered loudly. "The police are coming!" She poured the water onto his hanging head.

"Oof!" With a sweep of his undamaged hand the man knocked the bowl aside, staggered to his feet and shook himself like Monty coming out of a brook. "The police?" he sputtered, pawing at trickles of water running down his neck while he stared at her. "You"—he pointed a shaking finger at her and blinked—*"you* called the police? You don't know who I am—"

"But I do, and so do the police. Don't worry, Duke," Ann said gently, for the horrified glare of the brown eyes was unnerving, "I'm giving you a chance to get your grip and then make your own getaway." How easily she fell into the underworld slang! "Come on, I'm going to hide you until they leave."

Still eying her, the man pulled a handkerchief from his pocket, wiped water and blood from his face, and then wrapped it around his damaged hand.

"Well—thanks!" he muttered, gave an hysterical laugh and choked it off. "Promise you won't let them arrest me?"

"It's a promise." Ann grasped his arm and steered him on a wavering course to the hall.

There he clutched the newel post and huddled over it.

"Hold everything," he begged breathlessly, resting his forehead on the banister. His shoulders quivered. "Sue! Sue! What I suffer for you!" he moaned.

Still thinking of his partner, Ann told herself crossly. So the Tiger Cat was "Sue"—probably with a feline hiss! How could a decent man fall for a tough girl, let her lead him astray? The Duke might have remained an honest man but for that!

A cautious tap on the front door brought her heart into

her mouth and ended the moralizing. Ben Snowden at last! She prodded her captive savagely.

"Stand up!" she urged wildly. "The police are at the door! Up the stairs—quick!"

"Okay, I can make it," he mumbled. "Quit pulling me!"

As they staggered to the top the knocking grew louder and obviously impatient. Ann hurried him through the sitting room to her bedroom and switched on the light, steadied him to the bed and hastily twitched off the immaculate spread. The man stretched out with a grateful sigh.

"Don't make a sound, Duke!" she cautioned. "I'll lock the door and come back as soon as I get rid of them."

The brown eyes looking up at her twinkled.

"How come you keep calling me that?" he whispered.

"I told you I knew!"

Grinning, he shook his head in admiration.

"What a girl! Watch yourself now with the cops! And thanks!"

He might be a hard-boiled crook, with an accomplice named *Sue*—ugh!—but he was fascinating, Ann decided while she locked the bedroom door. The whole affair was incredible, her own reactions most of all. Would she awaken in the wing chair, and find, like Alice in Wonderland, that it was all a wild and nonsensical dream?

Voices below! The police were in the house! She scurried down the stairs.

The living room seemed alive with blue uniforms. Portly, grizzled Ben Snowden, with bulging eyes and outthrust head, resembled a bloodhound on the trail. He and a taller, swarthy patrolman were watching a third man wearing a sergeant's stripes as he stooped to inspect the dark water stain on the rug.

"Well, you *finally* arrived!" Ann was surprised at the cool detachment of her voice.

The sergeant answered the gibe with his own complaint.

"Why didn't you leave the front door unlocked, like Snowden told you? We had to come 'round to this broken one to get in! Held us up plenty, Miss Jerome."

"I did, but you were so long in coming that I was afraid and locked it again." A nifty comeback, Ann thought.

The sergeant grunted. "A big help!" He jerked a thumb at the French door. "Did you hear that smash?" His boots crunched on the scattered glass as he walked to it. "What busted it, anyway?"

"Probably the wind blew it open. It crashed right after I thought I heard someone on the trellis under my window."

She realized at once that she had made a stupid mistake as the sergeant's narrowed eyes fastened on her. She must cover it. Glibly she went on, "It could have been my hectic imagination—about the trellis, I mean. Nobody climbed into my room, I assure you. I was in it when I heard your voices and came down."

All perfectly true, she thought with smug satisfaction at her cleverness, and smiled at Officer Snowden.

"How have you been, Ben?"

"Okay," he growled, self-consciously putting the hand which gripped a large black revolver behind his back. "Look, we were all around the house and didn't see anyone, so he must've been inside. If you'd left the door open we'd have had him! Like I said, a woman can mess anything—"

"He had time to run a mile before you got here!" Ann reminded with spirit.

"All right!" snapped the sergeant, flushing, "so we were late. The Duke's a slippery one, though, and since we're here now, we'll give this place a check from cellar to roof." He strode to the hall while the others trailed after him. After a moment's survey he asked, "Any back stairs, Miss Jerome?"

"No."

"Good!" He nodded at the dark-faced patrolman. "Blaney, you take a stand here; you've got everything covered from this hall. Snowden, come with me; the cellar first and then this floor."

Blaney backed against the front door, fists on hips, his revolver ready in his right hand. He was still there, immovable as a statue, when the sergeant, Ben and Ann returned from their unexciting search of the basement, dining room, kitchen, and Mr. Jerome's study.

The party mounted the stairs and Ann wondered if the

men could hear the pounding of her heart. She'd better make conversation to muffle it!

"Do you know what the Duke looks like, Ben?" she asked.

"Nothing definite. We told you he's slippery; only been seen at a distance. Know more about his side-kick. They caught her once, but she got away."

"So I heard." Ann meant to continue the idle chatter but the sergeant silenced her with a scowl. Meekly she followed them through one bedroom after another. Then her sitting room, Sonia's room. And then the sergeant turned the doorknob of her own room.

"Hey, it's locked!" he grunted.

While the two officers stared at her Ann's brain whirled sickeningly. Why hadn't it entered her feeble mind that this would be the logical result of the search? How to explain the Duke stretched out on her bed, with the door locked and its key still clenched in her fist? Could they jail *her* for hiding him? Wait! They didn't know what he looked like; she'd claim he was her brother. Darn! Ben Snowden knew she'd never had a brother!

"Come on, come on!" rasped the sergeant. "Where's the key?"

Reluctantly she handed it to him.

"I—I guess I was too scared to know what I was doing—"

"Keep back!" He seemed to unlock the door and swing it open in one lightning motion. He and Ben stepped in together, their guns poised.

Fearfully Ann peered over the broad blue shoulders. The bed was empty, its spread back in place without a wrinkle. Not a sign that suggested anyone had been there. Where was he? Her eyes flew around the room and she flinched. Was that reddish smear near the doorknob of the closet blood? Did that furtive rustle come from the closet?

The men heard it, too, and the revolvers swung that way. Snowden glanced back at her and frowned.

"Get out, Annie!" His lips formed the words without sound. Noiselessly he moved toward the closet with outstretched hand.

The door was not shut tight; it jerked gently as though someone inside were pushing it. The sergeant's gun motioned Ben away and came back to the door.

"Come out with your hands up! You're covered!" he warned harshly.

Slowly, silently, the door was pushed open. A huge black cat gave it one final nudge, walked delicately to the edge of the rug and sat down. A pink tongue licked the ruffled fur to satin smoothness and then large topaz eyes regarded the two men and the girl with that stare of utter indifference which only a cat can manage.

Ann caught her suspended breath with a choking gasp, sank onto a chair and shook with nervous laughter.

"Think it's funny?" snarled the sergeant, lowering his revolver. "Been a real joke if I'd shot your cat, wouldn't it! I damn near did!"

Relief made Ann lightheaded.

"Don't shoot till you see the whites of their eyes, Sergeant!" she giggled, and went off into another burst of laughter.

Growling, the two men went on with their tour and left Ann to recover her poise. She regarded the stolid cat with a mixture of admiration and curiosity. A beautiful animal sporting an elegant collar of tooled silver links; obviously feline royalty. But how did it come to be in her closet? It must have slipped in at the window when her late prisoner slipped out; that had been his only possible way of escape.

Perhaps he, like the sergeant, had assumed that it belonged to her. However it had happened, she was relieved; the Duke was off her hands for better or for worse and the black cat would be easily disposed of. Just as well to do that now, before Monty came home!

Ann opened the window invitingly; the cat arose, indulged in a prolonged and luxurious stretch before leaping out to the porch roof and melting into the darkness, the rattle of the trellis indicating its course.

When the officers returned from a search of the attic, Ann followed them downstairs.

"Guess we lost him," the sergeant informed Blaney while all three holstered their guns. "Nothing more we can do here—unless we leave a guard outside. Want that, Miss Jerome?"

"What in the world for? We aren't sure there was anyone here, are we? Let's forget it and put it down to my lively imagination. I'm terribly grateful to you all and sorry to cause so much trouble."

Protesting their willingness to serve her, the men went out to their car and drove away. Ann replaced the trusty poker in its stand, retrieved the silver bowl and filled it with water in the kitchen. When the chrysanthemums again brightened the mantel, she started to jam the broken door shut. Before she could close it, feet pattered on the terrace and Monty trotted in.

"Just like a man!" Ann reproved the springer as she propped a chair under the doorknob and drew the hangings together. "Where were *you* when I needed help? Out gallivanting around town!"

XI

At ten o'clock on Saturday morning Myles Langdon turned his uncle's car into the Jerome driveway, stopped at the front door and and leaned back with a satisfied sigh. This was his maiden attempt at driving while one arm was out of commission. Up to now he had gone to and from town by the bus line at the end of the street; on other occasions either Sonia or friends furnished transportation.

This morning, however, Sunny had telephoned breathlessly that her car was in the shop, and she must attend a committee meeting at the Country Club. Ann was gone with her convertible; *could* she borrow one of the Leslies' cars? She was late, hurrying to dress; *could* Myles bring it over? Oh, thanks a million!

It had given a lift to his spirits to have her ignore his damaged arm; he would have liked even more to believe that she had forgotten it, but that seemed too much to hope for. Anyway, if he didn't intend to baby himself for the rest of his life, this was as good a time as any to try his wings. The success of even the short drive to the Jerome house had greatly increased his confidence.

When Sonia dashed down the steps he slid from the seat and grinned.

"Taxi, *señorita?*" He bowed her behind the wheel and took his place beside her.

As they raced toward town he realized for the first time since his return that Sonia hadn't changed in one respect. She drove with brisk competence but too fast, too determined to beat out the other driver, too impatient on the horn. He remembered always being nervous when she was at the wheel, his foot automatically stamping on an imaginary brake when she whisked too close to the car ahead or raced across an intersection in the face of oncoming traffic.

Today he sat relaxed; not a nerve quivered when she cut in front of a truck and swished around a corner on whining tires. Maybe what he'd gone through on the Loma job had insulated him against any violent emotion. Would it be permanent? he wondered, settling into a more comfortable position. Right now he felt as much at ease as though he were riding with Ann.

How different the sisters were in this respect. In his opinion Ann was the perfect driver—smooth, cool, considerate of others; he preferred to ride with her any day. Yet Sunny, so far as he knew, had never been in an accident while Ann's car had twice suffered damage. Queer how often Fate picked on those who least deserved misfortune.

Take the Loma bridge, for example. For months on that job he'd drilled caution and safety into the workers and was bringing them through without a single serious mishap. Then the rebels struck and, bang—five shattered men in the hospital! They were out now, thank God, all but Red Fallon, who wrote that he expected his discharge soon. The fate of the missing man was not known; still no trace of Walter Bruce, and it weighed on his mind.

Maybe he should have talked to Bruce, advised him against too much fraternizing with the natives because one could never be sure whether they were rebels or not—or even spies for one side or the other. But Bruce, although he acted like a kid at times, was actually only a few years younger than himself; it would have been presumptuous to ride herd on him.

When the car stopped he came back to the present with a start and held the door open as Sonia slid along the seat and stepped out beside him in the Country Club parking lot.

"This meeting won't take long," she advised as they walked toward the clubhouse, "but afterward I want to talk to Ellen Shaw about the Halloween dance program. Do you mind waiting?"

"At your service, *señorita*."

"Then amuse yourself here for perhaps an hour and you can drop me at the Harrisons' for lunch. After that you're free."

Myles sat before the smoldering fire in the lounge and idly leafed through several magazines without finding anything of sufficient interest to divert his thoughts. They were on a treadmill, endlessly wondering how much longer Sonia would insist on continuing this intolerable engagement.

He had believed that he loved her when he left for South America, but, as month after month dragged by down there, he became increasingly certain that he didn't. To return, demand an end to the engagement and meet her violent refusal was a shock he wouldn't forget. Not that he blamed Sunny. Under the circumstances, no doubt a lot of people would have called her a poor sport if nothing worse. Pretty stupid of him not to have anticipated that.

Myles welcomed an interruption of his gloomy musing when two men entered the lounge and one of them hailed him. Ben Turner advanced with outstretched hand.

"Hello, Myles, it's good to see you!"

Turner was a pudgy, round-faced lawyer with a shock of red hair beginning to show streaks of iron gray, an amiable fellow whose airy chatter camouflaged a steel-trap legal mind. He beckoned his companion to join them.

"This is Enrico Prestes from Brazil, Myles. I'm putting him up here at the Club a while. *Señor*—meet Mr. Langdon."

As Myles put out his hand he thought the slim, dark visitor's eyes widened as though in surprise or recognition, but he was certain he had never seen the man before. The impression faded when Prestes smiled and shook hands.

"This is a double-lucky meeting," Ben Turner announced, happily rubbing his hands together. "Myles is just back from your part of the world, *señor,* so you and he can sling Spanish at each other."

"Don't get your hopes up," Myles warned with a rueful laugh. "My Spanish is pretty lame."

Prestes grinned broadly, his teeth startlingly white in the smooth brown face.

"So we commence even, eh? Mr. Ben Turner forgets that my country speaks Portuguese."

Turner chuckled as they sat down in the big leather chairs before the fire.

"Typical southern courtesy to say I *forgot* it; I'm so dumb I didn't even know it! Anyway, Langdon has been building a bridge in your neck of the woods, so you two ought to have *something* in common."

"My job was on the west coast," Myles explained to the Brazilian, "in Loma. Rather messy country. Do you know it?"

Prestes shook his sleek head and blinked shining eyes, soft as black velvet.

"No, Mr. Langdon, I do not know that Loma. Personally I do not like the—what did you call it—the 'messy country.' Very good name; I shall remember it." He leaned back, crossed his legs and beamed. "I run export-import business right in the city, on the east coast, and let my partner, a much more fearless man than me, go and roam the jungles."

He accepted a cigarette from Ben with a bow and surveyed the room with approval.

"A pleasant place, Mr. Turner. I much appreciate being a guest here."

While Turner explained the Club rules, Myles studied the man with interest and liking. Prestes spoke English well, in spite of a noticeable accent, although his choice of words was often odd and amusing. Certainly he seemed different from the various types with whom Myles had come in contact on the job—the thin, nervously arrogant, chip-on-the-shoulder officials, or the equally unpleasant, oily and ingratiating businessmen who supplied native produce for the camp.

But it was unfair to judge Loma by them, Myles reflected. After all, a few money-hungry grafters did not make up a country. This man from Brazil probably more truly represented the South American citizen.

"Is this a business or pleasure trip, *señor?*" Myles asked when Ben finished his explanation.

"Both, Mr. Langdon. Never before have I been in the United States, so I wish to become acquainted with your country and your people. But in the meanwhile I check up on my representatives here, you may be sure, and perhaps find some new ones, eh?"

He spread his hands toward the fire which was now blazing steadily.

"That feels good, you know. Your country is not so warm as mine. Beautiful," he added hastily, "but not so warm."

"That depends on what part of this country you're in," Turner suggested. "Have you seen much of it?"

"Pretty much. I flew from Brazil, but then I travel by train and the bus. So interesting to see everything. Meantime I arrive here and your village is—" He checked himself and snapped thin fingers loudly, "—a thousand pardons, gentlemen, your *city* is so agreeable, so different and interesting, I think I stay here some while."

He tossed his cigarette butt over the fireplace screen and turned to Myles.

"So you built a bridge in—Loma, is it? Do you go back there soon to build more?"

"Not on your life!" Myles answered decidedly. "My engineering days are over, and I'm settling down right here in our 'agreeable' city."

Ben Turner snorted and slapped his knee.

"Don't you believe it, Prestes! He'll be off again any day, blueprints and transits are in his blood."

"Not any more," Myles denied gruffly, and tried to sound convincing. "Junketing to far-off jungles has lost its appeal. Give me Uncle John Leslie's nice solid, comfortable house on Camden Road—a nice smooth paved road—from now on!"

"Tell that to somebody who doesn't know you!"

Annoyed because Turner was so right, Myles growled his answer.

"Want to hear something and be convinced, wise guy? The company shipped my stuff home for me in one whacking big box and I haven't even checked to see if everything is there. It's still sitting right in my den where it landed."

"Unopened, of course?" Ben scoffed.

"Well, no. The men who brought it pried off the cover under my aunt's direction to make it easier for me, but I'm going to nail it back on and have the blamed thing put in the attic." He smiled apology at Prestes for his irritation. "I'm working in my uncle's bank now and hope I never see another bridge."

"Is it so? Well," the foreigner winked and smiled, "bridge makers are interesting to meet—if you need a bridge—but a banker is good to know always."

Turner nodded. "You'll never go wrong, *señor,* by cultivating bankers like Langdon and his uncle—who is president of the bank, by the way. Myles, we're having a drink and lunch shortly. Join us?"

"Thanks, but no can do. I'm waiting to take Sonia to some hen party, and then there's a special directors' meeting at the bank which will last all afternoon, I'm afraid. Have to grab a bite downtown, because Aunt Pam took her granddaughter off shopping for the day and I don't want to bother our maid to get lunch for one."

Prestes scratched his chin thoughtfully.

"You talk of your 'Aunt Pam,' and a little time ago you speak of 'Uncle John Leslie's house.' Is that where you live, Mr. Langdon?"

"That's right."

"One of the town's show places," Turner put in, and enjoyed Myles's instant protest against such exaggeration.

The Brazilian's black eyes widened in query.

"I do not know which man to believe, but I suspect that Mr. Langdon is being modest? Already I have seen some of the mansions of wealthy North Americans, but have not been inside one. It is large, this house, with many servants?"

He spread his hands in smiling apology.

"I ask too many questions, eh? Forgive, please. I only wish to learn all about life in your United States. So interesting!"

"That's all right," Myles assured him, "but Ben was joking. Uncle John's place isn't what you describe. Look, I just mentioned eating downtown so I won't make work for Mabel, our one and only servant. That doesn't sound like a millionaire's staff, does it?"

Prestes nodded, flashing his white teeth.

"I see Mr. Ben Turner was—kidding me—is that right? So, okay! I don't mind. That is the way we would treat him in—in my home town, eh?" He pulled himself up out of the big chair. "I have remembered something, Mr. Turner. Before we have that drink, could I make the telephone call?"

"Right through that door—see the booths?"

"Perfectly. I shall return quick." He departed humming.

"Friendly feller," Myles said. "Where'd you pick him up?"

Turner hesitated, rubbing his hands.

"Well—I'm glad you approve of him. I wasn't too keen about introducing him here, knowing so little about the man. Joe Snell asked me to fix him up with a guest card."

"Snell?" Myles arched an inquiring eyebrow at the other. "He turns up his nose at this Club, never has joined. Why would he want his friend staying here?"

Uncomfortably Turner explained, "Prestes isn't Joe's friend, really. He brought a letter of introduction from some customer of the foundry in Brazil, I think—and evidently Joe felt that he had to do something for him. So he called me about it, and it would have been rude to refuse."

"Especially as you are Snell's lawyer, huh?"

"I'm Laurence Parker's lawyer!" Turner corrected sharply. "He still owns the foundry, in case you didn't know."

"But Joe Snell has taking ways." Then Myles apologized, "That's an unnecessary, dirty crack, I admit. But

I'm glad your Brazilian isn't one of the Snell gang, so I can go on thinking he's a good egg."

"If you mean that crew Snell takes up to his cabin on the ridge for hunting, I agree with you," Turner growled. "The kind of hunting they do seems to require more bottles and wild women than wild game."

"Now who's making cracks?" Myles laughed. He saw Sonia beckoning from the hall and rose. "There's my passenger sending me the high sign, so I have to run; sorry not to give your guest a formal good-by, but I'll probably see him around town. So long, Ben, nice running into you."

As Sonia walked beside him to the car she studied his face with a worried frown.

"Am I being boringly possessive, making you squire me around and wait for hours?" she demanded.

"Honestly, I didn't mind. Had a pleasant chat with Ben Turner—first time I've seen him—and a friend of his."

"I'm afraid you're just being polite, as usual. Anyway, this trip ends your tour of duty for the day," she promised. "Until tonight, I mean. The frown returned. "Unless you'd rather not take me to the Club dance?"

"Of course I'm taking you!" It was Myles's turn to scowl while he added, "Or did you have someone else in mind? Maybe Joe Snell dances better than he bowls. Does he, by the way?"

"Why bring up that ancient history?" she evaded.

"Because he seemed more interested in you than in our match."

"My fatal charm," Sonia sighed dramatically. "And speaking of that bowling party," her tone dripped icicles, "you and that green-eyed, man-crazy Cecile certainly had yourselves a ball. Talk about childhood sweethearts reunited! I watched you!"

Myles snorted and opened the car door for her.

"You weren't the only watcher; she had one eye on Snell every minute! Could she be after the successful Mr. Snell with matrimonial intentions?"

"I wouldn't know!" Sunny started with an angry spurt which spun the wheels. "And let's not discuss that evening any further! It wasn't *my* idea, remember?"

When she whirled out of the parking lot Myles noticed

a dust-streaked sedan standing across the street from the Club entrance. A man in a sweat-stained brown hat sat reading a newspaper which he held spread across the steering wheel.

As they passed he lifted his head for a quick glance and dropped it as quickly, but the lightning look gave Myles an unpleasant thrill. There was something sinister, hawklike, about the eyes in drooping red-rimmed pouches. The deeply creased cheeks and hooked nose heightened the effect of a bird of prey.

Myles felt the same revulsion which the huge feathered carrion hunters of the jungle used to arouse in him. Why in the world, he wondered, was such a hard-faced character hanging around the Country Club?

XII

The directors' meeting did not last as long as Myles had expected, a happy circumstance because it enabled him to maintain a show of interest to the bitter end. That was no easy task, however; his enforced indoor life seemed to be making him tired and restless at the same time, and listening to elderly men drone on and on about debentures and bond issues was hardly calculated to snap him out of the doldrums. Too often he found his hand sketching bridge towers and spans on the pad of paper supposed to record his notes of the meeting.

When at last it ended he left the bank with the others by the rear door, where he declined several offered rides, insisting that he wanted to take a walk. Drawing deep breaths of fresh air, he went around to the front of the building and halted in surprise. A man lounged almost full length on the broad granite steps, a faded khaki cap pulled low over his face and dusty boots propped comfortably high.

Hearing him approach, the man pushed up his cap and grinned.

"Hi, boss, you sure put in long hours now!"

"Red Fallon!" Myles hurried forward as the other got to his feet and they shook hands with equal enthusiasm. "What in the world are you doing here?"

"Waiting for you. Stopped on my way through and called your house, and the girl said you were here. Sounded like *quite* a girl, by the way. What's her name, age, et cetera?"

Myles poked him in the ribs.

"You mean you didn't get all that over the phone? You're slipping, Fallon! And Mabel is as Irish as you, too!"

"I got *that* much myself. Mabel, huh?"

"Too old for you," Myles discouraged. "And that's lucky for us or you'd blarney her away, and after twenty years we'd miss her." Meeting his friend and fellow worker acted like a tonic on him, and he could see that Fallon was enjoying it fully as much. "So you finally escaped the clutches of that nurse—what was her name?"

"The old battler who chased you out of my room? Never wanted to know; she had a grip like a lady wrestler! Sure, they let me out, one leg in a concrete slab, but raring to go!" He picked up a cane lying on the step and leaned on it. "You look okay, too, boss."

"I'm coming along. But what brings you here? How about me buying you *mucha cerveza* while you tell me?"

Fallon licked his lips and grinned.

"After what's happened to me, when you speak Spanish—smile! But beer is beer and you're twisting my arm. Let's go!"

Myles led the way down the street and into the cool twilight of the Chop House. Mercifully the jukebox was not in operation.

"Ain't this like old times!" Red sighed, nursing his squat mug of beer with both hands. "Better than the dives in Condona, though. You still dead set against South America?"

"Definitely! Also against engineering. I'm sticking to my job here from now on."

Myles glanced around the dim restaurant, wondering if

he could bear the drabness, the monotony of a desk job in the city. He was startled to see, in a booth across the room, the same tough-looking man who had been parked at the Club. Not a local type, Myles felt sure; more the big city mobster. He turned back to the cheerful red face of Mike Fallon.

"Once more," he asked, "what lucky wind blew you this way?"

"Another bridge job for Carrington Construction, boss, but no jungle stuff this time. Upper New York state. I'm driving to the headquarters they're setting up there with one of the foremen and detoured to check on you. I'm to keep time and do other clerking jobs till my leg's okay." He hesitated, took a long pull at his beer and blurted, "The company'd like to have you on that job, boss. They wrote you about it, didn't they?"

"A couple of times." Myles frowned and leaned back in his seat. "I answered the first letter and tore up the other. When I left the Coast I told them I was through. Why can't they believe me?"

"They're not short of engineers that I know of, so it must be they figure you're something special, and want you."

"Very flattering, *Mr.* Fallon—if I believed you! Anyway, I've made my decision and I'm sticking with it. Or stuck with it," Myles growled. "Tell them to leave me alone!"

"You don't act happy about it and——"

"That's my business, Red. Sorry, but nothing doing!"

"Sounds like you mean it," Fallon sighed, "so I wasted the trip—except I'm damn glad to see you."

"Same here, Red—doubled in spades!"

Mike looked at an ornate gold watch on his wrist.

"Barney Danahy is over at Oldfield trying to find a rigger to ride up with us and is picking me up in half an hour in front of the post office."

"Oh." Myles sounded disappointed. "I thought we'd chin a while, have dinner here, and then go out to my house. I know my aunt and uncle would love to quiz you about our doings in S.A."

"Sorry. Sounds like a good deal, but we've got to keep rolling with a coupla hundred miles still to go."

Myles heard someone enter the room behind him and was surprised to see Fallon sit suddenly erect and bring his mug down on the table with a bang. The Irishman's eyes popped and his mouth hung open. Myles looked over his shoulder to learn what had brought on such a seizure and was in time to see his new acquaintance of the morning, Enrico Prestes, turn sharply about and hurry from the restaurant.

"Hey!" Fallon gasped. "Who was that?"

Myles laughed. "South America really gave you the jitters, Red, if the sight of a man from there throws you into a tailspin. That was Mr. Prestes, a Brazilian businessman who's sightseeing in the States."

"Oh, Brazil, huh?" Mike relaxed but his forehead remained furrowed in perplexity as he stared at the doorway where the man had disappeared. He grinned sheepishly at Myles. "I guess you're right, boss, I got too big a dose of the jungle and I'm still loopy. For a second I thought he was one of the guys who took Walter Bruce out of your shack the day the bridge blew."

Again Myles laughed at him, then shook his head sadly.

"You act *loopy,* all right. Maybe you've got what the doctors blame for my bad arm—traumatic neurosis."

"Huh? Sounds bad! What's it mean?"

"Oh, nerve trouble, caused by an injury—or fright. In your case, probably you were so badly battered that now anything unexpected can throw your subconscious back to that day. Not a very scientific explanation, I guess, but the best I can do. Subconsciously, Red," he teased, "you're still scared."

"Like hell! And I wasn't *scared* that day, either!"

"Sez you!" Myles jeered. "Just because a South American type walks in you throw a fit. Level with me, now. Did Mr. Prestes *really* look like your rebel friend—if he was a rebel?"

Fallon shifted uneasily and lowered his eyes.

"I—I don't know—I thought so. Of course the guy in Loma had a beard. But this feller's eyes hit me just the same way—and he was tossing some keys in his hand— car keys, I guess—just like that other man juggled the grenade."

"That was it!" Myles snapped his fingers in satisfaction

at the solution. "We've been talking about S.A.—the place is in your mind. You see that action with the keys and instantly your subconscious flashes back to a similar scene. Mr. Fallon, sir," he joked, *"you* are a sick man!"

"In a pig's eye! And lay off my subconscious, will ya? I just made a mistake, so forget it." He mitigated the force of his words by smiling; then stood up and stretched. "I like to take my time when I'm stumping along, so I'll buzz off now to meet the fellers. You're sure you ain't interested—?"

"I'm a banker, now, Red, and that's final. It was great seeing you, and if you come by this way again don't fail to look me up."

Myles went out with his friend to the street, and when he had hobbled out of sight, stood staring after him before he boarded a bus for home.

Much as he had enjoyed seeing Red Fallon, Myles regretted the meeting. It swung his thoughts even more firmly to the old life, which haunted most of his waking hours in spite of every effort to lose himself in the daily routine of the bank. There he could sometimes forget for a time, but when he was alone, as now, the memories crowded all else from his mind.

"Like a man who's given up smoking," he muttered, "and gets the craving every time he smells a cigarette!"

Walking down Camden Road toward the house, he sternly whipped his brain into reviewing various decisions of the directors' meeting. He missed a step and stumbled when a horn blared three rapid blasts behind him and a car shot past. Prestes sat at the wheel, waving gaily and pounding the horn again with staccato hoots.

Myles waved back, watched the car shoot down the street past the Leslie house to whirl around the corner, and pursed his lips in mild disapproval. The little man drove too fast but he was friendly as a puppy. Rather noisy about it, though.

There was a decrepit panel truck in front of his house and as Myles approached a hatless, red-haired figure in overalls hurried down the walk, jumped to the seat and took off with a clash of gears.

"If you're the long overdue plumber," Myles muttered, "and have fixed that dripping shower in my bathroom, blessings on your head! It was driving me crazy at night!"

This place was as bad as Loma, it seemed, for getting small, simple jobs done. After Aunt Pam had tried unsuccessfully for days to get her plumber to attend to it, Myles hounded the man by telephone and finally lost his temper. The ensuing battle of words had apparently succeeded in getting action; although, he thought grimly, after the bawling out I gave him he may charge us enough to put in an entire bathroom.

The man's obviously insincere promises had especially riled him. "Like to have him on a bridge job for a few days, I'd cure him of his 'tomorrow'!" he muttered. "Boy, wouldn't he have filled in nicely with that native crew and their eternal '*mañana,* boss—*mañana*'!"

Still muttering and absently massaging his numb arm, Myles went upstairs to check on the annoying shower. At the door of his room he stopped in amazement. The packing case had been moved to the center of the room and opened. Its contents were strewn and tumbled in piles around it.

His automatic thought was that little Kathy, overcome by curiosity, had made further exploration in the fascinating "treasure chest." A cute kid, but she needed a prompt and forceful lesson in manners.

"Aunt Pam!" he shouted, before he remembered that she and her granddaughter were out. Even so, his bellow was loud and angry enough to get a response. He heard a hurried shuffling on the stairs.

"What is it, Mr. Myles?" Faithful old Mabel panted to the top. "Your aunt ain't home. Can I do anything for you?"

"Who's been rummaging in my stuff?" he demanded. "Was Kathy in here?"

The maid peered past him into the room.

"Mother of angels!" she shrilled. "What's been going on? But it wasn't the gir-r-l, Mr. Myles, bless her! I dusted here myself long after the Mrs. and her went off to town, and everything was apple pie then! And don't scowl at me; I know better than to touch anything of yours, except to whisk a dustrag over it.

"Wait, now!" She wrung her hands and flushed brick

red with outrage. "Could it be the man who was just here, the villain? Is anything missing?"

"You mean the plumber? I saw him drive away—"

"The *plumber?*" Mabel sneered. "It'll be mid-winter before that lying, lazy, good-for-nothing gets here, Mr. Myles! No, this was a man from the phone company, come to fix the telephone, though I didn't know there was anything wrong with it."

"Neither did I. Why should he come in here?"

"Why, indeed, when the extension is in the hall? I should have stood over the rogue every minute he was in the house! I'm sorry, Mr. Myles!" she wailed.

"Nobody's blaming you, Mabel." He patted her shoulder reassuringly.

"It's my fault, just the same. I watched him while he fooled around with the phone downstairs and did nothing of any use that I could see. Then he asks if there's an extension, and I says, 'Up the stairs' and up he went, and I got back to polishing the silver in the kitchen—the more shame to me for being so careless!"

"Forget it, Mabel. There was nothing especially valuable in the box and I won't be using the stuff again, anyway. Don't know why I got so excited."

He began to pile the scattered contents back into the box until Mabel, seeing his one-handed awkwardness, elbowed him aside with a blustering, "Leave me clean up, 'tis no work for a man!"

Myles went to stare out the window, scowling as he tried to make sense of the affair. There had been only two articles of value to a thief in the packing case. The slide rule, which Ann had appropriated, and the binoculars, which he had removed.

If the telephone repair man was the culprit, he couldn't be very bright to waste time rummaging through a box of papers when Aunt Pamela's sterling silver vases and flower bowls decorated every corner of the house. Even in this room his expensive prism binoculars, so easily pawned or sold, stood in plain sight on the desk, but had been ignored.

Mabel finished her picking up, slammed the cover back on the case and retired with muttered threats against the suspected vandal should he dare to return. Myles was habitually neat, a trait which life in the jungle had further developed. Noticing the maid's careless replacement of the wooden cover, he fitted it into place and then stood a moment studying his firm's name stenciled on it.

Come to think of it, there were reports that the assistant engineer's shack at Loma and the office in Condona on the coast had been ransacked at some time after the destruction of the bridge. Now some unknown came frisking his box from the job. Could there be a connection?

"Boy!" he muttered scornfully. "That explosion must have really rattled my brain if I reach for a wild one like that!"

XIII

It was Ann's firm determination to miss the regular Saturday night dance at the Club rather than watch Myles and Sunny together for hours. When her father arrived unheralded from Washington at eight o'clock she greeted him effusively; here was the perfect excuse—a quiet evening at home with Dad. His response to the suggestion stunned her.

"Pass up the dance tonight? Not on your life!" Robert Jerome protested emphatically. "I cut an important meeting so I *wouldn't* miss it. Even bought a new dinner jacket!" He strode briskly up the stairs, swinging his suitcase, and called back, "Throw on your glad rags, pet, I want you to go with me!" He disappeared into his room before Ann could invent a plausible excuse.

On the ride to the Club she pondered this sudden enthusiasm. As long as she could remember—at least since her mother's death—he had avoided dances like the plague. Her father broke into her train of thought and threw her into confusion with a sharp question.

"Where are your pearls? I've heard they ought to be worn constantly, to keep their luster."

Ann's heart leaped into her throat. She hadn't thought of them since last night when, panic-stricken, she'd pushed the necklace under the chair cushion to save it from the prowler in the garden! Devoutly she hoped it was still there.

"That's true, Dad, but real pearls don't seem quite proper for a working girl to sport around the bank, so I can't wear them 'constantly.' And tonight they are taboo because they wouldn't go with these extra-long and luscious rhinestone earrings."

That disposed of the pearls without revealing their present unusual location and inviting further questions which might uncover her mad behavior of the night before. She thanked her stars that Old Charley could turn his hand to any odd job; by mid-afternoon he had repaired the broken door so that, except for the fresh paint, hardly a trace remained of the *"Affaire* Duke."

Mr. Jerome accepted her explanation and studied her with approval.

"Even without them, yours is 'the face that launched a thousand ships,' " he quoted, adding more prosaically, "you're looking like a million dollars tonight. I'm glad of that."

" 'Praise from Caesar!' " Ann laughed. "But just why are you *glad?*"

Mr. Jerome fingered his black bow tie.

"Have you met the new people who have rented the house next door?"

"I didn't know that it was rented." She wondered if his voice held a tinge of embarrassment, or did she only imagine it? "Haven't seen any lights on or anyone around there. Do you know them?"

"I—humm—met them in Washington last winter. In fact—humm—I suggested the place to them; knew they would be good neighbors. Bruce is the name, a brother and sister, and they moved in yesterday. Susan—Miss Bruce, the elder of the two, is—er—charming. A successful career woman. I'm sure you will like her. Already she likes you."

"What are you talking about?" Mystified by his manner, Ann slowed the car to glance at him. "How can she *like* me when we've never even seen each other?"

"I showed her your picture—doting father stuff, you know." He appeared even more uneasy and added hastily, "You are bound to like the brother, too. Peter Bruce —just the type of man I would pick for you, Ann."

She snorted derisively and trod on the throttle.

"The old matchmaker in person! Ann will pick her own man, thank you! What does this paragon of a brother do?"

"Peter is a lawyer, very handsome, *I* think. About thirty, I'd guess. You're twenty-five, aren't you?" At another snort from his lovely daughter Mr. Jerome quickly resumed his description. "They wanted to get into the country for a while where Pete can take it easy. Had a severe case of flu this spring—made more serious because he was overworked, I'm sure. Conscientious man, wouldn't give in."

"An earnest worker!" Ann scoffed. "Deliver me! And if the sister is older she won't be much fun, either."

"Several years older, yes. Susan is more in your gay young father's class."

Something in his tone stabbed Ann's heart, but the next moment she condemned herself for being selfish. He was such a dear; they had been pals since her mother's death ten years ago. Surely he had mourned the loss long enough and ought to marry again—if he found the right person. Would Ann approve his choice, though?

Her doubts lasted only as long as it took Mr. Jerome to find Miss Bruce in the Club lounge and present her to his daughter. Ann's heart went out instantly to the tall woman in a rust-colored moiré dinner dress with a softly draped neckline. Her brown hair swirled in the latest fashionable cut and level eyes sought Ann's with warm friendliness—but with a question, too. All the anxiety, Ann realized, is not on my side.

There was a touch of breathlessness in Susan Bruce's voice. "I hope we are going to be friends, Ann. Bob—" She bit her lip and corrected herself. "—Your father has told me so much about you that I'm sure of it."

"I am just as sure," Ann smiled, "although he hasn't

told me anything about *you*—until tonight. I can't imagine why."

Mr. Jerome interrupted hastily. "Isn't Pete here with you?"

"No, he's resting at home, doctor's orders." Miss Bruce turned to Ann. "My brother is convalescing from a virus, what the doctor lightly calls a 'low-grade infection,' and" —she hesitated, finishing with—"and complications."

"Would he be able to come over for tea tomorrow afternoon?" Ann surprised herself as well as her father and Miss Bruce by the sudden invitation, but something was urging her to lose no time in making friends. "I'll ask only a few of the neighbors to meet you, really just a family party."

She saw Susan's darting glance at her father and his delighted smile, which showed relief at Ann's instant acceptance of the woman in whom he was so interested.

"Of course they'll come," Mr. Jerome accepted promptly. "Pete will be on deck by then, eh, Sue?"

"We're right next door," Ann pointed out, "so he can go home whenever he feels tired, and we'll understand perfectly."

"What's this? Another invalid?" Myles Langdon joined them and was introduced.

"Where do you get that *'another* invalid'?" Ann reproved when her father had taken Miss Bruce off to dance. "Anyone would think you were bedridden, the way you talk!"

"Might as well be. I gave the arm a workout in a slow dance with Sunny but we quit before it ended."

"Myles Langdon *quitting?*"

He flushed at the gibe, the scar pale against his angry color. It distressed her unbearably to hurt him, but Aunt Pam had suggested that the paralysis of his muscles might be partly psychic, that sometimes an impulse stronger than his mental block would loosen them. If anger could do it Ann would be merciless.

"*I* didn't quit!" he protested. "Sunny—" He clamped his lips before he laid the blame on her, then added, "It wasn't much fun, with both of us trying to hold my arm up."

"I see she's getting along very nicely with Joe Snell," Ann prodded, hating herself but determined. "Did she bring him along for a spare?"

"No, he came with Cecile Parker, but it didn't take him long to shift his attention." Myles eyed the couple under discussion and swung about to face Ann. "Maybe *you'd* like to try dancing with a one-armed partner!"

The suggestion turned her knees to water, not at the thought of how awkward it might be, but at the prospect of being in his arms, so close to him. Yet refusal might make him even more bitter.

"Forget it!" he snapped before she could decide how to reply. "I've had enough *dancing,* if that's what you could call it, but you riled me for a minute with your snide remarks!" His devastating smile suddenly erased all trace of ill temper from his face. "Look, *amor mio,* how about us sitting comfortably at ringside—until some eager swain grabs you for a whirl?"

They moved out to the porch from which resting couples and some elderly members viewed the dancing. When they were comfortably settled on a scarlet cretonned glider he stretched out his legs with a satisfied sigh and lit a cigarette. Better switch to a noncontroversial subject before Ann started prodding him again, he decided.

"Had a burglary at our house today," he said, grinning, and told her about it, making the affair sound as ridiculous as it now seemed. "And the more I think it over," he ended, "the more I wonder if my little niece wasn't the criminal, with soft-hearted old Mabel covering up for her. Do you think Kathy could drag that heavy packing case to the middle of the room without help?"

"No, and she wouldn't do such a sneaking thing, anyway," Ann murmured, her heart thumping with apprehension. Although Myles treated it so lightly, it *had* been an attempt at robbery, she felt sure. And why was a burglar at large in their town? Because Ann Jerome fell for a handsome face and a smooth manner, went utterly insane and helped the notorious Duke to escape the police. Even if she wasn't accused as his accomplice she could be hailed into court for obstructing justice—if that was the correct term. It had an ominous ring. She felt small and extremely foolish.

"Ch-Charley Duval says there are—burglars operating in this area—" she stammered.

Myles snorted. "Has he been trying to scare you, too? He poured that cock and bull story into my unwilling ear when I kidded him about that oversized gun he's so proud of."

"But the police—that is, Charley says the police told him they were after them."

"Okay—so maybe there's a modern Raffles operating here, complete with Tiger Cat gun moll. But if he's the one who passed up all the valuables in our house for a go at my box of junk—he should have his head examined." He saw Sonia coming toward them, her hair and her dress a golden glow, and rose to his feet.

"Myles," Sunny whispered, "will you dance with me again?" Her color was high and both hands were tightly clenched.

"Why, of course!" He turned to stub out his cigarette in an ash tray.

"Myles Langdon!" It was a quavering call from a small, white-haired woman sitting near the doorway. "I haven't seen you before! How long have you been home—why haven't you been to see me?" A hand blazing with diamonds beckoned imperiously.

"I called Greystone, Aunt Louise, but your butler said you were out of town." With an apologetic nod to the girls he went over to make his peace with the old lady.

"Beloved by young and old!" Ann murmured.

"Myles is a dear," Sunny sighed. "I knew he wouldn't fail me. I couldn't stand dancing with Joe another second; people were beginning to stare at us!"

"I should think they might, especially if you were obviously enjoying it."

"I wasn't!" She heaved another sigh. "Somehow I don't feel as I did about Joe."

"Good! You're actually beginning to show some sense." Ann spoke lightly, but her heart ached. Exactly as she had foreseen and dreaded, Myles Langdon's charm was working on her weathervane sister, swinging her back to normal. Normal, because what woman in her right senses could prefer Joe Snell? Numbly she watched Myles lead her sister to the dance floor and glide away, Sunny looking up at him, smiling, sparkling—evidently not a care in the world.

Gritting her teeth, Ann whirled and hurried out of the sun porch into the open air of the broad veranda. With only the faint light of the stars she could let the tears flow—

"Bless you for coming out!" a man whispered from a shadowed corner. "Remember me?" He stepped closer.

Ann stared in horror at the too familiar face, decorated now with a strip of surgical tape across the forehead. The Duke again! What was *he* doing here? She had a momentary vision of Mrs. Ballentyne's jeweled fingers, of other women displaying valuable bracelets and earrings. Her hands flew to her throat. Thank heaven she wasn't wearing her pearls!

"I've been trying to figure out how to reach you," he smiled confidently. "Didn't dare walk in there without an invitation."

"You—you dare to even come here?" Ann gasped. Anger drove away her fears. "Go away! Unless you leave here this instant I'll—I'll scream!"

"Don't!"

The appealing hand he raised was bandaged, but that and the tape on his forehead were the only signs to remind Ann of their previous meeting. Tonight a gray tropical worsted suit had replaced the tan outfit. It fitted him perfectly, she noticed, and seemed quite as becoming as the other—eminently suitable for someone called "the Duke."

Her involuntary appraisal of the man increased her anger; what a time to be admiring his clothes! If she didn't watch out she'd be feeling sorry for him again, and once was enough!

He took a step nearer and smiled again.

"I want to explain about my busting into your house. You must have thought—"

"Stop it!" Ann ordered with such vehemence that his smile faded. "I meant what I said! Get out!"

"Take it easy," he begged, glancing toward the sun porch and its occupants. What he saw brought a dismayed grunt.

Miss Bruce brushed past Ann to face him.

"Are you out of your head, Peter?" she demanded in a voice low but tense. "You promised you wouldn't leave the house!"

"Don't be bossy, Sue!" the man growled. "It isn't becoming."

Ann backed against the veranda rail and clutched it with both hands. She steadied herself but not her whirling brain. He called her "Sue"—the name he had muttered last night! The Tiger Cat! She was far from the hardened gun moll which that name had conjured up for Ann, but of course the Duke would have no mere guttersnipe for a partner.

So *this* was the couple now renting the house next door, and at her father's suggestion, too! And he stood there, beaming fondly on this terrible creature, the "successful career woman" as he called her, who was reported to have put at least one policeman in the hospital.

Outraged as Ann felt she still fought down an hysterical inpulse to laugh at her honored parent, who prided himself on being an expert judge of human nature, particularly the criminal element.

Mr. Jerome moved nearer the couple.

"Don't be hard on the boy, Sue," he urged. "What young fellow wants to miss a dance? And since he apparently wasted no time in making my daughter's acquaintance, that proves there's nothing wrong with his eyesight at least." He peered more closely. "But what happened to you, Pete? You look as though you'd tangled with a threshing machine."

Susan Bruce sighed. "I'm afraid I am responsible for the bandages, Bob. Last night"—she hesitated and then went on with an apologetic laugh—"it's too silly to bear telling, so let's just say that I sent Peter on an errand. It was evidently a little too rugged for a man so recently recovered from the flu. He came home battered and won't tell me what happened."

"I'm not proud of it," said the man they called Peter. "But I was about to tell all to Miss Jerome when so rudely interrupted. If you two will kindly scram I'll do just that. Then she can use her own judgment about spreading the story." His grin at Ann was conspiratorial.

"The doctor told you to stay in bed," Miss Bruce insisted. "Please go home, Peter. I couldn't stand it if you have another relapse."

"You're so right, Sue, I know it's been tougher on you than on me." He patted her hand. "I promise to head for home in a minute—if you'll leave us alone now. I love you dearly, Susan, but let absence make my heart grow fonder."

"That's a hint, Sue," Robert Jerome suggested, and gravely quoted, " 'Not so deep as a well, nor so wide as a church door; but 'tis enough, 'twill serve.' These young people would be alone; come on, let's dance." As they departed he gave Ann a meaning wink.

"Matchmaker!" she muttered, and mentally added, "Serve you right if I fell for this second-story worker!"

"Now, Miss Jerome," Peter Bruce began, "or may I call you Ann on such short acquaintance—?"

Eyes flashing, Ann interrupted indignantly.

"The acquaintance is ending here and now, so you needn't call me anything! I can't understand how you and your—your *sister* wormed your way into Dad's confidence, but I suppose an unscrupulous woman like her can do anything with a man, and—"

"Hold it, right there!" he cut in sharply, his handsome face paled, his whole manner changed. The easy friendliness gave way to sternness which did not need his scowl to make it impressive. "I've treated this as a joke until now. When you bring in Sue with remarks like those, it's no longer humorous!"

"I never thought it was!" Ann retorted. "I must have been temporarily out of my mind when I hid you from the police; I can give no other explanation. But I'm not crazy tonight, and I'm not going to let you get away with anything here!" She took a step toward the sun porch.

He gripped her elbow.

"Listen to me before you make yourself the laughingstock of the Club." When she glared he nodded soberly. "I mean it, Ann! Thinking it over, while I hid in your room I began to make sense out of your wild remarks. I've done some checking since then, and made more sense. You thought I was a burglar."

"I knew! I saw you skulking through the garden!" She

tried to jerk her arm free but could not. His fingers were
gentle but inflexible. And again, just as she had made
mental note of his taste in clothes in spite of her anger,
an irrelevant thought intruded: Now I know the meaning
of "the iron hand in the velvet glove"!

"You thought I was the Duke," he chuckled. "But the
police inform me that your favorite housebreaker and his
consort, the Tiger Cat, were captured last night a hundred
miles from here and are both safe in custody."

XIV

It required several seconds for Ann to recover from
her surprise sufficiently to appreciate the relief which filled
her at Bruce's announcement. He and his attractive sister
were exactly what her father believed them to be, and
not a pair of crooks masquerading with evil designs on the
neighborhood. But with that fact established came the realization of her own behavior.

Ann sank on the veranda railing and regarded Peter
Bruce with dismay.

"Can you ever forgive me—especially for calling the
police?"

"Under the circumstances I admire your presence of
mind." He perched beside her on the rail. "But equally I
applaud the change of heart which allowed me to escape
a session with the boys in blue; at present that would have
been awkward."

"Why?" Ann demanded, and again suspicion stirred.

Peter Bruce laughed at her.

"From your tone you have an unbridled imagination,
but don't overwork it. Who would choose to have to explain my situation at that moment? Let's get back to *how*
I got into that position—if you care?"

"I'm panting to hear!"

He settled more comfortably on the broad railing and folded his arms. The distant orchestra hummed soft background music for his lowered voice.

"To appreciate the picture, you should know about our family which consists of Susan, me—and one pet. A few minutes ago, telling about the *errand* she sent me on, Sue almost let the cat out of the bag—and that's no mere figure of speech—but suddenly went shy and wouldn't admit to your father that she is a cat-loving old maid."

Ann sniffed and shook her head.

"If *knockout* Susan is an 'old maid,' then that's my ambition!"

"Which you will never achieve," Peter murmured with an admiring glance. "Although I understand from your father that you are still single. What's the matter with the men of this fair burg? Not that I object, believe me! I'm staking a claim right now!"

"Go on with your explanation, please."

"Crushed!" He grinned and obediently proceeded. "All right, as I explained, our family consists of us two and a cat, a many-times prizewinning cat which Sue calls 'Delilah,' and I address only as 'Scat!' On our first night in the new house that feline fiend slipped out and disappeared—looking over the neighborhood, I suppose. Natural enough, and all right with me!"

"Don't you like cats?" Ann asked.

"Sure, but Delilah can't stand *me*. She sits eying me with such cold contempt that I shrivel. Anyway, Sue began to worry when she didn't come home; you know that sort of hysteria—'the poor creature is lost!—wandering helpless in a strange place—devoured by that dreadful dog we heard barking next door!' "

Ann bridled. "Monty is not a dreadful dog, he's perfect!"

"Does he chase cats?"

"Well—of course. All dogs do."

Peter Bruce nodded and shrugged.

"Therefore *all* dogs are dreadful, quote from Sister Sue. Anyway, I was elected to go and find sweet Delilah— a black cat, in the dark, in surroundings completely unknown to me, mind you! It was pure dumb luck that I sighted her in your garden.

"Of course I knew it was your place, and as the house wasn't lighted, I sneaked over. Believe me, I'm not one to stir up strangers in the middle of the night probably backed by a load of buckshot!

"Well, to make a long story longer, I almost caught her; my dive under some kind of a prickly bush was a masterpiece, but the pesky critter was too quick for me."

"I saw that," Ann giggled. "I thought you were taking cover. And then two gleaming eyes glared at me through the French door!"

"Not I, but Delilah. I missed her again on your terrace and she started up the trellis by the door like a—well, like a space missile taking off. I jumped up on it, grabbed for her, something broke and I did a backward, sideways dive through your door. What I go through for Sue!"

"That's what you said when I was helping you up the stairs," Ann remembered, "and I thought you meant the Tiger Cat. For heaven's sake, why didn't you explain right off?"

"Explain?" he jeered. "For heaven's sake, yourself— what chance did you give me? I recognized you from pictures your Dad showed us, but was too groggy to realize that you wouldn't know me from Adam. Then you put on your ministering angel act by dumping a pot of ice water over me!" He shivered and hunched his shoulders reminiscently.

"I was trying to revive you. First aid lesson number one."

"Glad you didn't go any farther with the course. You revived me, all right, enough to hear you babbling about police coming to arrest me." He eyed her solemnly. "You sent for them. What made you change your mind?"

Ann had no intention of confessing that it was his attractive looks and manner, so she took refuge in a half-truth.

"I was disgusted with our guardians of the peace; I could have been murdered and buried before they arrived! Besides, you were *my* prisoner and to be disposed of as I wished. And, by the way, how *did* you make your escape? Down the trellis?"

"Right. No trouble at all, fortunately. Were you surprised to find Delilah taking my place? When I opened the window to make my getaway she lounged in as though she owned the house. With one hand damaged it was out of the question to lug her down with me so I shut her in the closet for safekeeping. Did she startle you?"

"I'll tell the world! But she nearly lost a few of her lives by police guns; would have if Ben Snowden and his sergeant weren't as slow on the trigger as they are answering a call for help." Ann shook her head in reproof. "In the mangled shape you were in, getting down off the porch roof was risky. You might have broken your neck!"

"I might have, but didn't. Also, my presence in your bedroom might have been misunderstood. Did you stop to think of that while you played Good Samaritan to the battered Duke? When I heard the tramping of heavy feet on the stairs and judged from your remarks that it was the loyal constabulary, I decided to avoid embarrassment for all and took off."

Peter slid off the railing with snapping fingers.

"Now that you know all, how about a dance?"

Ann shook her head.

"Thank you, but you're forgetting that you promised your sister to go right home. According to her, you should be in bed."

"Do you think one dance will kill me?"

"I don't intend to find out. And I'm not going to begin my friendship with your sister by abetting you in flaunting her authority. Please do as she asked."

"You talk like a nineteenth century novel," Peter chuckled. "Flaunting and abetting. Where did you ever learn such words?"

"You're trying to change the subject. My father is a lawyer like you, so I know even more impressive words, but I'll keep this simple for your benefit. *Please—go—home—at—once!*"

Peter Bruce failed to answer, being too busy staring toward the sun porch. He emitted a fervent but low-pitched whistle.

"Who is *that?*"

Myles and Sonia were walking toward them, the moonlight, which had suddenly flooded the veranda, highlighting her upturned, laughing face.

"*That* is my sister," Ann informed him, adding with a

flick of sarcasm. "I assume you weren't referring to the gentleman."

When an acquaintance stopped Myles for a welcome-home handshake Sunny joined Ann and was introduced. Bruce appeared stunned by her loveliness and stumbled over the usual polite phrases. Sunny seemed to find something unusual in him, too, for her blue eyes widened to a sleepwalker's dreamy stare. In fact the meeting triggered an electric shock so powerful that Ann herself could feel its waves. She still tingled from them while introducing Myles when he arrived.

Under cover of the general talk, Peter murmured to Ann, "The photographs didn't prepare me for this!" and wasted no time in preliminaries.

"Miss Sonia Jerome, I'm a stranger here," he said. "Would you care to show me around—as far as the dance floor, anyway?" He grinned at Myles. "Hoping that Mr. Langdon has no objections?"

"None at all," Myles assured him. "Go to it!"

"Well, I have!" Ann announced crisply. "Mr. Bruce is not well enough to stay here. He and his sister have taken the house next door to us, Sunny, and that's where he should be. In bed!"

"Ridiculous!" scoffed the invalid. *"Something* has rejuvenated me; never felt better in my life! Come with me, Golden One." He took Sunny's hand. "Before your sister can summon the police, her favorite remedy for any emergency," he added with a grimace at Ann. He led Sonia toward the sun porch, she skipping to keep up with his eager strides.

Myles took his place on the railing and stared thoughtfully after them.

"Nice-appearing feller; known him long?"

"No, I met him last—the other night. Very attractive, isn't he?" she added hastily, as she felt her face flush at her near slip of the tongue and hoped he would not ask her where.

"Mmm—" Myles considered her confusion and in his mind's eye reviewed the tender scene of parting which he had witnessed outside the Wilder home. So there went the party of the second part!

"You two sat here so long with your heads together that I thought you must be old friends," he said tartly.

"Unfortunately, no," Ann feigned regret with a deep sigh. "And since he's met Sunny I'm afraid he's forgotten me already. Like so many men I meet—ships that pass in the night!"

"I can't imagine any man in his right mind—" Myles stopped the words in time but mentally completed the thought, that no man would willingly pass up Ann for Sonia, or anyone like her. Aloud he continued, "Sunny certainly changes partners fast! First me, then Snell—now a new one. Although I imagine either of us is somewhat of a letdown after a package of he-man dynamite like Joe Snell."

"Somebody paging me?" The gentleman mentioned was lounging in the doorway of the sun porch, more handsome than ever in his immaculate dinner jacket, pleated crimson cummerbund and gleaming dress shirt.

If Myles was surprised, he concealed it successfully with a blunt statement.

"I wasn't paging you, Joe, I was describing you."

"Yeah, I heard. Dynamite. Very flattering."

Myles shrugged. "It wasn't meant that way. Since my recent disastrous venture in South America, dynamite is the thing I like least."

"Afraid of it, huh?" Snell moved closer, hands on hips and a sullen scowl on his tanned face.

"No-o," Myles drawled without stirring from his seat on the rail. "I simply don't like to have it anywhere around —if you know what I mean."

"I ought to take a crack at you for that, Langdon!" Snell's voice twanged with repressed fury. "Only I don't hit cripples—if you know what *I* mean," he added mockingly.

"If you refer to me, that's smart of you, Snell."

Myles still had not moved but Ann saw the brown eyes narrow in a danger signal well known to her. She slipped a hand over his where it gripped the railing and gave a cautioning squeeze.

"You must think you're in Anderson's Athletic Club, Joe," she said lightly. "We don't stage boxing matches here. When you appeared I thought—I hoped that you came to ask me to dance."

He was visibly taken aback and for a moment eyed her with suspicion.

"Huh, that's a switch!" he growled. "Thought you wouldn't touch me with a ten-foot pole. I still think so— you're just trying to break up this wrangle. But, by golly, I'll take you up on the offer! We ought to start getting better acquainted, you know—just in case." A crooked grin made the reference to his hope of joining the Jerome family painfully clear. He offered his arm. "Come on—if you're game!"

"A pleasure," Ann accepted with a forced smile, and allowed him to lead her toward the dancing. It would be anything but pleasant, she thought, but worth it to separate the two men. Although she marveled at Myles's exhibition of self-control, there was no point in testing it further.

Left alone, Myles continued to lounge there, smoking and observing the couples who swept past the tall windows. Appearing to watch them, at least, because he could not have identified a single person, so deeply was he immersed in thought.

He found it difficult to reconcile Ann's assertion that she had known Bruce only a few days with their absorption in each other before he and Sonia interrupted. Indeed he had personally engineered that meeting, impelled by curiosity about the stranger who was spending so much time with her. Simply from a brotherly sort of interest, he told himself firmly—and uselessly.

He came out of his brown study with a start when the man on his mind materialized suddenly and sat beside him on the railing with a weary sigh.

"I'm not as spry as I hoped," Bruce admitted. "Luckily some fellow cut in before I disgraced myself by falling flat on my face." He took a deep breath and wiped his forehead.

"Did someone say you've had the flu?" Myles asked, more to be polite than from genuine interest.

"Whatever the bug was, it laid me low for weeks. I understand you've had a rough time, too. Sonia tells me you were in that rebel attack on the Carrington Company's bridge down in Loma."

Myles grunted. "Sunny actually remembered the name of the company I worked for? Amazing!"

The sarcastic tone drew Bruce's questioning look.

"Well, no. But I knew it anyway because my cousin Walter worked as a clerk in your office."

"Walter *Bruce!*" Myles sat up in surprise. "Why, of course! Sorry, my brains are still mush; when you were introduced the name didn't cause a ripple, never connected it with him. You heard what happened to Walter?"

"That's what I wanted to talk to you about, Langdon. Your company has been investigating down there since the blow-up, of course, and we've done some checking on our own—" He stopped speaking, fumbled for a cigarette and took a long time lighting it.

"You and his family, you mean?" Myles asked.

"Yes—the family—naturally. So far nobody has found out very much."

"He wasn't blown up with the rest of us, if that's what worries you. According to my foreman, Red Fallon, Walter came into my shack after it happened and showed no damage. Red told me that in the San Diego hospital."

Bruce studied the ash on his cigarette and nodded.

"We got his story from the company. It is assumed that the two natives Walt left with were police, although the Loma headquarters denies any knowledge of him. From what you know of the officials down there, Langdon, would they be telling the truth?"

"Loma is so seething with unrest and intrigue that you can't be sure of anything. We found that out!" Merely thinking of the work and effort that had gone up in smoke gave Myles a sick feeling in the pit of his stomach, and discussing it with a stranger was even more unpleasant.

"Afraid I can't be of any help, Bruce," he said shortly. "Since I quit Carrington I'm completely out of touch with developments."

Peter stared at him in surprise.

"But it's the day of the dynamiting I'm interested in," he protested. "You were on the spot; haven't you any idea why Walter went with those men?"

"*I* don't know that he did!" Myles reminded sharply,

resenting the other's persistence when he must know that Myles had been knocked out at the time. "There's no use in pumping me—although I appreciate your worry about Walter. All I can give you is what Fallon told me, and remember, he was badly hurt, too. Red didn't know whether the men were friends, rebels or policemen. They both had revolvers; one of them was juggling a hand grenade. That made the deepest impression on Fallon," he said with a sour smile, "so much so that he's still sort of gun-shy."

"The fact that they were armed," Bruce mused, "doesn't prove anything. With rebels on the rampage anyone would go armed to the teeth, I imagine. Going back to the time before the bridge was destroyed, what do you know about Walter's friends down there?"

"Nothing." Myles scowled. "You *are* his cousin, aren't you? Because you act like a cross-examining lawyer."

"Sorry. As a relative I'm naturally interested, but I am a lawyer. Bruce, Weld and Bruce, 4 Court Street, Washington—if you want to check up on me. I'll postpone further questions until you do."

"My turn to apologize. Blame my rudeness on an aversion to even think about the Loma fiasco, let alone talk about it. Frankly, it still upsets me like the devil."

Myles made an effort at a friendlier tone. "I didn't see much of your cousin off duty; mostly he hung around the native workmen, at camp and in Condona, the seaport. Trying to improve his Spanish, I suppose."

"Improve—" Bruce coughed, stubbed out his cigarette and dropped it over the railing before he mumbled, "Yes, I recall that he was always interested in languages."

"Really?" Myles stood up to end a conversation which became more and more irritating. "Just the same, once or twice I almost cautioned him about the way he mixed in with the natives. Didn't think it was a good idea in that turbulent country."

"Evidently you were right," Bruce agreed soberly.

XV

For a spur-of-the-moment party it was going very well, Ann decided, as she moved from one group to another in the living room at Sunnyfield. In spite of her intention to make this a small family tea, somehow the guest list had grown by leaps and bounds until now there were at least thirty friends and neighbors on hand.

That increase, of course, meant a hectic day of preparation, although no one would have guessed it from viewing the perfection of Ann's cranberry-red sheer wool sheath, her satin-sleek dark hair and her happily relaxed manner.

Elderly Laurence Parker was the first to comment on her appearance when she came on him seated in a corner near the doorway. His round, childlike face and round glasses made him resemble Mr. Pickwick, and he possessed that character's air of perpetual enjoyment, as he munched the crackers and cheese supplied by his daughter. Cecile always looked after him with patient good humor; it was one of her characteristics which Ann could sincerely admire.

"Looking sharp today, Ann—mighty sharp!" Mr. Parker emitted a squeaky wolf whistle. "Got your Ma's pearls on, too!"

"Special occasion, sir; I'm dolled up regardless—" She stopped in surprise when Joe Snell came in with a cup of tea which he presented to the old gentleman. Not only was the courteous act unlike Snell, his presence at her party was unexpected. Ann's suspicions immediately centered on Sonia until Cecile drew her aside.

"Hope you don't mind my bringing Joe," murmured the green-eyed Parker girl smugly. "He dropped in at the house—and he'll help me look after Father."

"That's fine." Ann nodded and smiled at Snell, waved good-by to Mr. Parker, and went to the dining room. There was no longer any doubt in her mind that Cecile meant business; she was training Joe as a dutiful husband, and he seemed to accept the treatment. Did it mean that he realized he'd lost Sunny to Myles and so turned to an earlier love? Better forget the implications of such a shift and concentrate on her duties as hostess, particularly in the food and beverage department.

The mahogany table, extended to its full length, bore a deep-green linen cloth which set off the gleaming silver, Wedgwood china and the massive Sheffield compote dripping purple grapes and heaped with crimson apples and yellow pears. Round silver trays of crackers, each with its bowl of Roquefort or chutney-cheese spread, and platters of cheese twists toasted to mouth-watering brown were being constantly replenished by Sarah with the excited help of Kathy Flood.

For the lover of sweets there were flat Italian baskets of luscious date-walnut bars and rich chewy brownies and Ann wondered again how Sarah, with all her other duties, had found the time to make them. She watched with amusement while John Leslie finished one of each, licked his lips in approval, and after a furtive glance to make certain Aunt Pamela's attention was diverted, took two more.

Mrs. Leslie was too busy to notice him. It was an inspiration on Ann's part to install her at the steaming coffee urn which balanced an equally imposing teapot at the other end of the table.

Aunt Pam, eyes sparkling to rival the diamond pendant on her sapphire-blue dress, believed that a party, like cake batter, should be kept well stirred. She knew almost everyone on a first-name basis, but whenever a stranger did appear she lost no time in learning all about him or her.

With this information gained she scanned the company, summoned suitable individuals to meet the newcomer, steered the talk to some mutually agreeable topic and abandoned them to pounce on another prospect. No one within reach of her darting eye and alert ear remained a stranger for long.

When the Bruces arrived Ann held her breath while Mr. Jerome presented Susan to Mrs. Leslie, and found it encouraging that Aunt Pam did not immediately look around for kindred spirits to whom she could introduce her. Instead, after a few minutes of animated conversation, she imperiously waved Mr. Jerome away, dismissing him with some remark which seemed to amuse and fluster him equally, and gave her full attention to Susan Bruce. Taking her cue from that, Ann did not join them but retired to give Aunt Pam every opportunity to size up the new neighbor. There was no one whose opinion she valued more.

On the terrace, where the sinking sun slipped long shafts of dusty gold through the trees, Ann found Myles and Sam Wilder in a huddle with bald, red-faced Ted Rand from around the corner. Since Rand, like Myles, was an engineer and Sam a designer, Ann knew their discussion would be far over her head and was leaving them when there was a minor interruption to the atmosphere of good fellowship at the party.

Delilah, Susan's cat, appeared in the garden. No doubt she missed her family and proposed to join them at the festivities but Monty promptly chased her back to her own grounds—and beyond, to judge from the gradually diminishing sound of his furious barking.

"Hope Monty doesn't feel that way about all the Bruces," Myles said jokingly to Ann.

"He's only met Peter, as far as I know, and is *crazy* about him. We all are." How true, Ann thought, when turning back to the dining room she saw Sonia at the far end of the terrace wall where she might have been overlooked except that her hair and gold brocaded dress were as bright as the patches of sunlight. Peter Bruce sat beside her, and even at that distance there could be no doubt of their complete absorption in each other.

"Sunny really bowls them over!" Ann muttered, and felt a secret hope that sometime—perhaps *this* time—the bowling over would work both ways. Then she forgot that wish in apprehension as Joe Snell stepped from the living room doorway, unhesitatingly picked out the golden hair and dress and headed for them with an ominous scowl.

"Men!" Ann groaned. "I thought he was back in

Cecile's clutches, but you can't count on men!" Rather than watch what happened she retreated to the house.

Evidently Aunt Pam had released Susan to Mr. Jerome because Ann saw them circulating among the guests in the living room.

"Please, old friends," she murmured, "like her very much—for Dad's sake."

Mrs. Leslie did, for one, and let Ann know it without delay.

"That Susan—delightful!" she beamed. "I'm so glad! Everything about her is exactly right—for your father, I mean!"

"You—know about them?"

"Doesn't everyone? Your father never wears his heart on his sleeve, but it's in his eyes when he looks at her. And she considers him something special, too."

"I hope so. How do you know?"

"Asked her, of course."

"You didn't!" Ann was used to Aunt Pam's directness, but not to this extent. "The minute you met her?"

"Certainly not, although I was dying to. But I knew the answer, anyway. I want to see some more people." Mrs. Leslie stood up. "Get Sonia to take over here, my poor fingers are worn out from turning the spigot on your gigantic coffee urn." Without further words she headed eagerly for the hall.

Ann suspected that if Snell had acted true to form Sunny would be in no mood for the task and instead beckoned to Betty Wilder. The young couple had been among the first of Mrs. Leslie's protégés this afternoon and had thereby acquired a sizable circle of acquaintances, but at the moment Betty stood alone.

"Will you pinch-hit here for Aunt Pam, Betty?" Ann asked. "I'm sure she'll be back soon, she likes this post of command too well to stay away."

"I can serve the coffee," Betty laughed, "but don't expect me to shuffle the guests the way she does! She introduced us to half a dozen nice people, then discovered that Sam is a designer at the foundry and dragged up two men—I didn't get their names—and the three of them soared off into technical jargon which left me gasping."

"They are still hard at it out on the terrace," Ann said, and turned, as a hand twitched her arm, to find Kathy beside her.

The little girl pointed at Betty, seated at the table.

"Isn't that Mrs. Wilder, huh?"

When Ann confirmed it, with a whispered correction of her manners, Kathy grinned.

"I forgot 'mustn't point'—I usually do. Anyway, Mrs. Wilder, there's a man at the door asking for you. A first lieutenant, Medical Corps," she added from the depths of her Army experience. "Hey, here he comes with Grandma!"

At sight of the man in uniform whom Mrs. Leslie ushered into the room Betty and Ann cried in chorus, *"Henry Little! What are you doing here?"*

"You must have rehearsed that greeting," he laughed, "although I'd prefer a little less surprise and more delight in your tone." His big hand flipped Kathy's pony-tail playfully. "Left me cooling my heels on the front stoop, didn't you! But this charming lady rescued me." He turned to smile at Mrs. Leslie but found that she, having delivered him to friends, was already yards away in search of other neglected souls.

"Why aren't you somewhere in Europe?" Betty demanded.

"Feed me and I'll talk." The lieutenant accepted coffee and a brownie which Kathy rushed to him. "A couple days after we landed Mother had a heart attack—a very minor one it turned out, Betty, so don't throw a conniption—so my old man gets the wind up and cons the Red Cross into flying me home. Nice trip, Mother is okay and I'm on my way back to duty."

He set his coffee cup on the table and accepted a plate load of delicacies from Kathy with a "Thanks, pardner, you're a hoss to ride the river with!" a TV bromide which nonetheless thrilled the wide-eyed little girl.

He selected a nut bar and munched enjoyably while he studied the faces about him.

"Couldn't pass within a few hundred miles of my favorite cousin without saying 'Hello,' could I?" he asked smoothly, his eyes on Ann. "One of your neighbors told me where you were, Betty, and here I am." He bowed. "Am I outlawed for crashing the party?"

"Anything but!" Ann assured him. "It's nice to see you again, Hank, and it gives me a chance to thank you for the most impressive display of roses I ever received."

"A very inadequate expression of my admiration for you, Ann. I can't decide whether I prefer you in blue— like the other night—or in this red dress. Both make you look out of this world!"

"Oh, brother!" Betty Wilder snorted. "When Hank starts with the flowery compliments, look out, Ann. He's in his Don Juan phase. Remember, I warned you."

"Yes, you did!" Ann scoffed. "The day *after* your party, at the bank. But that night you brazenly encouraged him to lead me on!"

"Hold everything!" Little ordered. "I didn't come here to be insulted by my cousin. Ann, let's you and I retire to the garden I see out there while I convince you of my sincerity."

"As hostess I mustn't desert the party. Let's see if we can't find a place to sit in the living room, I want to hear about the trip overseas and what your assignment is."

She was somewhat surprised at his prompt acceptance of the suggested subject and a little piqued that he didn't again get personal. Evidently his cousin had been right about his lack of serious intentions toward the opposite sex. Which was just as well, it saved her the embarrassing duty of explaining that he would waste his time as far as she was concerned. Her heart was too full of Myles Langdon for any other man to make an impression, no matter how hopeless her chances with him seemed.

Nothing is hopeless, she insisted to herself, until the last gun is fired! That thought was reinforced when Myles came in from the terrace, saw them in the corner and after an impulsive step in their direction did a quick about-face and strode to the hall.

He was frowning, Ann noticed with a pleasant throb of satisfaction. To be sure, at the moment Hank happened to have her hand in his, but it was merely to prove by the length of the life line across her palm that she would be safe in driving his sports car. If Myles chose to see anything intimate in the gesture—more power to him!

With that on her mind, as well as a nervous conjecture about how Sunny, Peter and Joe Snell were getting along, Ann could not give Little's conversation the attention it deserved. It was some time before he realized her abstraction, and then he mistook the reason for it.

"I've monopolized you long enough," he announced presently and stood up. "You're worrying about your guests, I can tell, so come on." He led her to the dining room and was moving toward Betty when he halted and snapped his fingers. "Oops, your fatal beauty has made me forget my manners, Ann! I haven't even said 'Hi!' to Cousin Sam. Where is he?"

"Sam Wilder?" It was Myles who answered. He and Peter Bruce were sampling the refreshments. "Sam's out on the terrace." When Ann introduced them he set down his plate to shake hands. "Haven't we met before, Lieutenant?" he asked, sure that something about the man seemed familiar.

"I doubt it," Ann said. "Henry only makes flying visits here."

"Must have been two other fellows," Little suggested with his infectious grin. "However, I'm pleasured to—" He looked past Langdon and his eyebrows shot up. "Pete Bruce! You here?"

"Hello, Hank!" Peter joined them. "We seem to run into each other in all sorts of places, don't we?"

"I'll say! What are you up to—anything exciting?"

"A rest cure, if that fits the description."

"I'll bet it's a *rest cure!*" Little jeered.

"Just that. I'm getting over a flu bug." Bruce spoke lightly but with an almost imperceptible frown, which Ann noticed. "You know there's rarely anything *exciting* in trust work, Hank."

"Oh?" Little blinked. "That's right, you're a lawyer, aren't you."

"So my diploma says. Come on out back and see Sam Wilder. I've been talking to him, but didn't know you were cousins."

"By a happy marriage," Henry explained as they left.

Ann wondered if she had imagined a touch of restraint in Peter's conversation. It seemed odd that Henry Little, who seemed to know Bruce well, should not remember that he was a lawyer.

"Young lady!" Myles spoke so suddenly behind her that she jumped. "Just how many admirers are there in your string? From your tête-à-tête with Bruce at the dance I guessed that he had the inside track, and now this Lieutenant Little is entertained with noticeable enthusiasm!"

"Good old Hank!" Ann laughed. "Merely a friend—"

"I know that line—'ships that pass in the night,' " Myles growled. There was sharpness in his tone because he was confused. The man who took such loving leave of Ann that night at the Wilder home had seemed very tall, a description which certainly fitted Little like a glove. But Bruce stood well over six feet, too, and from a distance and at night—who could judge? "And which of your ships," he demanded, "leaves dozens of roses in its wake?"

"Roses—poof!" Ann dismissed them with an airy wave of the hand, and increased his confusion of thought by adding dreamily, "Dear Pete, *he* knows a modern girl expects more than flowers; that's only the beginning!"

"So Bruce sent them!"

"So what?"

The abrupt retort confirmed Myles's suspicions; it wasn't like Ann to resort to caustic slang, so she must be deeply involved. With sinking heart he muttered, "Thank goodness you're not serious about that man mountain in uniform, anyway!"

"Have you anything against Hank except that he's bigger than you are?"

"But he's only a boy—"

"Peter Bruce isn't! What have you against *him?*"

Ann surprised herself by the heat in her voice. What had begun as a lighthearted attempt to keep Myles guessing had suddenly become an inquisition which set her nerves on edge. It was strictly none of his business; he was engaged to Sonia, wasn't he? Why should he dare to interfere with her? He was behaving like a jealous suitor, and how fervently she wished he had the right. Better to end

the interview before she either screamed at him or burst into tears. She walked out onto the terrace.

But Myles would not be shaken off. He followed her
with a sincere apology.

"If I spoke out of turn, Ann, blame it on lifelong—
friendship." His hesitation before that word was only momentary and he rushed on, "I want nothing but the very
best for you!"

So do I, she thought with aching heart, but I can't have
him. Perversely she burned with anger against Myles and
with an urge to hurt him.

"Am I to understand," she demanded with all the scorn
she could put into the question, "that you have appointed
yourself guardian of my love affairs? Really, the progress
of your own is far from encouraging!"

An explosive laugh startled her. "That's telling him,
kid!" jeered Snell, who came striding up the steps from
the garden.

His face was hotly red, his eyes glittered with fury; his
whole manner told Ann that he had emerged from a
stormy session with Sonia and now was ripe for trouble
with whoever crossed his path. His next snarling speech
confirmed that.

"Langdon's got a nerve, advising you on romance!"
Joe's mouth twitched in a sour grin. "Shucks, he was no
competition for *me,* and I wasn't even half trying."

Ann caught her breath at the sneering reference to his
pursuit of Sunny. She saw the color drain from Myles's
face until the scar on his cheek, which she never noticed
now, stood out an ugly purple streak. His jaw muscles
ridged and his right hand balled into a fist.

Then to her relief he controlled his anger, slipped his
hand into his pocket and stood at ease.

"You mean, I suppose, that you think you've cut me
out with Sonia," he said evenly. "Competition from a
man a couple of thousand miles away *wouldn't* worry you
much, I guess, Snell." He laughed without mirth. "You
disappoint me, though. I knew you were a mighty hunter,
we hear so much about that fancy lodge you have in the
hills. I *didn't* know you were a poacher!"

"Anything goes in love and war, doesn't it?" Snell

growled, his face redder at the insult. "I get what I want, Langdon, no matter who stands in my way."

"At the moment you don't look flushed with *success*."

"I said 'what I want,' wise guy!" It was a weak parry, and Snell realized he could not compete with the other's gibes. He switched to another line and lifelong resentment roughened his voice. "I've done all right so far, and without any rich uncle to slip me into a soft berth if I flopped on my own! I worked my way up in the foundry until I'm manager, and in a little while I'll—" Some remnant of caution penetrated his anger and stifled the boast, so that instead he muttered, "—I'll do better than that!"

Myles studied him with narrowed eyes.

"What did you start to say? That you'd take over the foundry in a while?"

"I said what I meant, and you keep your nose out of my business." Snell hesitated, and with an effort smoothed some of the harshness from his tone before he said to Ann, "Nice party. Thanks for letting me come. We'd better take Mr. Parker home now." He turned on his heel and strode into the house.

"I'll have to see them off," Ann murmured, adding the contrite apology, "Forgive me for what I said, Myles, and for setting Joe off on such a tantrum."

His heavenly smile made her heart pound.

"I'll forgive you anything, *Ana mia*," he said softly, "and *you* didn't start it. I saw him talking to Sunny in the garden, and I judge they have parted permanently. Run along in and speed the departing guests."

When she had gone he sat on the wall and wondered glumly how many other people in town were making comments on his noticeably lukewarm engagement to Sonia Jerome. How had he ever slipped into that entanglement before he went away? Confusion of mind, probably; all their lives he and Ann and Sunny had been inseparable companions and he must have been subconsciously in love with both. Golden-haired, mercurial Sonia had blinded him for the fateful moment when they became engaged —and the damage was done.

It was not the sight of Ann with her damnably attractive suitors which had brought him to his senses. The months in the Loma jungle did that long before, forced maturity on him, and with it the knowledge that it was Ann who meant everything to him. Lovely, steadfast Ann was the woman with whom he wanted to share his life, wanted it with such intensity that his heart raced at the thought.

Raced—and then sank to a leaden weight when Sunny's bright face intruded. Had her reason for keeping on with the engagement been pride or sympathy? If she really loved him could she be interested in these other men? Whatever it was that moved her, she held him trapped for the present!

And meanwhile, how much did that good-looking Peter Bruce mean to Ann? Her indignant reaction to Myles's questions gave a disturbing answer.

XVI

Myles paused in his task of inspecting a customer's file and looked up at the man in immaculate gray flannel and jaunty porkpie hat who stood in the doorway.

"Señor Prestes!" Myles left the desk to shake hands with the Brazilian. "Glad to see you again."

With a roguish shake of his finger Prestes warned, "I told you that I should cultivate bankers. Especially you, Mr. Langdon, now that I find you to be a man of such importance that you have a sumptuous office like this!"

"That's misdirected flattery," Myles commented with a smile as he pushed forward a chair. "This happens to be Treasurer Connelly's room and I'm only using it while he's on a business trip to Chicago. How have you been getting along since we met? Comfortable at the Club?"

"Oh, very indeed, and Joe—Mr. Snell has been most kind, including me several times when he entertained his friends. Most enjoyable. I really have been quite busy or

I would have called on you some days ago as I wish two things from you, Mr. Banker."

"Happy to oblige in any way I can. Just name it."

Prestes extracted a wad of paper money from an inner pocket.

"First, I want to exchange these hundreds of contos into dollars, if you are so kind. And next I would open up the—the"—he snapped his fingers at a loss for the word—"the account to keep my dollars in—"

"A checking account?" Myles suggested. When the South American grinned and nodded he took the foreign currency. "I'll figure the exchange, and then we can arrange the account." Holding down the money with his numb left hand, he thumbed through the pile and noted the amount. From a desk drawer he took the exchange listing and his slide rule.

Awkwardly he fumbled the rule from its plastic case, then glanced up at Prestes with an apologetic smile. At sight of the other's face the smile faded.

The Brazilian was white, his black eyes were wide, fixed on Myles's hands. He drew in a shaky breath.

"*Señor*, are you ill?" Myles asked.

"No, no!" Prestes took a long breath and tapped his chest. "It is only a fever I have had before; sometimes it comes back like a chill, eh? Thank you, I am quite all right now."

Myles leaned back in his chair and nodded.

"You do look better. You had me worried, my friend!" With some embarrassment he explained, "I thought my crippled arm had given you a turn. No strength in it since the bridge smash-up. Maybe Ben Turner told you about it?"

"Yes—yes! Mr. Turner did say you were hurt, but I assure you, Mr. Langdon, I did not notice your arm; not at all. I would not be so rude."

"Nothing to worry about. I can still figure your exchange correctly, believe me." Myles made his calculations and then helped Prestes fill out the required forms and signature cards for his checking account. "Now," he suggested, "let me take you to a teller, get what cash you want, and I'll place the rest to your credit."

When that business was attended to Myles waved away

Prestes's effusive thanks, walked to a front window, and smilingly watched the South American hurry down the steps. He climbed into a sedan at the curb, and Myles recognized it as the same car which he had been driving on Saturday.

"Wonder if Snell supplied him with that, as well as entree to the Country Club," Myles muttered. "If so, whoever introduced him to Joe must be a very good customer." And, Myles wondered further, do you suppose Prestes has a driving license?

The Brazilian turned the car out into the traffic and took off with his habitual speed. Across the street another car left the curb, made a swift U-turn which brought a squeal of brakes and shouts from an oncoming truck, and sped after Prestes.

Myles stared. The dusty car looked familiar—even more familiar was the intent, hawk-faced driver, the man he had seen parked outside the Country Club on Saturday. Why should he be trailing the inoffensive foreigner? Lucky that Prestes had turned in most of his money to the safe-keeping of the bank if Hawk-face had robbery in mind!

Myles snorted in derision at his own foolishness; these days everything he saw seemed to suggest danger and crime! He'd go over to Ann's window and wipe away such thoughts with pleasant conversation. Talking to her never failed to soothe his troubled mind, and she'd enjoy hearing about his newest customer.

It was no more than an hour later when Ann saw Señor Prestes come into the bank again and recognized him from Myles's amusing description. The Brazilian's felt hat sat at a jaunty angle, his hands were thrust in the pockets of the gray flannel suit, and his chest swelled importantly. She noticed another, younger man who entered behind him, but apparently they were not together.

Prestes went through the railed enclosure and down the short hall to Myles Langdon's temporary office, while the other man stopped at one of the counters set in the middle of the room for the use of the customers. There he leaned on his elbows and apparently studied the various deposit slips arranged in the racks. From her window Ann idly watched the broad shoulders twitch under the leather jacket and wondered what was the matter with him.

Prestes came back, half-leading Myles and talking volubly.

"Only one moment, Mr. Langdon, if you will come look at this car. I think I have found just the one for me to buy, but I would like your judgment on it first."

"I'm afraid a year in the jungle hasn't fitted me to judge a modern automobile," Myles protested, and winked at Ann as they passed. "Is it the car I've seen you driving?"

She did not hear Prestes's answer because a customer appeared at her window as they went out. While she cashed the woman's check she caught a glimpse of the man in the leather jacket. He was walking down the hall between the private offices; at Myles Langdon's door he paused and then when in.

Busy counting out money Ann gave only part of her mind to the rough-looking stranger. Why should he go to that room when he must have seen Myles leave with the Brazilian? she wondered. Of course it was possible that he had an appointment and still didn't know Myles by sight, but he had gone straight there without asking directions, as if he knew the way.

She caught Charley Duval's eye and beckoned. The old man came over with a grin.

"Someone went into Mr. Langdon's office, Charley," she said, "but he's stepped out with that South American."

"I seen him go out, Miss Ann. They're looking at a car."

"Why don't you find out what this man wants. Tell him Mr. Langdon will be back shortly."

"Sure thing." He squared his shoulders and marched toward the office.

Another customer claimed Ann's attention with a batch of checks and cash for deposit. She was deep in calculation when the businesslike calm of the bank was shattered by a furious yell from Duval.

"Get out of that desk, you!"

There was a commotion in the hall, the clatter of running feet, and then an explosion which seemed to rock the building. Ann clutched the counter, the customer at her window screamed, clapped both hands over her ears and went on screaming. The leather-coated man darted from the hall, leaped the rail, and dashed for the rear door.

Another explosion, but this time Ann knew it was a shot echoing thunderously in the marble-walled room. Duval skidded into view, still firing at the running man, the automatic jumping with each shot. A bullet ripped across the counter near Ann to glance off the wall with a horrifying screech. The banking room was a bedlam of shouts and screams.

An arm closed around Ann, pulling her down behind the counter and Myles Langdon shouted, "Duval, hold it!" But as the running man pulled open the door to the parking lot and hurtled down the steps, Charley sent another slug crashing after him.

"*Stop shooting!*" Myles bellowed.

Ann had not seen him come back into the building and now stared up in frozen surprise at his white face bending over her.

"Are you all right?" he panted.

"I—I think so. Yes, of course I'm all right!" She fought to control her voice. "That bullet—one of them—hit the counter—" The memory of its terrifying whine as it glanced past brought a sob and a gasp.

"Okay—okay! Forget it—it's all over." His hand trembled as he helped her off the floor, brushing the dust from her dress. "Better go to the rest room and lie down for a while."

"I don't need to. I tell you I'm all right—just—just scared."

"Who wasn't? If that old fool had hit you—" Myles choked on the thought, rubbed a hand across his eyes and shook his head like a groggy fighter. "Please get out of here for a few minutes; I'll take care of everything."

"Heavens!" She succeeded in laughing lightly. "You seem more upset than I, and I didn't know you were in the bank!"

"I got back in time to see you in the front line." His voice was still shaky but he forced a grin to match her light touch. "Now that I'm sure you're okay, I've got to get hold of Duval." He patted her arm reassuringly and hurried away.

The guard, still aglow and sparkling-eyed from his moment of heroism, brushed aside Myles's vehement protests.

"I went to your office, like Miss Ann told me, and this guy is pulling out the drawers in your desk. When I yelled at him he lit out like a scared rabbit. Nearly knocked me down, so I tried to stop him. Ain't that what they give me a gun for?" he demanded crossly.

"You darn near hit Ann Jerome!"

"But I *didn't,* did I? I know how to handle a gun, Myles Langdon; knew how before you were born! I'll tell you something else," he growled, his large ears bright red with anger. "If you hadn't made me wear my gun under my coat I'd have got it out a sight quicker and might've winged him!"

"You *keep* it under your coat, do you hear? That may have saved a few lives," Myles said caustically.

"What are you so worked up about? Nobody got hurt, did they?"

Myles preferred not to explain why he was so "worked up"—a gross understatement of his feelings—and abandoned further argument with the veteran.

"We'll have to report this to the police, Charley," he said. "Can you give them a good description of our visitor?" Before the other could answer Myles had a swift flashback to the previous call of Señor Prestes and the man who seemed to be watching him from across the street. He snapped his fingers. "It wasn't a thin-faced fellow with a big beak like a bird, was it?"

"Where was *he?*" demanded Charley. "Waiting outside —the lookout, huh?"

"No, no! I saw him earlier. No connection, probably."

"That's what you think! You don't know how these crooks operate. I'll have the cops check on him, too, believe me! The guy in here was about twenty-five, short and stocky; had kind of a round, moon face with no nose at all, hardly." Duval scratched his ear and frowned. "You know, Myles, he looked sort of familiar; maybe I've seen him around town. If he's local, it'll make it easier for the cops to locate him."

"All right, Charley, I'll leave the police to you."

"Do that, son. And Myles"—the old man grinned and winked—"you better go take a walk in the fresh air, you still look mighty peaked. None of them slugs went near you, did they?"

"Report to the police and never mind me," Myles snapped as he turned away.

He was still pale when with order restored and business functioning normally he faced John Leslie in the president's office.

"That was a frightening thing, Uncle John," he said slowly, staring at his white-knuckled hand gripping the edge of the desk.

"Dreadful!" Mr. Leslie agreed, making two attempts to light a cigar before his shaking fingers succeeded. "We *never* had any trouble before. I don't know what things are coming to when a bank like this can be invaded in broad daylight! Just can't believe it happened!"

"I'm not talking about *that*," Myles corrected sharply. "I mean Duval's reaction! That man was only a sneak thief—but *Charley!* My God, someone might have been killed!"

Mr. Leslie pulled nervously at his cigar.

"The way he cut loose with that gun scared the daylight out of me, I'll admit. But with the steady diet of shootings we get in the movies and on TV I suppose we have to accept it as run of the mill. Duval is used to handling a gun, at least—"

"Used to it!" Myles growled. "He darn near wrecked the place! Did you see what his slugs did to the doorway—where they ripped up the counter in front of Ann's window?" He drew a shaky breath. "I've looked into the wrong end of a gun a few times, Uncle John; it's bad enough when the man behind it is an expert—if he's a fool—just thinking about it gives me the creeps."

"Duval is no fool, but I *will* do something about him. We have trouble getting guards, you know; I guess we have the choice of their being no good in an emergency or trigger happy. I don't know which is worse."

"I do—and you've got one of the worst!"

"You're taking this hard, Myles."

"Because it's serious! If any of his bullets happened to hit metal you could have had ricochets all over the place. Nobody would have been safe. And suppose that crook had started shooting, too!"

"We were very lucky," the president admitted, rubbing his face wearily. "Apparently he was a sneak thief, as you say, and not an armed robber. Duval caught him rifling your desk. Can't imagine why he picked that room, though. What is there to steal there?"

"Nothing as interesting as the five or six thousand dollars lying around the tellers' windows."

"Very strange. Do you suppose he was hunting for a note he'd signed, planning to tear it up? No, that's fantastic!" He sat for a moment in puzzled silence. "Nothing missing!" he muttered.

"Oh, yes, there is!" Myles's laugh was sarcastic. "My slide rule is gone, case and all. If he took that he's a real big-time operator." He stood up, walked to the window and spoke over his shoulder.

"Let's forget all that, Uncle John. There are just two people in this bank who mean much to me, you and Ann. You *have* to be here, and this office is pretty well protected from anything such as happened today. But Ann is out there in the open, right in the line of fire!"

"Oh?" Mr. Leslie grunted. "So that's it."

"That's what?" Myles did not wait for an answer. "It's all very well to say this is the first time such a thing has happened, and probably the last. Suppose it isn't!" He swung around to glare at his uncle. "Ann mustn't take the chance! Damn it, man, if one of those shots had gone a few inches to the right she could have been killed!" he shouted in his desperate anxiety.

John Leslie sank back in his chair and gave his nephew a long probing look before he spoke.

"Um, yes—I see what's on your mind, my boy. I agree with you, Ann is mighty precious to me, too, you know. And she doesn't need the job here, as the others do. I'll speak to her later, tell her she must give it up." He sighed. "She isn't going to like it, Myles."

"Probably not, but you can make her see the wisdom of it. But for heaven's sake, Uncle John, don't let on that I had anything to do with it!"

The banker nodded, studying the ash on his cigar.

"I understand, Myles. Mustn't have her thinking you take too much interest in your fiancée's sister, eh?" Under lowered lids he watched Myles flush uncomfortably. "Quite right, my boy. I'll take all the blame for firing the girl; I'm used to it, you know. Let's settle down to banking now, if the gunfighters will let us." He waved his nephew out of the room and then sat staring unseeingly at a print on the wall and smiling to himself.

As he left, Myles wondered if he had been too vehement in making his point. Not that he didn't mean every word, but his uncle's speculative expression seemed to suggest some secret and amusing knowledge. Was he another who suspected that the romance between his nephew and Sonia Jerome did not sail a smooth course, and had he his own ideas about the reason for it? He'd better be careful with John Leslie; a man didn't become president of a bank unless he had plenty on the ball in the way of brains.

XVII

Ann came to the end of the business day with mingled relief and satisfaction. In spite of Myles Langdon's demands and Uncle John's suggestions she had stuck to her job with grim persistence until the regular closing time. She could not help sounding a little triumphant in her "Good night" to Thomkins, the other guard, who let her out the back door.

His respectful air amused her; naturally he had received a glowing account of the day's adventure from Charley Duval, whom he replaced at noon, and his admiration extended to anyone present at the shooting, no matter how small their part in it.

She started across the parking lot to her car but then turned resolutely away to the street. It had been her intention to do some errands after work and a slight case of nerves was no excuse for neglecting them. Although she still felt shaky, the crisp fresh air was a welcome tonic and the always absorbing interest of shopping would complete the cure. "If you feel low," ran a favorite Jerome prescription, "go out and buy something."

This time, however, the remedy was not wholly successful and when at five o'clock she started for her car she regretted her tentative date for supper with Peter Bruce. The shock and terror of those few seconds in the bank must have taken more out of her than she suspected, because she simply did not feel equal to an evening with a new man, even one as attractive as Peter.

Fortunately he had not been sure how well *he* would feel and was to telephone in the late afternoon to confirm the arrangement. She could phone Sarah at once and trust that loyal soul to make her excuses for her. She went into the neon-spangled drugstore across from the bank, and found an unoccupied booth.

Ann dialed the number and while waiting stared through the smudged glass door at a young couple who were enjoying sodas at the counter. They sat close together, swishing the long spoons in the creamy concoction and talking, talking, talking. The man said something which made the girl laugh and glance up at him, and the adoration in her face made Ann's heart throb in sympathy. With that one look the two became, for her, Myles Langdom and Ann Jerome sitting together, sipping delicious frothy ice cream sodas on his last night in town over a year ago.

She could remember every detail of the scene, every word spoken, and her own feelings—better forgotten now. Myles had waited for her after a charity musical show in which she sang several numbers, and insisted on treating her on the way home. Sonia? Oh, yes! Sunny was laid up with a cold; that was why Myles appeared alone.

Halfway through their sodas Myles turned his head

to stare soberly at her, and his words sounded clearly in the stuffy phone booth twelve months later.

"You looked beautiful on that stage, Ann, and you have a wonderful voice. You know that, I guess. Just as you know your new hair-do really does something for you—but I mean, *something!* Right now your eyes have stars shining behind them—" He stopped, gulped some of his drink and laughed. "Guess I'd better switch to another wave length quick! You'll be getting a swelled head!"

The dream shattered at Sarah's high-pitched "Hello!" in her ear. Ann dragged herself bodily back into the present.

"It's Ann, Sarah. Any messages for me?"

"No message, but some fellow called, asking for you. Sounded real nice; wanted to know when you'd be home, but I told him it was no use calling again because you were going out to dinner with an old friend after you got home, which would be late because you were going shopping after work. Just what you told me, Miss Ann, and—"

"I didn't tell you to *broadcast* it!" Ann interrupted the monologue which she knew from experience might run on indefinitely. "Who was it that called?"

"He didn't give his name, but he sounded nice—"

"So you said." Ann had a disturbing thought. "Why did you tell him I was going out with *'an old friend'*? I distinctly said a *new* friend when I told you."

Sarah chuckled. "Thought he might get more interested if he knew he had some competition, that's why. What's the difference?"

"Just this," Ann informed her severely, "it was probably Mr. Bruce, calling to say our date was on for tonight, and you bluntly tell him I'm going out with someone else!"

"Heavenly days!" Sarah groaned. "How'd I know it was him? I'll phone him right away and—"

"Don't you dare! It's all right, because I'm too tired to go—but I could have turned him down a little more subtly, I think."

Ann hung up and stared moodily out of the booth. Slowly her eyes focused on the back of a man who sat at the counter from which the young people had departed. After her recent dreamy excursion into the past it was a shock to recognize Myles Langdon.

His chin on his fist, he scowled down at the counter and seemed as deeply lost in thought as she had been, Ann decided, when she perched on the adjoining stool without disturbing his preoccupation.

"This is the late-late show on TV," she announced softly, causing him to jump and cock an inquiring eye at her. "Where they rerun ancient movies," she explained with a smile. "This one is a real oldie, called 'Sodas For Two.' Remember?"

"You bet I do! I even know what flavor they were." He crooked a finger at the counterman and ordered, "Two chocolate sodas, pal—with double scoops of ice cream!"

"You do remember!" Ann wondered how much more of that evening stayed in his mind while she made automatic protest. "We shouldn't, really; it will spoil our suppers."

"Seems to me that has a familiar ring, too," Myles laughed. "I'm sure you said something like it. Maybe we can run through the whole script!"

"We'd better not!"

At her decisive tone his eyes flicked to her face and after a moment's study turned away.

"You're probably right. To the best of my recollection I talked too much that night, so now we'll stick to the present tense." He waited until the clerk had served them and retired to wash dishes at the farther end of the counter. "How are you, by the way, after your Wild West morning of gun play?"

"Quite recovered, thank you, sir." She plunged a spoon into her glass and smacked her lips. "This should be the finishing touch!"

"If it isn't, try some of Aunt Pam's latest prescription— whatever it is. They're compounding it now in the back room; that's how I happen to be here. Something she recommended for my *nerves!*" he jeered, spooning up chocolate soda between sentences. "It must be that I'm showing the effects of my Loma ordeal more than I realize," he added bitterly. "Behold the wreck of an engineer!"

"You are *not!* You stop talking like that, Myles! Remember Aunt Pam's slogan, 'Think success and you invite success.'"

"You've always been my most loyal cheering section, Ann."

"If you were the wreck you keep harping on you wouldn't have got to me so fast when the shooting started," she reminded. "You were there before I had time to be afraid—and then I wasn't."

"You were the only one in the bank who wasn't, then," Myles muttered. "I was shaking like the proverbial leaf until I found you were safe. And while I don't want to accuse you of handling the truth carelessly, it seemed to me that you were *plenty* scared."

"Not after you came; then everything was all right."

"You make me sound like your knight in shining armor," Myles growled without looking up from his glass. "But you're not fooling me. Not after seeing you with some of your flames, and how they fling long-stemmed roses around by the dozens."

For a heart-lifting instant Ann imagined that his grumbling indicated jealousy, but then common sense pricked and deflated her ballooning hope. Her sister's fiancé was only being humorous in his heavy-handed masculine way.

"I don't consider sending *me* flowers 'flinging them around,'" she retorted. "And you certainly were a friend in need when the shooting started."

Outside the drugstore a car's brakes squealed harshly and Ann waited for the noise to subside before she continued her praise.

"You have a most comforting way about you, solid and dependable, and—"

She stopped again as in the mirror behind the counter she saw a hatless man hurry through the door and hesitate.

"Why, Myles!" she murmured, "isn't that your South American friend standing in the doorway?"

Langdon glanced over his shoulder and then swung on his stool to wave.

"Hello, Prestes. You look jittery. What's the excitement?"

The man came forward, showing his teeth in a mechanical smile.

"Excitement indeed, Mr. Langdon. I have just heard what happened at your bank after I left!" He took the stool next to Myles, whipped a gaudy handkerchief from his hip pocket and wiped his face. "I hear only a little piece of the story, and I was so afraid something happened to you, my good friend! Then as I drive by I see you through the window—and you are all right! Good enough!"

"Nice of you to worry," Myles grinned. "I wasn't even on the firing line, but this young lady was." He introduced the man to Ann. "Miss Jerome is one of my best friends as well as one of the major attractions of the banking business, *señor*."

"I agree very much!" Prestes bowed to her with all the dignity he could manage while perched on the stool. "Miss Jerome will allow me to smoke?" he asked. When she nodded, he drew a case from his pocket, proffered it with a flourish, and when they refused, took out a brown cigarette. "After the shock I must quiet my nerves," he explained solemnly.

"Nothing to get worked up over," Myles assured him dryly, wondering if the other always made such a production of his feelings. "Just a run of the mill robbery attempt." Briefly he told of the sneak thief's visit and his precipitate retreat under fire.

Prestes waved smoke away to fix his black eyes directly on Myles.

"And after all this trouble he got nothing, eh?"

"Only one very secondhand slide rule, as far as we know."

"Your rule?" Ann exclaimed. "I didn't know that!"

"Forgot to mention it."

The Brazilian touched his arm to get his attention, and the brown face drew down into lines of reproach.

"This—you call him a sneak thief?—stole your ruler only, you say? I think you are making a joke with me, eh?"

"No, no, I'm not kidding you, Prestes."

"But *why?* I saw you using it at your desk; it is just a ruler. You have been an engineer, I know; you would have a dozen like it, maybe? This one is not so special that the thief thinks he can sell it for big money?"

"If he thought that, he's the stupidest crook we've ever had in town and—" Myles stopped, struck by an idea which seemed almost too far-fetched to be seriously considered. The idea of a stupid thief recalled his feelings on that afternoon when someone ransacked his stuff from Loma, his conclusion that a person who ignored Aunt Pam's various treasures in favor of searching a packing case, contents unknown, should have his head examined. Today's occurrence certainly indicated an equal lack of common sense on the part of the would-be bank robber. It might not do any harm to ask the police if they knew some local character of subnormal intelligence with a record for petty theft.

Prestes broke in on these thoughts, insistent on pursuing his own line.

"Perhaps this criminal fellow believes you have a very good rule, worth much money, and thinks the one in your desk is it?"

"But why should he have such ideas?"

"*I* do not know that," with a helpless shrug, "only the whole affair is so strange. You do have other slide rules?"

"I have another," Myles admitted impatiently, "but even if he stole that expensive one—you borrowed it, Ann, for Sunny to try out—he couldn't possibly get more than a few dollars for it in a pawnshop or secondhand dealer's."

"That reminds me," Ann said, "Sunny wouldn't bother with it, Myles, so I'll have her bring it home tomorrow to replace the one you've lost. I know how a person gets to depend on a thing like that."

She noticed how intently the Brazilian was listening, his black brows furrowed in concentration, so she explained.

"My sister works at the Parker Foundry here in town, Mr. Prestes, and has to do a lot of figuring. I thought the slide rule might help her. But Myles shouldn't have lent it; it's too valuable as a souvenir of his bridge building days."

"I need nothing to remind me of *that*," Myles growled.

Prestes did not appear to hear the remark; he continued to stare at Ann.

"This is so interesting for me, Miss Jerome," he said. "So very unusual, eh? I mean, you Yankee girls"—he waved expressively—"*all* the North American girls seem to have jobs of work! And your sister is at this foundry?"

"You've probably seen her," Myles suggested. "Sonia Jerome is secretary to the manager—your friend Joe Snell."

"Aha, my very good friend Joe! Then your sister must be the so beautiful girl with golden hair? Right in the office with him, eh?" He kissed his finger with a knowing leer. "What a very interesting arrangement!"

"A business arrangement," Myles retorted sharply. "She is Snell's right-hand man—or girl—from all I hear."

Ann slid a look at him under her lashes to see if there might be a hidden meaning in the remark, but his face remained impassive. On the other side of Myles she saw the South American watching him as well.

"She appears quite—efficient—that is the word?" Prestes murmured. "When I drop in at the office to see Joe she seems always so busy. No time for pleasantries with me, you know." He shrugged and grinned. "But perhaps I should not make pretty speeches to the working girl—is that so? Joe did not seem to like it, either. Would he have a reason?"

Myles snorted. "Perhaps you Latin Romeos work too fast for our girls," he suggested, and deliberately turned the conversation away from Sunny. It seemed to him that Prestes was becoming overly inquisitive about matters which did not concern him, and he wondered how the man would take to similar probing.

"You are learning a lot about our country, Mr. Prestes, and I trust that your business is progressing as satisfactorily. I understood Ben Turner to say that you brought a letter of introduction to Snell from some customer of his?"

"That is so, Mr. Langdon."

"Someone you knew in Brazil?"

"No, in New York. I buy some things from him—what you call novelties, I think—for my trade."

Myles nodded. "One of your suppliers, huh? And he also does business with the foundry? Exporting castings and so on? Rather an unusual combination, isn't it?"

"I do not know his business with the foundry, Mr. Langdon; I did not ask. Shall I ask, since you wish to know?"

Even Ann noticed the altered tone, the chill undercurrent in the smooth words, and glanced at him in surprise.

Myles was tracing his initials on the counter with a wet straw, his face carefully blank, but his mind pondered the change. It was the first time he had heard anything but open, rather effusive friendliness from Prestes and the shift was disturbing. Enlightening, too. It suggested a character which might have much in common with Snell's ruthless arrogance and the reason that they seemed to have become close friends. Hardly a recommendation for the South American.

Almost at once Prestes recovered his habitually easy manner and attempted to cover up his rudeness with small talk.

"You know, Mr. Snell has been most kind to me, a stranger, putting me in your very comfortable club and introducing me to many of his friends. We have been once or twice to his hunting lodge, too; very good fun. You go there with him, Mr. Langdon?"

"No."

The curt reply drew a frown from Prestes.

"Is it that you do not hunt, or you do not care for Mr. Joe Snell?"

"I'm not much of a hunter," Myles said, and let it go at that, as he took the small white paper-wrapped package the druggist handed him and stood up. "Okay, Ann, we'd better drift along."

He helped her off the stool and nodded to Prestes.

"See you around, *señor.*"

On the sidewalk he paused and looked at his companion.

"Run you home, Ann?" he offered. "Oh, you have your own car, haven't you."

"Yes, in the parking lot. I'm glad you're driving again."

"I'm coming along slowly. Have to pick up Sunny at the plant and thought it would be an easy workout for the arm. Glad you mentioned that slide rule, by the way; I'll get it from her now—before some half-wit steals that, too."

XVIII

A telephone call interrupted Myles Langdon's breakfast with the Leslie clan and he returned from it with a preoccupied frown.

"Mr. Parker, at the foundry," he explained to his aunt and uncle. "He's got trouble."

He sat down and thoughtfully studied the bacon and eggs that remained on his plate.

"It seems," he continued, "that I told Ann about my packing case being rummaged; she told Cecile Parker, about that and the trouble at the bank; and Cecile told her father."

He raised his head and gave his listeners a wry smile.

"Evidently, by the time the story reached the old man, each of the lovely ladies had added her bit to make it more exciting, so that a couple of puzzling incidents have turned into the makings of a crime wave. And Mr. Parker is more sure of this, and sounded very much upset, because the same thing has happened at the foundry."

He ate a piece of bacon and nodded at his rapt listeners.

"Yes sir! Last night somebody went through the desk drawers in Snell's office; dumped everything on the floor. Since I was in on the other incidents, Mr. Parker wants me to come out there and compare notes with him."

"Sure he was *at* the foundry?" Mr. Leslie asked. "I didn't think he went there much now; he leaves everything to Joe Snell."

"So I understand," Myles muttered. "Do you think it's misplaced confidence?"

The banker pursed his lips and shook his head.

"Joe is honest, for all his rough, tough manner."

"What made you ask that, Myles?" Aunt Pamela eyed him over the rim of her coffee cup. "It isn't like you. I hope you aren't listening to a lot of idle gossip about Joe."

"What gossip?" demanded Kathy without looking up from her bowl of cereal.

Myles and his aunt exchanged rueful glances; they were still not accustomed to the child's presence in the house and the need to guard their tongues. He ignored the question and diverted her with, "Have to get moving. *Qué hora es, gatita?*"

After an instant's hesitation Kathy remembered that lesson and ran to look at the tall clock in the hall.

"Ocho, señor," she said from the doorway.

"Son las ocho!" Myles corrected with a wink and turned to his uncle. "It's early enough so I can see what's eating Parker and still make Boston in time to take care of your business, as we planned."

"You're not driving all that way!" Mrs. Leslie wailed. "I know I've advised you to use your arm, but gradually, Myles!"

"Calm yourself. I'm picking up Fred Markham, he'll spell me at the wheel when I feel tired. *If* I feel tired," he amended with grim determination.

"Who's Fred What's-his-name?" asked Kathy, back in her chair.

"The man I'm picking up, nosy." Myles patted her fondly on the top of her head and went to get his coat.

The Parker Foundry lay on the edge of the city, a sprawling cluster of buildings which showed by the variety of their wood and brick construction how the business had grown year after year. Its expansion from a two-bits operation was one of the things which contributed to Laurence Parker's habitual look of wonder; he still found it hard to believe that he owned a million-dollar enterprise.

Myles drove into the yard, left his machine in line with the cars parked there, and stood for a moment looking about. A police cruiser almost blocked the office doorway and beyond it Sonia was getting into her car. When she saw him she waved and hurried forward, her cardinal red coat standing out like a bright blossom against the huge pile of iron scrap in the background.

"Hi!" he called, going forward to meet her. "Where are you off to?"

"Home!" Sunny's cheeks were pink and her eyes sparkled with indignation. "I'm fired!"

"Cheers!" was his unsympathetic response. "Did Snell have to call a load of cops to throw you out? I saw you having a set-to with him at the tea party and he was mad enough to bite afterwards. Did you give him the final brush-off?"

"I don't know what you mean by that!" Sunny's color deepened until it almost matched her coat. "I told him to stop pestering me because I'm engaged to you."

"I'll bet that surprised him," Myles could not resist the chance for sarcasm. "So good old Joe was mad enough to fire you? With him, that figures."

"I guess that's the reason," she muttered, "although he pretended it was on account of the trouble here. Somebody broke in last night and generally messed things around in our office. But they didn't steal anything as far as we know."

"Didn't crack the safe?"

Sunny's blush returned and she looked down at her feet.

"They didn't have to because I forgot to lock it when I left yesterday. That was Joe's excuse for firing me."

"Not a bad one, if you ask me," Myles conceded with a grin. "Well, you run along home and I'll go in and see how old man Parker is bearing up."

"He's all right; having the time of his life watching the police look for fingerprints. That antique Ben Snowden has a special camera in case they find any. Can you imagine *him* as a detective?"

"Maybe not the popular private eye type, but there's plenty of bulldog in old Ben," Myles differed. "I'll bet he'd hang on a case till he cracked it."

"Well, they hadn't found anything for him to *crack* by the time I left, and the place was crawling with police!" Sunny scoffed and departed. Myles went into the office.

Her description of it as "crawling with police" had been more vivid than accurate. Only Snowden and a plain-clothes man were examining the premises, while Mr. Parker dogged their every move with breathless interest, as though he were watching a crime movie on TV. Joe Snell was gathering up scattered papers from the floor and sorting them into piles. At Myles's entrance he straightened and scowled.

"What's the idea?" he rasped. "A snooper from the bank to see if we're still in business?"

"Mr. Parker asked me to come," Myles informed him shortly.

"That's right, Joe!" Mr. Parker snapped. "You mind your tongue!" He spared a moment from watching the police work to shake hands. "Sorry to bother you, Myles, but I thought we ought to get together on this. I want to see what these officers find, so get the dope from Joe, will you?" He went back to the policemen.

"Really nothing to it." Snell continued his rescue of the papers from the floor. "Might have been kids. They didn't take a thing."

Myles leaned against a desk and watched him.

"Was there anything here, except the office equipment I see, that a crook could turn into money?"

"Nope. Not even five dollars' worth of stamps and petty cash. Which is damned lucky, Langdon, seeing that your girl friend didn't have sense enough to lock that safe last night!" He vented some of his irritation by slamming a handful of pencils into a drawer.

Myles ignored the criticism of Sunny, appreciating that under the circumstances Snell's anger was justified. He had just had a disturbing thought and lowered his voice.

"Maybe they weren't after money, Joe. Do you have any government work—classified defense contracts?"

Snell stood up, his hands full of papers, to stare at Myles.

"Do you know any plant—in most any line of work—that isn't mixed up in government projects? But I get you; we *are* turning out stuff which might be damned interesting to—er, to foreigners. You think someone might have been after blueprints or specifications?"

"It's a possibility, isn't it?"

"Could be—but they wasted their time in here." Joe glanced across the room, where both officers and the old gentleman were in a huddle, and moved closer to Myles. "We keep everything like that in another safe," he murmured. "It's a small vault—off the drafting room."

Myles nodded. "Good idea, and I hope not too many

people know about it. In fact, I wish you hadn't told *me!*"

"Oh, come now! I hate to admit it, Langdon, but you're one guy I'd never suspect of any crooked work."

"Thanks," Myles laughed. "I only meant that the fewer people who know about such things the better."

"Sure. Anyway, you've come up with the only sensible explanation of this fool business. I'm going to talk to some of the men, see if they have any ideas about who might be blabbing about our work."

"Do it carefully, Joe." Myles looked toward Mr. Parker, who continued to impede the efforts of the police by his close supervision. Ben Snowden had to elbow him aside to inspect something on the inner surface of the safe.

"Joe," Myles whispered with a nod in their direction, "I wonder if the old man has been careless?"

"Forget it!" Indignation made it a bark, but Snell instantly lowered his voice. "He may be getting along in years but he's still on the ball. For the love of Mike, he's been mixed up in defense work since before World War II, when you and I were kids! That's what built up this foundry, and he didn't get those jobs by shooting off his mouth. He hasn't changed, either!"

As Snowden adjusted his camera the foundry owner picked that moment to turn and beckon.

"Come and watch, Myles," he called. "See this gadget to photograph fingerprints? Mighty clever! Show him, Ben."

Snowden uttered an impatient grunt.

"Leave us alone, will you! Give me elbow room! Move over!"

"Lay off, Ben!" Snell ordered roughly. "Mr. Parker happens to *own* this place and he is certainly entitled to watch you if he wants to. Stop crabbing, do your job and get out of here!"

He glared for a moment at the muttering policeman who was again bending over the safe, gave a satisfied nod, and turned to Myles.

"The way bird-brain Snowden acts," he murmured, "you'd think my boss was a doddering old fool. I'll bet he could draw you a diagram of how that camera works right now! No sir, if anyone's been gossiping about our secrets it isn't Laurence Parker!"

When Myles left he felt confident that the foundry was

in good hands, and he had a new respect for Snell. Rough and tough he might be, but the young manager's evident fondness and admiration for Mr. Parker was as heartwarming as the sight of an alert dog protecting a helpless child from danger. And now that Joe was warned, anyone who entertained further ideas about stealing from the foundry had better look out.

At Sunnyfield Ann was enjoying the unusual pleasure of a late breakfast and an idle morning. She stretched luxuriously and settled lower in the glider on the terrace, causing Monty to groan and push against her thigh to keep his comfortable position. Gently she tugged a fold of her amber jersey skirt from under the dog and moved over. Monty accepted the added room and snored softly.

Sunshine was creeping closer across the flagstones as relentlessly as an incoming tide. Evidently it was going to be one of those hot Indian summer days; she ought to move back into the cooler shade but put off making the effort. Too comfortable to move. That excitement yesterday had left her more shaken than she realized, although part of her lassitude might be blamed on letdown, the realization that she was through at the bank.

Last night's interview with Uncle John Leslie had been stormy, indignation on her part, stubborn insistence on his. Ann Jerome was not to be further exposed to danger, or as she angrily put it—Ann Jerome was *fired* from her first job for no reason at all, and how would that look to her friends? All her protests were wasted breath; Uncle John proved strangely adamant.

Remembering Myles Langdon's white face as he dragged her to safety, she wondered if he was the force behind the usually indulgent Mr. Leslie. And having succeeded in "protecting" her—would Myles miss her at the bank? She bit her lip and pushed that thought back into the innermost closet of her brain.

How long would it remain there, though, when she saw him so frequently? When just a look from his grave eyes sent her heart pounding into her throat and her pulses throbbing? No matter how often and severely she told herself to forget him, that his engagement to Sunny made an insurmountable barrier between them, the mere mention of his name sent an uncontrollable shiver over her body. This emotional tempest could not be allowed to continue. Perhaps Uncle John was right, it was better to give up her position at the bank—not for her safety, but for whatever peace of mind it might bring.

Again she considered going away, breaking all ties— and maybe her heart.

From beyond the garden wall drifted a woman's voice raised in song, the rich brogue making up for the lack of tune:

> "O'Ryan was a man of might
> Whin Ireland was a nation . . ."

The Leslies' Mabel trudged across their garden toward the kitchen door carrying a basket.

> ". . . But poachin' was his heart's delight
> And constant occupation."

The slam of the door cut off the song.

Ann shook her head in smiling censure. That Mabel was certainly a character, but what wonderful care she took of the Leslie family and their home! The house was always spotless, glowing like a newly scrubbed face. Ann studied it with fond approval.

Sunshine filtered through the branches of the two immense oak trees, patterned the ivy-grown brick walls and the gray slate roof with fluttering shadows, stenciled the broad brick steps with wavering designs of gold. One of the trees brushed its leaves against the wrought-iron balcony above the side entrance. Many a time she had swung from its railing to the biggest branch and clambered to the ground to escape a tag in the riotous games she played with Sunny, Myles and the other children. Once Myles had outguessed her, lain in wait and caught her when she slid to the ground—

Myles again! Gritting her teeth, she sat up straighter and with determination opened the diary he had lent her. If it was no use trying to forget him she might as well enjoy his company in the comparative safety of the written word.

She was deep in the pages, enjoying without understanding the running account of technical difficulties, when footsteps on the terrace brought her back from the jungle with a start. Peter Bruce advanced, smiling.

"Good morning! Hope I'm not intruding?" he asked. "Heard about the hold-up, called the bank and they said you were taking the day off to recuperate. That sounded bad, worried me, so I thought I'd better check up."

"Thank you, but you needn't have worried. And I didn't *take* the day off—I was discharged for my own safety! Silly, isn't it? Otherwise I'm perfectly fine."

Bruce leaned against the table, hands in his pockets.

"Well, I figured you must be in fair shape if you could go out to dinner with—with someone last night. Sorry I was late in calling."

"I'm the one to apologize," Ann said hastily, "and I did *not* go out. That was a very garbled report Sarah gave you, but such things are to be expected from her and you'll have to get used to it." She studied him speculatively, realized that she was weighing him as a possible replacement for the unattainable Myles, and flushed. "I mean," she added quickly, "you must get used to it if you're going to try again."

"That I am!" He pulled up a chair and sat down facing her. "Glad you left that possibility open; you didn't look as though you would. You certainly size a man up with those big beautiful eyes, don't you! Is it my face you don't like, or are you still mad at your favorite jewel thief?"

"Nothing like that; as a matter of fact I was wondering why I liked you so much—and so suddenly. Even when I believed you were a burglar I was—fascinated."

"Me, too!" he admitted with an engaging smile. "Seems as though we ought to do something about it."

"I don't understand what you mean by that; I thought you were starry-eyed over Sonia."

"You mean at the dance? Blame that on my weakened condition."

Ann raised her brows in mockery.

"You appeared in excellent health at my party, but I noticed that you monopolized her at every opportunity."

"Ah?" he jeered. "So you were watching me! Beware of jealousy, the green-eyed monster—"

"You flatter yourself. As hostess, I watched *all* my guests to be sure they were entertained. Which you certainly were."

"All right, I admit it. You ought to post guards around that girl, she's dangerous. I've seen all I could of her since, until I found out that she's engaged. That meant curtains for Bruce! I don't go in for romance-wrecking. Nothing left of my heartache now but scar tissue, so"—He ogled her with exaggerated ardor—"you fascinate me more than ever!"

"Well, really! The second fiddle thanks you, sir!"

"That was a blooper, wasn't it!" he groaned. "How do I square myself now? Let's see—"

Before he could attempt it a black cat appeared on the wall, dropped to the flagstones and padded softly to him. Peter laughed with relief.

"Thanks, Delilah," he said, scratching the sleek head. "You saved an awkward situation. Glad you followed me—"

A whirlwind of charging spaniel erupted from the glider; a flurry of black fur whipped across the terrace.

"Monty!" Ann shouted. "Stop it! Come back here!"

The last command was as useless as the others; the dog was racing across the garden in fine voice, in the wake of the rapidly vanishing feline.

"If you're worried about our cat," Peter said when the uproar had subsided, "I assure you Delilah can more than take care of herself."

"She had better not come barging in here, just the same. Monty resents intruders."

"He must get that from his mistress, but at least he doesn't call the cops! And you haven't, this morning, so I must be making a little headway. Am I as fascinating by daylight as in the dark—and half-drowned, at that?"

"Even a second fiddle can look at a king."

Bruce shook his head and sighed.

"I can see it's going to take me some time to live down that unfortunate remark. Let's abandon personalities in favor of intellectual conversation. What were you reading when I arrived?"

"Myles Langdon's diary." She held up the weather-stained book. "No, I'll be technical if it kills me to remem-

ber. He called it his daybook; the daily account of what
went on at that bridge-building job in South America. He
warned me when I borrowed it that most of it would be
dry reading, but I think it's thrilling!"

Peter sat forward and reached for the book.

"Sounds very interesting. May I see it?"

"Well—" Ann hesitated, then dropped the book in her
lap. "I'd rather not show it to you without his permission,
Peter."

"For heaven's sakes, why not! It's just a record of the
job, isn't it? Nothing personal?"

"I don't know. He wrote about his life there, too, things
that happened to him, his impressions of the jungle and
the people. It's a personal diary as well as a construction
record, and perhaps he wouldn't care to have everyone
read it."

Peter's frown suggested that he resented her refusal, but
a second interruption prevented him from continuing the
argument. Kathy Flood galloped up the steps from the
garden with Delilah in her arms.

"Lookit!" she panted. "Isn't she the loveliest thing! I
found her in your apple tree, Ann. Hi, Mr. Bruce! Say, it's
the tree you and Sonia were parked under at the party!"

Bruce smiled at Ann's look of surprise.

"Evidently the perfect hostess missed that," he murmured.

Ann made a face at him and turned to the girl.

"Be careful she doesn't scratch you, dear. Was my
Monty there, too?"

"She wouldn't scratch—she loves me!" Kathy stroked a
black ear and the yellow eyes closed in rapture. "Monty's
over in our garden, digging in a hole. Mr. Duval says it's
a woodchuck burrow. This poor thing must be lost. Who
do you suppose owns her?"

"I know," Peter said. "A very nice lady who lives next
door and gives cookies to girls who return her wandering
pet. Her name is Delilah, by the way. The cat's, I mean.
The owner's name is Miss Bruce."

"Oh, your sister? She was at the party. I'd better take
Delilah right home so she won't worry."

"How come you're not in school today?" asked Ann.

Kathy shifted the animal to a more comfortable position and shrugged.

"Teachers' convention, or something. Should I go to the back door, or the front, Mr. Bruce?"

"My sister isn't there; the cleaning woman will let you in. Tell her I said to give you your reward. I suggest the back door, it's nearer the cookie jar."

Kathy drew herself up to her full height, little as that was, and gave him a haughty stare.

"I wasn't thinking of that! I merely wished to save anyone the inconvenience of coming to the front door in case they happened to be in the kitchen." Still nose in air, she departed, crooning to the cat.

"*That* for me!" Peter chuckled. "What a command of words!"

Ann laughed with him. "She reads books."

"The encyclopedia, for a guess." Without hesitation he resumed the subject Kathy had interrupted. "About Langdon's daybook you have there. I'm not being merely curious, I have a reason for finding out all I can about what went on down in Loma. My cousin, Walter Bruce, was Langdon's clerk and disappeared after the rebels wrecked the bridge."

"How dreadful! And you haven't located him?" She remembered what Myles had told her about Walter. "Why, he was 'the Jukebox Troubador'—that's what the men called him—the lovesick boy who wrote poetry." She smiled at the memory, glanced at Peter and then snapped her head around for a closer look. "What *is* the matter?" she gasped.

He was leaning forward in the chair, white-knuckled hands gripping the arms, his lips a thin hard line in a colorless face as he glared at her.

"What do *you* know about his poetry?" he demanded harshly.

XIX

The violence of the question shocked Ann; it took her a moment to collect her thoughts sufficiently to answer.

"His—his poetry?" she stammered. "Why, I only know what Myles told me. There was one of the poems slipped between the pages of this book when Kathy unearthed it from his engineering stuff. We read it. I understand that your cousin wrote them to a girl he was in love with."

"You still got it there?" Involuntarily his hand reached for the daybook, but he withdrew it and sat back.

"No, Myles threw it away." Ann searched his face with anxiety. "You're white, Peter; don't you feel well?"

"Must be the flu bug kicking back, but I'm really all right. Do you happen to remember the poem?"

"Why, I'm afraid not."

"Try, please. See if you can; I'm very much interested in anything to do with Walter."

To humor him she did try, frowning in the effort of recollection. It had been a silly verse; they had laughed at it; the first line had been something about calling love grand—

"I'm getting it! Ah! It started:

'The Spanish call love something grand,
    But I don't know the lingo'

"Then there were some Spanish names I don't recall, and it ended with 'by jingo,' to rhyme with lingo. It was pretty awful stuff, really!"

"I got that," Peter sighed and then added quickly, "I mean—I got that it was punk poetry."

Perversely Ann defended the Jukebox Troubador.

"Well, of course it wasn't the finished product. Myles said Walter used to copy them carefully before he mailed them. This was a rough draft on—on the back of a shipping list. I think that's what Myles called it."

"A shipping list?" Peter's fingers drummed on the chair arm. He gave Ann a long searching look. "You know Myles Langdon well, don't you? I wonder if you'd do something for me—without letting him know I asked you."

It was Ann's turn to stare appraisingly at the handsome face and level eyes fixed on hers. Surely there was nothing but honesty in them.

"What is it you want me to do?" she demanded cautiously.

"I want you to get me some information—which Langdon may be able to supply."

"Why not ask him yourself? He won't bite."

Bruce shook his head.

"I tried at the dance. He doesn't like to talk about Loma—to me, anyway. Can't say I blame him, it must have been a terrific blow to see all his work go up in smoke. I have an idea that *you* are the one person he'll open up to."

At her impulsive objection he held up his hand commandingly.

"I'm not forgetting his fiancée, either. I still say you are the one, and never mind why I think so. Will you question him—delicately—about some things which went on down there?"

"What things?" She was still on the defensive.

"To explain, I'll have to tell you a secret and ask you to keep it to yourself. And I mean just that!" He spoke with sober intensity. "Not a word to *anyone!* I know I can trust you."

"How impressive!" She clasped her hands in dramatic fervor, then laughed. "If your secret is anything less than world-shaking, my friend, you're overacting! But go on! Continue! Tell me! Of course you can trust me! 'Great Day,' as Sarah says—have you forgotten that we already share a deep, dark secret? That a certain eminent lawyer —from Washington, no less—was involved in a breaking and entering episode in the dead of night?"

Ann pointed her finger at him and smiled.

"No one else knows about *that,* I assure you, unless *you* have talked."

"Heaven forbid! I'm not so proud of that fiasco that I've blabbed it around. But this is a deadly serious matter, Ann! Please, take this seriously."

The gravity of his tone and the steady regard of his narrowed eyes impressed her.

"Well, all right, if you insist on making a federal case of it." With a last attempt at levity she crossed her heart in the childhood gesture. "Hope to die if I tell—unless I talk in my sleep."

"I'll chance that." He produced his wallet and held it a moment while he seemed to deliberate. "Don't accuse me of 'making a federal case' of this, Ann; but that's what it is." He flipped open the wallet and held it toward her.

Ann stared for a moment and then recoiled as though a snake had struck at her. "Federal Bureau of Investigation! You? *FBI!*"

Bruce snapped the wallet shut, returned it to his pocket and sat back in his chair.

"Actually I'm in the Washington office and not usually involved directly on investigations; this is something of a coincidence. I caught the flu and was on leave of absence when Sue rented the house here. I came with her to kill two birds with one stone: recuperation and the possibility of picking up some information."

"We're back to that," Ann said eagerly. "From Myles?"

"I hope so. It's a long story, so make yourself comfortable. To begin with, you probably know that there is a lot of unrest in South America, a series of revolutions and attempted revolts in the various countries. Because of the general poverty there none of these disturbances could last long—unless they received help from outside."

"Communist help?"

"We don't need to pinpoint the source, it's the effect which concerns us. The situation there and in the Caribbean at present is like a smoldering volcano, a serious threat to world peace. We hope to avert any local explosion which might trigger wholesale war. That is why we investigated the tip that there is a considerable amount of illegal shipment of arms and ammunition—generally called 'gunrunning'—from the States to South America."

"To Loma?"

He settled more comfortably in his chair and nodded.

"Among others, yes. Anywhere, in fact, where there's trouble—and troublemakers to use the guns. Our government must stop it, of course, and my department has the job. The first step was to locate the shippers in this country and we investigated various possible sources of supply. No luck. Then an agent was sent down to the west coast of S.A. to try and dig up information from that end. He found out definitely that the stuff was coming into the port of Condona from New York, but for some months couldn't discover who was shipping it."

"This *is* exciting!" Ann swung her legs off the glider and sat facing him, chin in hands. "Go on! Wasn't it queer, though, that they should send guns from New York to the far side of South America? Why not from San Francisco or Los Angeles, they're so much nearer?"

"That's a good question, and I'll admit we wasted some time checking those ports in the beginning. Probably the shippers figured we'd do just that, and get nowhere. Anyway, distance isn't important, the added cost would mean nothing to them because the profits are enormous on deals like this. Getting the goods there safely is what those crooks want. They are crooks, you know, if they smuggle contraband, even if they control freight lines and appear respectable."

"Did your man down there find out who was sending the guns?"

"No. What he did find out—" Peter stopped, hesitated, then stared out over the garden, his face grim. "He found that the contraband was coming into Loma hidden among the cargoes consigned to the Carrington Construction Company."

There was a moment of utter silence and then Ann flashed up from the glider and faced him with blazing eyes.

"Do you mean to insinuate that Myles Langdon would—You're detestable!"

"Control yourself!" Bruce lifted a placating hand and laughed. "I never knew anyone who jumped to wrong conclusions as fast as you do. First you tag me for a crook, now you accuse me of maligning your future brother-in-law. I didn't *insinuate* anything, Ann, I merely gave you a cold *fact*. Nothing to do with Langdon; probably the same goes for his company. Somebody took advantage of their shipments, that's all. Personally I like your friend Myles very much."

"Well, that's better!" Ann smiled and sat down. "Hurry up and tell me more! I'm thrilled to death and have a thousand ears. To borrow from 'The Ancient Mariner':

> " 'The Wedding Guest sat on a stone,
>   He cannot choose but hear!' "

"That's my situation."

"Do I 'hold you with a glittering eye'?" Smiling, Peter capped her quotation, and then became serious again. "There isn't much more to tell—yet. The last word from the operative in Loma was that he had a sure lead, a contact able to give him the names of the ring in New York who are behind the shipments and he would send them in his next report. With that list we could gather in the men and break up the gunrunning for good. Well, it never came; there was never another message from him."

"What happened?" Ann demanded, breathless with suspense.

"After a while another man went down there to investigate and I received his final report a few days ago." Bruce sat silent a moment, scowling at his clenched fists. "He found that the rebels had carried off the other agent and killed him. They tortured him first."

"*Tortured!*" Ann gasped. "The beasts! Why would they do that?"

"To find out what he had been up to, what he knew."

"But—but—you mean they *knew* he was an FBI man! I thought you people always worked under cover, so how could that be?"

Peter shrugged. "Who knows? Maybe they intercepted some of his reports, which were in a very simple code—so simple that no one should have suspected them. No need to keep it secret now, it won't be used again. His reports were poems to a nonexistent girl named Alice in New York."

"*Alice?* But your cousin wrote to her!"

Bruce nodded soberly.

"Walter was the agent in Loma."

If Peter expected a reaction to his announcement Ann felt certain that she satisfied him. For a long moment she sat open-mouthed and, she was sure, goggle-eyed while she stared at him. Slowly she got her breath back, and with it some of her composure. She shook her head in reproof.

"Why do you spoil an exciting story with absurdities, Peter? That lovesick boy an FBI agent? And planted as a clerk in Myles Langdon's office without his knowing it? Really, neither Myles nor I are as stupid as you seem to assume!"

"There you go, jumping to the wrong conclusion again —several of them, in fact." He raised one finger. "First, and most important, I think you are anything but stupid, which is why I've told you all this. From observing you in various circumstances, including the capture of a danger-ous jewel thief like the Duke, I would say you have one of the quickest minds I've ever run into."

He reinforced the compliment with a smiling bow and lifted another finger.

"Second, Langdon, after short acquaintance, impresses me as knowing what the score is every minute." He low-ered his hand. "I'll run out of fingers before I'm through. As to getting an agent into Langdon's office, the Federal Bureau, because of the type of men used and their thorough training, can infiltrate anywhere. Ninety-nine per cent of the time without detection."

"I suppose that's true," Ann conceded. "But that *boy!*"

"Walter looked a lot younger than he was, which can be a definite advantage sometimes, and he was selected for that South American assignment because he speaks the language like a native." Bruce smiled reminiscently. "I got a kick out of Langdon's suggestion the other night that Walt talked a lot with the workmen to improve his Spanish. Luckily I didn't laugh; he was touchy enough without that. Now I'm asking you to find out from him all you can about what went on down there. It won't be easy."

"I know; he certainly hates to talk about it."

Peter waved aside that obstacle.

"He'll open up to you, I'm sure. That isn't what I meant, it's the particular information I want that may be hard to get. Here's the situation; Walter was to get the names of the kingpin smugglers in New York from some-one down there. Either he didn't have time to get the in-formation and relay it to us, or his report was intercepted. We must find that informer and try to get the list of names, even at this late date.

"I want you to get Langdon talking about Loma. Things he's forgotten now but may remember as he talks. Es-pecially anything about the people that Walter spent time with."

"Well, I'll try," Ann said doubtfully, "but I keep think-ing about your cousin being tortured—it gives me the shivers!"

A touseled head popped up over the wall and Kathy Flood's round eyes gleamed with excitement.

"*What* gives you the shivers?" she demanded breath-lessly.

"Nothing really, dear, I was just talking with Mr. Bruce. Did you get Delilah home safely?"

"Yup! And the cookies were yummy! Golly, I should have brought you some but I ate 'em!" She climbed onto the wall and walked along it, balancing with the grace of a circus queen of the high wire.

"Be careful!" Bruce half rose from his chair.

"Don't worry about her," Ann advised calmly. "I used to do that when I was her age, and before. Even if she managed to fall off she couldn't hurt herself. Kathy is the adventurous type, as Aunt Pam is learning at the cost of a few more gray hairs. She never knows what the child will try next."

They watched her reach the far end of the wall, turn with a pirouette and start back, before Ann resumed the interrupted discussion.

"Of course you want me to get the information as soon as possible, don't you? Suppose I drop in at the bank, very casually, as though I just couldn't bear to leave my former haunts? If I go now I can catch Myles before he leaves for lunch."

"You can't!" Kathy, who had heard the last sentence, announced from the wall. "Uncle Myles drove to Boston. I heard him talking to Grandpa about it. Bank business," she added importantly.

Ann sat up with a worried frown.

"You mean he's *driving* that distance with only one—?" She smothered the alarmed question.

"One arm?" Kathy supplied cheerfully. "Yup, he says he's getting pretty good. Just the same, he's taking—uh—Fred Somebody from the bank to help him. Do you know Fred?"

"Fred Markham? Yes, he's the assistant treasurer."

"Well, they're driving up together. Just when Uncle Myles was ready to start he had a phone call from Mr. Parker to come up to the foundry right away. Something happened there last night, but I don't know what."

Peter chuckled. "I'm surprised that you missed anything!"

"So Uncle Myles has gone to Boston," Kathy continued, serenely ignoring him, "so it's no use your trying to see him. Hey! There's Monty with his nose all covered with dirt!" she squealed, leaping into the garden. "I wonder if he caught Mr. Woodchuck?"

"Kathy!" Ann called after the running girl. "When will Myles be back?"

"Tomorrow afternoon!"

"There goes the intended interview," Bruce sighed, starting to leave by the terrace steps. "Please try and see him tomorrow, and let me know what you get as soon as possible, will you?"

Ann stood up and saluted.

"Operative 13 will report at the earliest moment!" she promised with pretended solemnity.

Bruce whirled and for a moment studied her under frowning brows. Then he relaxed.

"Okay, Operative 13! But I did hope that I had impressed you with the seriousness of this business. If it's a game with you, it's one with a good many human lives at stake!" He walked quickly into the garden.

It took Ann a moment to recover from that verbal spanking and by the time she did he was out of sight.

"Sorry, Peter!" she called, but there was no answer.

"Too little and too late!" she murmured, resolving to make a proper apology as soon as she could bring him some worthwhile information.

Wholly absorbed in his tale of jungle intrigue, whose long arm stretched to the States, and thrilled to have even a minor part in the investigation, she had for a moment completely forgotten that the murdered agent in Loma was his cousin.

She sank down on the glider and stared glumly at her clenched hands.

"Peter has remarkable self-control," she sighed, "or he would have thrown something at me. I wonder if he still considers me 'anything but stupid,' as he so gallantly put it?"

XX

Determined to leave no stone unturned in her efforts to help Peter, and thereby retrieve his good opinion, Ann lay back and tried to remember everything that Myles had said about his clerk. He had joked about him when they found the verse in the daybook, but had talked seriously about this young man far from home and in love with a New York girl, when he let himself go at Aunt Pam's supper party.

She remembered that he had been troubled by Walter's association with the natives, although he misunderstood the reason for it. Perhaps his diary would mention some-one with whom Walter was particularly friendly, someone who might have been able to supply him with the informa-tion about the contraband.

Determinedly she picked up the book, found her place, and began to read. She was deep in the fourth month of construction work when a car whirled into the drive and skidded to a stop. She heard the front door bang shut and Sonia strode out to confront her.

"Greetings, loafer!" The pink of indignation still colored Sunny's cheeks. "Have you room here for another ex-wage-slave?" At Ann's amazed stare she laughed scornfully. "Don't glare at me that way! *You* were fired, weren't you?"

"Joe fired you?" Ann gasped, and then realized that she should have expected it to happen. "Was it because you finally gave him the gate at our tea?"

Sunny's cheeks flushed still more, her eyes narrowed.

"How did you know that? Did *he* come running to you and—?"

"Hardly, my dear!" Ann interrupted sarcastically. "Mr. Snell doesn't favor me with any confidences since the day we lunched at the Chop House and I gave him my unflattering opinion of"—She remembered Myles's gibe—"of poachers. No, he didn't need to tell me; he was the picture of baffled rage when he came in from your interview."

"He *was* boiling," Sonia admitted with satisfaction. Ignoring the chair Peter had vacated, she pulled a chaise nearer and dropped into it. "I expected he would be, so I got him out of range of our guests—out under our apple tree."

"Really? I heard it was Peter Bruce you had there!" Ann countered tartly.

"Afterward, yes." Her sister jerked upright. "Who told you that?"

"Little Kathy. Sees all, knows all. But back to Joe Snell. Did he actually have the nerve to fire you because you dropped him flat?"

"Oh, he made up another excuse, but I'm sure that was the real reason." Sunny told of the break at the foundry and was annoyed when Ann hooted with laughter at her confession about the safe.

"There's never anything valuable in that old box!" she defended stubbornly. "And they didn't take a thing from our desks, either; they just messed papers around."

Before Ann could take issue with her on a secretary's duties Peter Bruce came hurrying through the garden.

"Anything wrong, Sunny?" he called and took the terrace steps in a leap. Then he seemed to realize that his impetuous arrival suggested undue interest in an engaged girl, and became nonchalant. "Saw you drive in here, when you're supposed to be at work—wondered if anything had happened."

"Nothing to unsettle that scar tissue you boasted about," Ann said, repressing a smile at his confusion. "Sunny has just joined the unemployed."

She watched with amusement while her sister once more poured out the tale of her dismissal. Peter's expression, as well as she could judge, mingled anticipation of sharing some of Sonia's new leisure time and curiosity about the attempt to rob the foundry.

Even in a demure office dress of honey-brown wool with a white piqué collar the golden-haired girl made a mouth-watering picture where she lounged on the chaise. Most men, Ann thought, would be spellbound. Now that she knew Peter's connection with the FBI, however, she was not surprised to hear him swing the conversation back to the crime.

"You say there never was much cash kept in the safe," he observed, tilting back in his chair and lighting a cigarette, "because the help were paid by check? You employ several hundred, don't you, so that fact must be general knowledge in town? Who would bother to break in, then?"

Ann snapped her fingers.

"Could it be that thief the police were looking for—the Duke, wasn't it?" she suggested with a sidelong smirk at Peter. "But I hear he was captured."

"More than once," he agreed, smiling and rolling his eyes from Ann to Sonia. "Anyway, the Duke's only interested in valuable jewelry, I understand, and there was evidently none of that in the office."

"How about the dope who tried to rob our bank?" Ann offered, and told of that futile effort.

Bruce shrugged it off.

"That sounds like a sneak thief acting on impulse; in this foundry case someone went to a lot of trouble to break in." He thought for a moment before he asked slowly, "A foundry could be—" He looked inquiringly at Sonia. "Any classified defense work going through your plant?"

"Yes—no! I'm not supposed to talk about it."

"The perfect secretary!" Ann jeered. "You'll have to

watch your tongue with this man, sister dear, he's a—"
She caught herself in time and finished lamely "—he's a
lawyer, a demon at cross-examination."

"How do *you* know?" Sonia snapped, annoyed at her
own carelessness. "What's he been trying to pump out of
you?"

"She's only trying to flatter me," Peter soothed, with
a disgusted glare at Ann. "But I'm really interested in this
foundry business and would like to discuss it—without
prying into secrets. Your sister was reading," he pointed
out, "so why don't we two adjourn to the living room
where we won't disturb her?"

"You won't bother me," Ann protested.

"The sun's too hot out here," Sunny decided, quitting
her seat with noticeable eagerness. "Peter, will you drag
Ann's glider into the shade, I'm sure she'll be more comfortable."

"Good!" Ann applauded. "Then I won't be tempted to
come in and bother *you*."

Grave-faced but inwardly rocking with laughter, she
rose to permit him to make the suggested change. When
they left she dutifully tried to lose herself in the day-by-
day account of life in the Loma jungle and close her ears
to the murmur of conversation in the living room. Until,
that is, it grew too loud to be ignored.

"Conversation?" she jeered, keeping her eyes on her
book. "It sounds more like an argument! And I'll bet it
doesn't concern the trouble at the foundry." In spite of
herself she couldn't miss hearing her sister's desperate protest, "No—I won't, Peter—you know it wouldn't be fair!
Please—!"

While Ann struggled with the urge to break up whatever
was going on she was saved from making a decision by
the front door chimes. They produced instant silence,
broken a few moments later by Sarah's excited tones, and
the maid, trailed by Sonia and Peter, came scurrying to
the terrace.

"A telegram!" she panted, waving the yellow envelope.
"For you two girls! A boy just brought it on a bike!"

"You open it, Ann," Sunny suggested. "Those things
always make me nervous!"

"All right, let's have it," Ann ordered calmly, swinging

her feet to the ground and sitting up. "I wonder why they didn't telephone it as usual."

"I asked the boy that!" Sarah shrilled, "and he says they had strict orders to deliver it by hand—so it must be terrible important!" She peered over her glasses as Ann ripped open the envelope. "The Lord preserve us from bad news!" she muttered fervently.

Ann stared at the message, gulped and shook her head to clear her brain.

"Brace yourself, Sunny!" she warned, and read it aloud:

SUE AND I MARRIED THIS MORNING. FORGIVE US FOR NOT LETTING YOU IN ON IT. QUICK AND QUIET SEEMED THE BEST WAY. TELL OUR FRIENDS BUT NO FORMAL ANNOUNCEMENT. QUOTE: GOD'S IN HIS HEAVEN, ALL'S RIGHT WITH THE WORLD.   LOVE, DAD.

Robert Jerome's love of the dramatic would have been well satisfied by the reception accorded his bomb. After an interval of stupefied silence there was a chain reaction of delighted exclamations from the three women.

"Married?" squealed Sunny, clasping her hands.

"To that lovely Susan Bruce!" Ann cried.

"The very one I picked for him!" Sarah was in tears, but tears of joy.

"You picked her?" Ann gasped. "And when was this?"

"The minute I laid eyes on her, coming into the house with him. There's a winner, I said to myself!"

"Well," Ann admitted, "I guess we all felt that way."

"I did!" Sunny nodded happily. "I suspect that Dad was pretty lonely at times—perhaps that's why he stayed away so much. Maybe now he'll feel like making this his real home."

"If they decide to live here."

"They will," Sarah announced. "Else why did he have me show her everything about the house when she was here? And she loved it all—or so she said."

"How could she help it?" Sunny demanded. "It's perfect! I do think Dad might have told us, let us throw a party for the wedding!"

Ann settled back in the glider and shook her head.

"No, I think this was the better way. When they come home everyone who wants to can have welcome parties."

Sarah let out a startled yelp.

"Great day! He'll be bringing her here, won't he! And this house is a sight!"

"Don't be foolish!" Ann laughed. "You keep this place as neat as a new pin; two new pins, in fact! I feel guilty every time I touch anything for fear I'll leave a smooch!"

"Little you know how a new wife will look in the corners and try the banisters for dust!" was Sarah's dire prophecy. She took off her glasses to wipe damp eyes and replaced them with a determined shove. "None too much time to put the house in shape," she muttered and trotted inside as though she expected the bridal couple to appear on the doorstep at any moment.

With her departure Peter, who had allowed the deluge of talk to roll around him with exemplary patience, ventured to put in a word of his own.

"Unless my ears deceive me," he remarked, "you are all pleased with the event?"

"And how!" the sisters chorused. Ann passed the telegram to him with an anxious, "You approve, don't you?"

"With cheers," he smiled, reading it for himself. "To paraphrase a famous remark, never have so few words given so much pleasure to so many. I like the poetic touch, too."

Sonia laughed. "Trust Dad to get in a quotation and hang the cost." A new idea caused her to clutch Ann and point at Bruce with theatrical amazement. " 'Child!' as Sarah would say—do you realize who this gentleman is? He's our Uncle Peter!"

"Why, so he is! Imagine that! Wouldn't he look more the part, though, if he were a little fatter, slightly bald, hair becomingly touched with gray at the temples?"

"I'm afraid," Peter sighed, "that I will take care of all those details in the course of time."

"I like Uncle Peter just the way he is!" Sonia objected.

"Blessings on you for that, niece-in-law. I suggest that this happy event demands a celebration. How about a day at the beach, sunning ourselves with fur coats handy, followed by dinner at some swanky eating place—all on Uncle Peter, naturally?"

"Let's go!" Sunny applauded.

"It will get really cold if the east wind comes up," Ann warned, "but it does sound like a lot of fun. Too bad Myles isn't here."

Bruce sobered and looked at her uncertainly.

"You think he'd object to—to my taking his fiancée to dinner?"

"For heaven's sake—why?" Sunny pouted. "You're chaperoning us, sis, if that worries you."

"I only mean it's too bad he's missing this family celebration—he might have been able to get off from his job."

"Well, yes," Sonia conceded reluctantly. "But after all, he's not a member of the family."

"Not yet."

She chose to ignore the implication of Ann's remark and persisted in the argument.

"I'm sure Myles would feel out of place at our family celebration."

"Then it would be the first time," Ann retorted, remembering the years of close comradeship between the three of them. "While you're getting ready, I'll run over and tell Aunt Pam the news. She and Uncle John should be the first to hear it."

"Don't be long, then, or we'll miss the best part of the day. Whose car are we taking?"

"Mine!" said Peter firmly. "And I'm driving; too precious a load of youth and beauty to trust with an excited Jerome girl today."

"I've never had an accident!" Sunny protested indignantly.

"So I hear," Peter said with a grin, "but after riding with you I'll never understand why. For your information, this is old Uncle Peter's party all the way. Climb into your sporting clothes, ladies; I'll come around and blow my trumpet before the castle gate—and don't keep me waiting!"

The afternoon and evening were as crammed with pleasure and luxurious living as Peter had promised, so that Ann should have enjoyed every minute. But, in spite of Sunny's arguments, she did miss Myles. The thought that he wasn't in on their fun, as he had been so many times before, was a constant undercurrent of regret. But only for her; Sunny, with Peter Bruce constantly attentive, had not seemed so carefree for weeks.

"I never believed in that old saying," Ann mused bitterly, "'Out of sight—out of mind,' but my little sister makes me wonder if it's true. No, it can't be—how can the heart forget?"

Late that night, when she and her sister were preparing for bed, Sunny insisted on reviewing all the events of the party until Ann called a weary halt to the monologue and suggested sleep.

"We can sleep all morning," Sonia objected, "now that we are both without jobs. Farewell, foundry!"

"Lucky you're through there; it might have been uncomfortable under the circumstances."

"Working for a man after I'd given him the air?" She shrugged. "I intended to quit, of course. Being fired is what burns me, but I'm glad to be clear of Joe Snell in any way!"

Ann, who had been compelled to hear his praises sung for so long, could not resist a sarcastic, "So you can devote yourself to Myles, you mean?"

"That sounds like a nasty crack, but I forgive you. Let's drop that subject and discuss something interesting—like our future."

"As ladies of leisure, I suppose?"

"Not me," Sunny announced. "I'm going to find another job. Aren't you?"

Ann nodded. "Certainly. Sitting around and being useless has no appeal. I've been thinking of spreading my wings, faring forth into the wild blue yonder, as the song has it. Perhaps New York or Boston. Get an apartment—"

"Leave Sunnyfield!" It was an incredulous gasp. "But why?"

"We can't stay here forever." Carefully avoiding any hint of her true reason, Ann pointed out, "This house has a new mistress now; it's hers. And you'll be marrying Myles soon, and want a place of your own, won't you?"

"I—I hadn't thought about it."

"Well, you'd better!" Ann advised curtly. "Or do you intend to keep him dangling forever? Good *night!*"

XXI

Myles Langdon waded grimly through the accumulation of work which he found on his desk when he returned from Boston. Lunch had been a sandwich snatched on his way to the bank; with no interruptions he hoped to finish in time to get home for dinner. He wondered if in this short time he had become so valuable to the bank that all these matters must come to him. Or had Uncle John arranged it to keep him busy and so content with this humdrum job?

That bridge in upper New York would soon be under way; Red Fallon breaking in a new crew—

A knock at his half-open door shattered his daydream. His annoyance at the interruption doubled when Joe Snell poked his head in. Rain beaded his tan coat and dripped from his hat.

"Busy, Langdon?" he asked.

Myles shrugged. "Come in, Joe." A possible reason for the call straightened him in his chair. "Something new on that burglary?"

"No, don't know any more than I did." Snell approached the desk and hesitated, rubbing his chin and clearing his throat. "Listen, Langdon, it's tough to say, but I apologize for the way I carried on at the Jerome tea." He drew in a nervous breath. "I got damn mad, acted like a fool! I'm sorry."

The speech was so unexpected, so out of character that Myles stared wordlessly. Then he jumped to his feet and shot out his hand.

"Forget it, Joe! I said a few things I regretted, too."

Snell's sigh of relief was audible as he shook hands.

"While I'm about it, I apologize for yesterday morning at the foundry."

"That didn't bother me; a burglary is liable to upset anybody."

"Sure, that's what I told 'em and——" Snell stopped, flushed and then spread his hands in surrender. "Might as well admit that I caught hell from both of them—Cecile and her father—for the way I've been acting. She overheard us at the tea party and, of course, Mr. Parker was right in the office when you were there. They ganged up on me last night," he sighed, "and I guess what they said is true—I'm a roughneck. I've heard that from Cecile often enough and laughed it off, but the old man knows how to make it sink in, believe me, and I ain't laughing!"

"He's had years of experience in handling all kinds of men and I understand he used to be a fire-eater."

"Yeh, and he hasn't lost his touch!" Joe grinned sheepishly. "So I guess I reform—or else!" He drew a relieved breath. "Now that's off my chest, I really came about something else. Wanted to ask if you know where that guy Prestes is."

"Why, no. He's your friend, not mine. Sit down, Joe."

Snell shook his head violently, as he took the customers' chair.

"Count me out. I took care of him because a good customer sent him, and I've entertained him some; but I can't stand the friends he's picked up lately. One of them from New York looks like something you'd find under a rock —long and thin and creepy!"

He swept off his hat, shook it violently, and dropped it on the floor beside him.

"Anyway, Prestes has been using my cabin and I want the keys in a hurry. I phoned the Country Club but they haven't seen him today. I sent a man out to the shack and it's locked up tight as a drum. I understand that Prestes comes in here off and on and thought maybe you'd see him and tell him I want the keys for a feller who has to look at the cabin tomorrow morning, if he's going to buy it."

"You're selling it?" Myles demanded in surprise.

"Yup. Cecile says——" Embarrassment halted him but

he shrugged it off. "She says for me to get rid of it and cut out the wild parties. She won't marry a poker-playing bum."

"Good for her! And good luck to you, Joe."

"Thanks." He picked up his hat and edged toward the door. "Don't forget about Prestes, will you, huh?"

So that, Myles thought as he went to work, explains Joe's crack about being in a better position than manager at the Parker foundry. And I suspected he meant to pull a Uriah Heep and squeeze the old man out. My mistake. Joe Snell is evidently what they call him, rough but a genuine diamond after all.

It was long after banking hours and the employees had left when another caller broke in on Myles at work, although this time he enjoyed the interruption because Ann caused it. Never had she looked lovelier, Myles thought, nor more desirable.

"Welcome, but how did you get in?" he asked as he placed a chair for her.

Ann opened her coat and shook off the raindrops before sitting down.

"Charley Duval threw wide the postern of this fortress, kind sir. No, the front door would be the *portal,* wouldn't it?" she asked doubtfully, dazzling him with a smile. "Why is *he* on the afternoon shift?"

"Uncle John changed his hours because there are generally fewer people to be shot at then," Myles explained smiling. "Still raining when you came in?"

"It's practically stopped. Oh, before I tell you why I came—I suppose you've heard about Dad and Susan Bruce?"

"Aunt Pam told me when I stopped on the way here. Wonderful news. At least I think so. I hope you do?"

"Of course. Nothing could please us more! And Aunt Pam and Uncle John were so delighted." She sobered at a thought and fixed Myles with a probing eye. "Speaking of Uncle John, was it *his* idea that I'd be safer out of the bank, or did you put him up to it?"

Although Myles considered Ann's directness one of her charms, at the moment it was disconcerting.

"When did John Leslie ever need advice on how to run his business?" he evaded with a careless wave of the hand.

"What lucky chance brings you here dressed in your best?" He leaned forward, elbow on the desk, to inspect her. "Ann Jerome, you are a sight for sore eyes at any time, but in that—that cornflower-blue suit and perky hat you—you look delectable!"

He meant only to shift from the delicate subject of her dismissal but his feeling for her betrayed him. The admiration and yearning in his tone shot responsive shivers of fire through her veins. With trembling fingers she smoothed out the flaring skirt.

"Imagine a mere man knowing the name of this color!" she murmured. "Another proof that men like blue."

Somehow the word "another" conjured up a tormenting picture in his mind, a girl and a tall man embracing in the Wilders' driveway. The man, of course, must have been Bruce—there was no question as to the identity of the girl. Unhappily he leaned back and forced a casual tone.

"Well, Miss Jerome, what can we do for you today?"

Ann was as willing as he to veer away from the dangerous waters of personal discussion.

"It's about this." She produced the daybook from her bag. "I've read only part of it and it's perfectly fascinating. Maddening, too, because it mentions so many things briefly which you could tell me much more about."

"If I could forget the whole mess I'd be happier!" His lips stiffened to an uncompromising line. "I'm through with engineering! Or anything connected with it!"

"No, it isn't right for you to give up what you've always wanted."

"Sometimes you have to," Myles growled, but he was not thinking of his profession when he said it.

The desolation in the words made her heart ache and she determined not to hurt him with further discussion. Let Peter do his own probing into the events at Loma. The most she would attempt would be to give him the help of the diary.

"Would you mind if I let Peter Bruce read this?" she asked. "He hopes to get a lead from it, to learn more about his cousin."

"I feel guilty about the way I brushed Bruce off at the dance," Myles admitted. "I was tired and he prodded me with cross-examination on an unwelcome subject. I'd like to make it up to him."

"Then you don't object if he borrows this book?"

"Not at all, although I doubt if he'll find anything to help." He took it and leafed through the pages, reading briefly here and there. "I don't remember mentioning young Walter particularly. Anyway, there's nothing I wouldn't want read by anyone. I'm sure I never bared my soul in it," he said with a smile. "The record ends abruptly, doesn't it, the day before the blow-up. Hmm, what's in here?"

He flattened the book on his desk and with difficulty removed a folded slip of thin paper which had been tucked deep between two pages. When he opened it he shook his head.

"Another of our would-be poet's efforts," he remarked soberly, and spread it on the desk where Ann could read with him.

> "Dear Alice, I enclose this noat
>   Inn lether bound best seller,
> To tell you that your charms have smote
>   This poor old homesick feller.
> Dreaming of you I let my duties slied
>   And rool out every outside pleasure,
> For may boss may come and the bos may go
>   But, sweetheart, I'll love you forever."

Myles shook his head again and grunted.

"Up to his usual standard, which means pretty bad." He went back to scanning the daybook.

"*'Dear Alice,'*" Ann repeated under her breath. Her heart skipped a beat and began to race. According to Peter Bruce the poems his cousin wrote to Alice were code messages for the FBI. There was no way of telling when this one was written, because Myles said Walter made a rough draft on any scrap of paper and then copied it more carefully to send to Alice. It was likely that he dated the final draft—Ann sat up suddenly and gasped.

"Myles! Was this poem between pages that you'd already written on?"

He leafed through the book and held it up.

"Right in here; my last notes are on the left page. The rebels fixed me so I never did get to the next. Why?"

"Then it must have been slipped in *after* you wrote that, or you'd have found it."

"Probably." He picked up the poem, reread it, and tossed it back on the desk. "Walter certainly was the champion poor speller of the year. Imagine—n-o-a-t, note!"

"And missing on *slide* and *rule* down here," Ann pointed out, "when there were slide rules all over the place!"

"He might see them, but not spell them. He wasn't an engineer, you know," Myles reminded, once more reading his book. "Here's a day I well remember; a bulldozer backed into the river!"

Ann did not hear that last sentence above the pounding of her heart. No, Walter was not an engineer! Being what he was, could he possibly spell so badly? Peter had said the poems contained a code—a very simple one. Suppose the mangled words made the secret message? She held her breath while she studied the eight lines.

Note—in—leather—fellow? Perhaps not fellow, because it had to be spelled feller to rhyme with seller. Next came *slide* and *rule*. Then *boss* near the end. The "may" before the first boss must be *my*. Her excitement mounted as she considered the sentence she had constructed. *Note in leather slide rule my boss.*

Walter's boss was Myles Langdon, who did own a rule in a handsome leather case! She remembered him telling how he kept it on his desk in the shack so everyone could admire it. Very handy if his clerk wanted to slip a "noat" in it. But Myles owned two slide rules; perhaps the other had been just as handy—

"Myles! Did the slide rule stolen from here have a leather case?" she asked.

Immersed in the daybook he took a moment to adjust to the question.

"No, plastic. The one the staff gave me was leather."

"Where is it now?"

He looked up. "Sunny returned it the other night."

"Where is it now?"

With a puzzled frown he put down the book, and stared at her.

"Mind telling me what this is all about? You're pink with excitement or something and your eyes are blazing blue diamonds."

"Your imagination is working overtime," she accused. "I—I would like to borrow your rule again, that's all."

He shook his head in disbelief.

"Wrong number! You ought to know better than to try to fool *me*. I've known you too long—and too well. There's something on your mind. Let's have it."

"I can't tell you."

Myles lit a cigarette, deposited the burned match carefully in the ash tray, and leaned back to study his visitor.

"From your sudden change of expression," he mused, "I gather that what you are up to is pretty serious. Since my slide rule is evidently involved, don't you think it would be fair to trust me with the details?"

The appeal almost wrecked her resolve to keep faith with Peter, and she longed to let him know how fully she relied on him.

"It isn't my secret," she temporized, "but I guess I can tell you a little—without breaking my promise. Peter Bruce is a lawyer, you know, and Walter was getting some important information about—about a case he's interested in. Peter expected a report in code from—from his cousin, but never received it; he thinks it was intercepted by the other side.

"Now read this!" Her trembling finger underlined each misspelled word in the poem. "Get it? Walter must have suspected trouble and put this in your book, feeling sure that Peter would check it for a clue if he disappeared."

Ann's words set off a chain reaction in Myles's memory.

"So that's what Red Fallon saw him doing after the explosion! And then those men took him away—" He slapped the desk. "This information he was after must be tied in with the revolt in Loma!"

At Ann's nod he leaned forward, scowling.

"Gunrunning to the rebels?"

"You knew about that?"

"Heard talk, but didn't pay much attention to it; we

had a bridge on our minds. Not all of us, evidently. So Walter Bruce was playing with fire besides clerking for me—a fire that turns him up missing!"

"Peter says he's dead!" She shivered. "The rebels tortured him before they killed him!"

"*Tortured* him? To make him tell what he was up to?" Myles jumped to his feet and glared down at her. "Then someone down there knows about this message!"

"We don't know that, and what difference does it make as long as we get it to Peter?"

"*We?*" He slumped into his chair and eyed her with knitted brows while his mind made a swift connection of seemingly unrelated events. "From now on, Ann, *you* keep out of this—but strictly out!"

"I should say not! Remember who broke the code, as they say? I'll finish the job. It's the most thrilling thing—"

"No!" A warning finger was aimed at her. "This may have seemed fun to you but it's anything but that now! Good Lord, Ann, I won't let you take the chance—I can't!"

She blinked in surprise.

"Chance of what?"

"Who knows? They tortured Walter to get what they wanted and then killed him, remember? That means the information he had was pretty important to somebody and they don't want anyone else to get it. Someone here in town is after that note!"

"That's ridiculous! You're only trying to scare me."

"I hope I do," Myles growled. "You think it's ridiculous? I would have, too, an hour ago, but this makes a difference." He tapped Walter Bruce's poem. "Now I know why that slide rule was stolen from my desk at the bank, and why someone got into my room at home and rifled the packing case.

"I blamed both those attempts on a bungling sneak thief." He laughed scornfully. "Bungling, my eye! They knew what they wanted." He frowned at her for a moment. "Not only that; someone broke into the foundry office where my rule had been—until I picked it up that night I called for Sunny!"

Ann felt an icy hand squeezing her heart tighter at

each addition to the evidence. Myles was right, this was no exciting game—it was real danger.

"Where is the slide rule now?" she whispered as though the unknown menace might be eavesdropping.

"I won't tell you; the less you know the better." Myles stood up. "You are going home as fast as you can. Tell Bruce I'll be right along, bringing what he wants. I hope he knows what to do with it!" He slipped the poem into the daybook and thrust it into her hand. "Give him this and tell him to wait."

"My car is out front, why can't we go together?"

"Because I don't want you anywhere near what I'll be carrying—it may be more deadly than dynamite! You know if anything happened to you, Ann, it would—" He clamped his lips shut and waited until he could steady his voice. "Come on, I'll see you out!"

Tucking the book into her bag, Ann followed him through the deserted main banking room. She tried to tell herself that his alarm was unfounded, but in her ears rang the near hysteria of his voice when he exclaimed, "If anything happened to you—" It wasn't like Myles to panic without reason—or to panic at all. Perhaps the jungle had sapped some of his nerve. Uneasily she felt it threatening her, too, even here in the quiet bank.

As Myles unlocked the front door and let her pass she saw the Brazilian gentleman crossing the sidewalk toward them. He smiled and lifted his hat to her, then smiled more broadly at Myles.

"I hoped to find you, Mr. Langdon. Can you tell me when my account—the checking account—will be ready for me to use?"

"I believe it is processed now, so go ahead," Myles answered.

Prestes drew the new checkbook from his pocket.

"Would it trouble you—just a moment to show me how—how you North American bankers wish the checks drawn—if that is the right word?"

Ann could see Myles waver between politeness and an urgent desire to get on with the delivery of the slide rule. After a momentary hesitation he shrugged and held the door open for Prestes, then waved to Ann and followed him into the bank.

Politeness wins, Ann thought with amusement as she went to her car and got in. She had started the motor when the door next the curb swung open and a man slid into the seat beside her. Slamming the door he pushed something hard against her ribs.

"Step on it, sister!" he snarled. "Get going—or I'll use this gun!"

Too stunned with surprise to think clearly, Ann reacted with automatic obedience; her foot stamped on the throttle. The car leaped forward and was racing down the street before her amazement gave way to indignation and alarm.

"Slow down!" the intruder ordered harshly. "We don't want the cops after us. Just keep driving sensible." He strengthened the suggestion by jabbing her side again.

With her heart pounding and the blood like ice water in her veins Ann looked wildly ahead for possible help. It was too late in the day; the darkening street with its streaks of wet from the rain lay deserted. Had *everyone* gone home to supper? And did he really have a gun, or was he bluffing? Not that she had any intention of making him prove it; her stomach shriveled painfully at the idea.

"Turn here!" The man removed the pressure on her ribs long enough to gesture to the right—and long enough for her to see that it *was* a revolver in his hand before the muzzle thrust once more at her side.

From the corner of her eye she glimpsed his face and shivered; a lean, bony profile, cheeks furrowed by deep creases, nose a menacing hook and an eye glittering between puffy red lids.

That face multiplied her terror, although she fought vainly to steady her throbbing nerves, driving all the while at a fast but legal rate when all her instincts were to put on maniacal speed. At a red light she sat rigid, powerless to make a move when it changed; drove on automatically at the jab of the gun.

Soon they were passing through the residential part of the city on a long road which led to open country. If she meant to do anything, she told herself fearfully, it must be here—before they reached woods and empty fields. But there were no cars in sight, no people outside any of the houses. A mile. Another mile.

In desperation she attempted a diversion.

"Has thumbing rides become so difficult that you have to use a gun?"

"Shut up!" As though anticipating attack he slid away on the seat and half-turned to watch her, the revolver still threatening. "All right now, get some speed out of this crate."

"What do you think you're going to do——"

"I said, *shut up!*" The coldly murderous expression on his thin face silenced her more effectively than the command. He glared at her a moment, then looked ahead. "See that side road into the woods? Take it!"

Ann shuddered. Well's Hundreds was a desolate section of timberland with no houses for miles except a few hunting cabins scattered along the ridge. If she disobeyed——? But he wouldn't dare to *shoot* her! With every nerve tensed for the worst she put on more speed and drove straight forward.

"Damn you—*slow up!*"

His foot kicked hers off the accelerator as he lunged across the seat and the revolver, now in his left hand, hurt her side. His right hand wrenched the wheel until the car swerved around the corner.

"Now you can step on it!" he snarled.

Numbed by fear, she raced along the dirt road. The machine swayed and bounced in the ruts and potholes, scattering muddy water like spray from a speedboat. Here the last of the daylight barely filtered through overhanging maple and oak branches. Ann reached forward to switch on the lights but he stopped her with an explosive curse.

In a moment he rasped, "Slow up now—watch it!"

Suddenly, as though a brief instant of sanity flashed through delirium, she guessed where he meant to take her. Just ahead the road crossed a white-painted bridge over a deep ravine where a brook boiled and foamed among boulders and ledges. On this side of the bridge a narrow cart track turned to the left up the hill to Joe Snell's cabin on the crest of the ridge.

It must be that! There was nothing else near here. She would not go up there, no matter what happened! Gritting her teeth, she drove faster.

With another oath the man dropped the gun in his lap

to seize the wheel with both hands and swing into the cabin road. The car skidded sickeningly on the wet surface, swerved wildly, and the revolver slid off his knees to hit the floor with a thud. Instinctively he took one hand from the wheel to snatch for it at the instant when Ann, blinded by terror to what might happen, braced herself and drove her foot down on the brake.

Even with arms and legs stiffened to meet the shock she was catapulted forward, her forehead striking the wheel with a force that sparked lightning flashes in her brain and thunder in her ears. The man beside her was less fortunate; being helplessly off-balance his head smashed against the windshield and he crumpled into a heap between seat and dashboard.

With motor stalled and forward motion stopped by the locked wheels the car spun completely about and careened broadside across the road. Ann saw the white rail fence which edged the ravine come leaping toward her and shut her eyes in horror. But she could not shut out the sickening crash of metal and splintering wood as the car struck the fence, broke through, pitched drunkenly downward—and then hung suspended in the grip of the broken rails.

The convertible lay tilted at such an angle that when Ann opened her eyes she could look down at the wet black rocks and foaming water far below. Dislodged stones clattered as they fell. She shuddered and made a convulsive grab to open the door beside her. At the movement the car slipped farther toward the drop, the broken fence rails screeching against the steel sides until they caught again and held.

That spine-chilling sound which followed the frightening lurch was the last straw. Already the savagery of the abduction and the violent ride had strained Ann's nerves to the breaking point and now she froze in a helpless paralysis of fear, her eyes riveted on the stunned man. If he came to and tried to struggle up from his cramped position it could jar the convertible enough to send them hurtling into the ravine.

XXII

Myles felt a bit disgruntled as he led Señor Prestes into the railed enclosure where he could show the Brazilian how to make out his checks. He had been keen to get on with the delivery of the slide rule to Bruce and this delay was aggravating, but he supposed it was part of his boring job to humor the customers. He reached for a check-book lying on a desk.

"We go to your office!" said Prestes behind him.

"No need of that." Myles turned with the book in his hand. "I can show you—" The words trailed to silence as he took a startled step backward.

Prestes had halted a few feet away and now stood leaning forward with an automatic in his hand. The muzzle pointed unwaveringly at Myles's chest.

"No trouble, please," he murmured. "I said we would go to your office!" The pistol muzzle jerked in that direction and returned to its target. "March!"

"Are you crazy?" Myles snapped, staring in utter disbelief. "Put that thing away before someone gets hurt!"

It seemed impossible that the man was serious and Myles searched the tanned face and black eyes for any sign of humor. As he looked, his heart chilled for he could find no trace of the friendly South American to whom Ben Turner had introduced him at the Club, the courtly, smiling *señor* who opened checking accounts and begged his judgment of secondhand cars. The face now was a bronze mask and the eyes glittered feverishly.

"If this is a stick-up, you *are* crazy!" Myles sneered. "The money's in the vault and the time lock is on until tomorrow. So—"

"Your office, *fast!*" the other cut him short. The menace in the harsh command and a quick glow of fury in the dark eyes warned Myles to postpone any further argument.

Tossing the checkbook onto the desk, he stared at Prestes speculatively for a moment, then walked unhurriedly to his office, hearing the soft pad of feet follow. As he went in he resisted the temptation to slam the door in the other's face; frosted glass offered a poor shield from a bullet. He swung to face the Brazilian, who had stopped to reach behind and push the door almost shut.

"What's the idea, Prestes?" he demanded. "What do you want?"

"I am not a bank robber, Langdon." A faint twinkle of amusement lighted the black eyes and vanished. "I only want something from you. Give it, and there need be no shooting."

"You can't get away with this!"

"I think I can. After you give me what I want we will walk out together, just as we did the other day."

"Not quite," Myles corrected sharply, "because I intend to yell for the guard—and he's trigger-happy, you know!"

"So am I," Prestes whispered with chilling intensity. "Remember that, please. I am not an amateur at this sort of thing, Langdon, and have made sure that we are very much alone. Your guard is out in the parking space at the back, oblivious of your welfare while he holds a friend of mine spellbound with an account of his exploits in foiling that sneak thief. Do you think me foolish enough to do this otherwise?"

"You're a fool to—"

"Enough! If you give me any more argument I shoot you—only a little, but painful. Listen! You have a slide rule in a leather case—not the one that was here—another one. I want it!"

Myles blinked at him for a moment unable to believe his ears. Then, as the unexpected demand finally registered, he backed to the desk, sank into his chair, and tried to steady his churning thoughts.

Only a short time ago he had guessed that someone from Loma was in town looking for Walter's message, and here stood the man. In the rush of enlightenment it was odd that his first coherent thought should be an apology to Mike Fallon. Red had spotted this character for what he was as he entered the Chop House, only to abandon the idea when Myles accused him of having neurotic fancies bred by fear. Brawny, unimaginative Mike was as liable to give way to nerves as one of his bulldozers.

"We waste time!" Prestes growled. "Where is that rule?"

Myles stared at him without answering, still sorting out the memories which stormed through his mind. The day Prestes came in to open an account he had suddenly become ill; probably the unexpected sight of the slide rule on the desk had given him a turn. And later he decoyed Myles from the bank while an accomplice stole it. Even before that he learned of the packing case from Myles at the Club and must have been warning a confederate—the "telephone repair man"—the day he drove past the Leslie house with deafening blasts of the horn. Myles snorted at his own persistent stupidity in failing to recognize the character of this man. Looking at him now, he could see nothing but deception and cruelty in the scowling face.

"You're out of your head!" Myles exclaimed contemptuously, tilting back in the swivel chair. "I know what you are after, Prestes—if that is your name, which isn't likely—and you don't get it!" He saw the black eyes dart to the desk drawer and shook his head. "It isn't here, and you can't find it."

The automatic jutted forward as the other moved nearer.

"If you are dead, you will not stop me!"

"If I'm dead," Myles mocked his threatening tone, "you never will find it."

Prestes nodded slowly, his lips curled back from glistening white teeth.

"This I was afraid of, Langdon, so I have what you call a—a ace in the hole, eh? Attend me! All this talk of shooting is useless." He dropped his gun hand to his side and scowled. "You will give me the rule, or take me to where it is hid, and then you will let me go, because—"

Myles broke in with the heartiest, most scornful laugh which he could manage and leaned forward in his chair as the other took an angry step forward. If he could goad the South American to come a little closer a flying tackle, before he could raise the gun, might be the end of this. Risky, but what else could he do? It worried him that Prestes came no closer but waited patiently until Myles had his laugh.

Then Prestes went on as though there had been no interruption.

"—Because *someone else* will suffer, if you don't do as I say. My ace in the hole is a hostage. I have an organization, Langdon, and by this time one of us has the hostage safe and hidden, just as you have that rule put away. But unless I come soon—*with* what we want—she will not be safe long!"

"*She?*"

"Oh, yes." Prestes smirked at the other's startled reaction. "A *señorita*—a young lady—makes so much better a hostage than any man, eh? You Yankees are so gallant, certainly you will want no harm to come to one I think you like so much. To Miss Jerome, in fact, who just left here and—"

"*Ann?*" Myles sent the swivel chair flying backward as he erupted to his feet, his fist clenched and legs tensed to spring. The whiplike report of the small automatic was followed by the sound of shattering glass and a thunderous crash which shook the room. His involuntary glance over his shoulder revealed that his chair, rolling from his upward surge, had smashed the lower doors of a cabinet and catapulted a pile of heavy ledgers from its top. He also noticed the small round hole in the glass of the upper door and realized that Prestes had fired over his head, but it was enough to chill his mad impulse to attack. He turned his head and glared at the other in silent fury.

"You see, as I told you, I am trigger-happy," Prestes jittered. "Better not jump so." The undercurrent of tension in his voice was as ominous as the warning shot. "As for your Miss Jerome; one of my comrades got in the car with her and she has driven to the place he tells her— because of something like this." His left hand patted the extended pistol and he nodded violently.

Myles sucked in a tortured breath. It might be all bluff, but even the suggestion that Ann was held captive by anyone connected with this madman turned his heart to ice.

"Do you know what *kidnaping* will get you in this country?" he warned.

"Nothing! Because I will be gone before Miss Jerome is found, believe me."

"It won't take that long, Prestes! There aren't any secret hideouts around here."

"Too much talk!" The South American made a threatening gesture with the pistol. "Enough. She is hid until I come there with the rule. If I do not come—" He shrugged. "My *compañero* is like me, trigger-happy, as you call it. So we get the rule, quickly, eh?" He stepped back and waved his pistol at the doorway.

His voice and eyes warned Myles that he was not bluffing, that Ann *had* been kidnaped. Sick with apprehension, he told himself that all the secret messages in the world could not weigh against her safety. He must give this character what he demanded and Bruce could chase after him if he felt it was so damned important. Getting Ann back outweighed anything else.

"What guarantee do I have that you will release her—?" he began, and stopped.

The office door swung open and Charley Duval looked in. Prestes spun to face him, but Myles was quicker. He left his feet in a headlong drive, driving his shoulder against the other's hip and sending him to the floor with a crash. As they fell he felt the gun cold against his cheek and snatched for it with his good hand, gripped the barrel and twisted with all his strength.

Half-stunned, he tried to jerk the gun away, realized foggily that the other was too powerful for his single hand, and sighed as the barrel cut his fingers when it was whipped free. There was a thud, Prestes grunted and rolled slackly away. Myles shook the dizziness from his head and staggered to his feet.

Charley Duval, grinning complacently, stood over the prone figure, his heavy gun poised for another blow if it were needed.

"Was out back talking to a guy when I thought I heard a noise in here," he explained blandly. "I start to investigate and he grabs my arm and tries to stop me. Otherwise I'd have been here sooner."

"Thanks for investigating," Myles said between gasps for breath.

"My pleasure! Seems like there's a lot of funny business going on around here all of a sudden."

"How right you are!" Myles stooped to seize Prestes by the shoulder and shook the unconscious man savagely. "Wake up, you!"

Duval snorted. "You ain't going to rouse him for quite a spell. I gave him a healthy swipe with this"—he weighed the .45 on his palm—"and it ain't no feather."

"We've got to bring him around! He had Ann kidnaped and I want to know where she was taken!"

"You're fooling!" The old man's watery eyes bulged in amazement. "Kidnap Miss Ann? That's crazy; where could he hide her around this town?"

"That's what I must find out!" Myles caught up the Thermos of water which stood on the desk and dashed the contents into Prestes's face. The jug was almost empty and the cupful of water made no visible impression. "Charley, fill this quick!" He handed over the Thermos, dropped to his knees and slapped the expressionless face furiously.

"Take it easy, Myles," Duval protested, "you've gone haywire!" He bent to stare at the unconscious man. "Looks like that foreign feller that Joe Snell goes around with! What do you know!"

"Stop babbling and get some water!" Myles shouted.

"Okay—okay! But it won't do any good," Duval muttered as he shuffled out. "I wasn't fooling."

Myles gave up trying to get a reaction out of the inert body, slipped Prestes's automatic into his jacket pocket, and then stood scowling down at him in a fever of impatience. Every minute of delay increased Ann's danger wherever she might be. The foreigner had threatened that, if he didn't appear with the slide rule, she would suffer. How long was her captor to wait? Myles gritted his teeth and pounded a fist on the desk in helpless fury. Damn Joe Snell, who had made it easy for this thug to meet and trap them!

He stopped hitting the desk and stood motionless, glaring down at the unconscious man. Snell had loaned this character the keys to his cabin. Why should the South American want to use a hunting lodge in the middle of nowhere? He knew it from tramping past; had never been inside. It was deep in the woods on the ridge, solitary, at least a mile from any other camp, as secluded as any movie gangster's hideout.

If Prestes had the keys here, the idea which had flashed into his mind was a washout; if one of his men had them it might be the answer he was looking for. His heart pounded with sudden hope as he dropped to his knees, went through the other's pockets, rose to his feet without finding what he was after.

At that moment Duval came in and with evident pleasure dumped the jugful of water on Prestes.

"Won't do no good," he growled. "We just gotta wait till this guy recuperates natural."

"I can't wait!" Myles gripped the old man's arm and shoved him toward the desk. "I think I know where Ann is—it's worth a try, anyway! I'm on my way. Use that phone to call the police to come for this crook. How about the man who tried to stop you out back?"

Duval looked disgusted. "He run off holding onto his head. I must be losing my touch!"

"Okay, forget him! Tell them about Ann being kidnaped, too, and get them started hunting for her—I may be on the wrong trail. And, Charley, watch this man— he's dangerous as a snake!"

"He ain't so dangerous right now; I guess I can take him in."

"Don't you try it, and telephone *right now!*" Myles yelled as he ran from the room to pick up his car.

Speeding down the street which led to open country, he swore at a traffic light which flashed from yellow to red as he approached. Must he lose time here? He darted a look at the cross street, saw only one car a block away on his left and raced through the intersection.

Once clear of the city he drove at full speed, his right hand clenched on the wheel and his left curled into a weak fist in his lap. As he slowed for the turn onto the side road, which he knew led to the bridge below Snell's cabin, he saw a red light blinking far behind and thought he heard the wail of a siren. If it was the police looking for

Ann, Charley had certainly wasted little time in alerting them.

A terrific bump brought Myles's thoughts back to his driving and he slowed still more, wrestling one-handed with the wheel to keep the car on the rough road. It was really dark under the trees and he braced the wheel with his knee for a second while he switched on the lights.

Rounding a curve he stamped on the brake to halt at Ann's car where it hung sideways in the broken fence. With a muttered prayer he ran forward and felt his heart leap at the sight of Ann's pale face in the glare of the lights.

"*Myles!*" It was a husky gasp. "Keep away! Don't touch the car!"

"Take it easy, dear! I'll take care of everything. Are you hurt?" He reached for the door handle.

"Get back!"

The hysterical whisper stopped him in his tracks, while relief at finding that she was apparently unhurt turned to apprehension as he stared at her. The blue eyes were wide with terror in a drawn and colorless face, the cheeks streaked with tears. He had never seen the poised, self-confident Ann like this; it would take more than a crack-up to shatter her nerve so completely. Could her fear be for him; was her abductor hidden somewhere near with a gun ready?

Braced to feel a shot, Myles slid a hand unobtrusively into his pocket and gripped Prestes's automatic.

"Where's the man who snatched you?" he whispered.

"He—he's in here on the floor—knocked out! I jammed on the brakes—he hit the windshield—he may come to any minute!"

"Then get out before he does," Myles advised reasonably. "I'll take care of him when—"

"You don't understand! I don't dare to move—there's nothing but the fence holding us!" Her wail of despair was suddenly muted to an agonized whisper. The strain of waiting in the poised car had shaken her so that now she feared even a loud word might start the avalanche. "I tri-tried to open the door and—and it made the car slip farther over!"

"Then for God's sake don't move until I can think!" His mind was a blank except for the horrifying thought of what such a drop might do to her, helpless in the inferno of rending steel and glass. As he spoke it seemed that the wheels slid another inch and he heard gravel rattle down the steep slope.

Ann smothered a gasp of hysteria and clenched her hands in her lap. Concern for him swamped her own fears.

"Myles, keep away!" she commanded, trying to keep her voice steady. "If you try to help me you may be caught and carried down!"

Her heroic unselfishness was an electric charge striking through his frozen veins and turning his blood to fever heat. Without conscious thought he tore open the door, sensed rather than felt the car tilt away from him, heard the sickening screech as the broken fence lost its grip.

He braced his feet in the mud while his arms—both right and left—shot forward to clutch Ann by the shoulders. He dragged her out as the car dropped away, crushed her body against his and heard the ton of steel go clanging and crashing down the slope to the bottom of the ravine.

It took him a moment to realize that they were safe and to catch his breath. He backed away from the gaping hole in the fence, still clasping Ann in a bear hug whose force was doubled by overwhelming relief. Even when he grew calm enough to realize that he was crushing her and loosened his hold, she clung sobbing in his arms.

"Ann!" he whispered, his lips against her hair. "You're safe, dear! Everything's all right!"

She was beyond speech and snuggled against him, gaining strength and composure from his nearness. She could feel the furious pounding of his heart under her cheek and her distracted mind could think only that he was exhausted—had overtaxed his one good arm to save her.

But he hadn't! Now she realized that her shoulders ached from the grip of his two hands when he dragged her from the car. And there was nothing halfway about his embrace at the moment. She leaned back to lift a radiant face to his.

"Myles, darling! You used your *left* arm!"

He released her and stepped back, holding out the once useless member and staring at it. Not until that moment was he aware of the fiery needles of pain shooting through every nerve and muscle. Tentatively he opened and closed the fingers, then made a fist and shook it in triumph.

"Well, what do you know!" he grinned. "Stings as if it were asleep, but it works!"

"You never could have pulled me clear without it!"
He nodded. "I guess I knew that. I had to use it."

"I was sure your arm would come right sometime," Ann boasted happily. "Aunt Pam hoped so—but I knew! What do you suppose cured it so suddenly?"

His hands were on her shoulders again, drawing her close. His engagement to Sunny was forgotten, there was no thought of her apparent romance with Peter Bruce. He was about to answer, "Danger to the one I love," when a harsh bellow interrupted him.

"Hold it, you two!" A uniformed figure strode toward them, silhouetted by the lights of Myles's car, and a police cruiser beyond it.

Myles released Ann to greet the newcomer with a laugh.
"Looking for a kidnaped lady, officer? Here she is."

"I'm looking for *you!*" was the grim retort. "Jumping a red light in town and breaking the speed laws like a crazy man!"

XXIII

Ann had been through too much to take more than a misty, impersonal interest in the scene which followed the arrival of the law. Myles was trying to convince the stubborn officer that he had more urgent duties than arresting a speeder. Unintentionally he complicated his task by producing the automatic from his pocket, a move which sent the startled policeman's hand flashing to his own gun.

Fortunately the kidnap alarm came through to the cruiser while they argued and at a bellowed explanation from the driver the first officer consented to look down into the ravine. His reaction was satisfyingly profane and he dropped, sliding and stumbling, to the convertible.

From that point onward the proceedings baffled Ann's exhausted mind with their speed. It was a blessed relief at last to find herself beside Myles in his car and heading back toward the city.

"Is it—all right for us to leave?" she asked hesitantly.

"Nothing we can do, dear. There's a police lieutenant here now and he's called for a wrecker and an ambulance."

"Then he—that man—isn't dead?"

"Far from it, worse luck! He was battered but game; came crawling out of the wreck just as Bentley reached it. Bentley is the dumb officer who gave me such a time, in case you care. If he had argued with me for one more minute the thug might have escaped."

"He had a gun—in the car."

"And came out with it," Myles growled, "though he was too shaky to use it before the cop took it away."

Ann shuddered. "Did you see him—the man, I mean?"

"Yes. He's the hard-looking case I've noticed around town; for a while I thought he was spying on Prestes. When I think of what he tried to do to you—!" Myles spoke with sudden savagery, "I don't know why they called an ambulance—they should have handcuffed him behind their car and dragged him in!"

He laid his hand on Ann's and gave it a gentle squeeze.

"Sorry. I shouldn't blow off steam to you after the emotional crisis you've been through."

"I'm p-perfectly recovered." The tremor in her voice gave the lie to her boast but she could not control it. When he put his hand back on the wheel she shivered, drawing away to the far end of the seat. Emotional crisis I've *been* through! she thought miserably. As though anything could equal the strain of sitting beside him now, still feeling the clasp of his warm hand and reliving that instant of hysterical joy when he appeared at the convertible. Her eyes filled with tears and she furtively brushed them away.

"You're crying!" Myles peered at her in alarm. "Is it that bump on your forehead, dear?"

"Oh—yes!" She seized on the excuse gratefully, fingering the swollen place tenderly. "My head hit the steering wheel when I slammed on the brakes and knocked out that dreadful man. Good grief! I must be a sight!"

"You look wonderful to me," Myles answered soberly. "Want to give me a run-down of what happened?"

"I'd rather not talk about it yet."

"No wonder. Anyway, I think I know pretty much the whole story, at least how that damned thug snatched you, and what for. Guess who told me. That charming cavalier and extrovert, Señor Enrico Prestes!"

"The Brazilian? How did he know?"

"You remember, *after* you alerted me by decoding Walter's message, I figured that someone was in town to get the slide rule? Well, he's the one who came up from Loma to get it."

Myles gave her a vivid description of what had happened at the bank, relieved to see that it took her mind off her own experience, if only for a few moments. He was able to bring the story up to date, too, because he had listened in on the police car's radio. Charley Duval, carrying out orders with an old soldier's thoroughness, had delivered Prestes to a detail from headquarters, and the Brazilian was now occupying a cell there.

"And he didn't get the rule!" Ann sighed her satisfaction. "Where is it?"

"Right where it's been since Sunny gave it to me when I picked her up at the foundry." He reached to tap the glove compartment. "Lucky she did. It was Prestes who had the place burgled that same night." He caught Ann's hand when she started to snap open the small door.

"*Ah-ah*, mustn't touch! It's caused you enough trouble. Bruce ought to be shot for mixing you up in such a dangerous game!"

"He didn't know of the danger."

"Then he's stupid!"

Ann sniffed and tossed her head.

"Anything but! You'd better be careful what you say about Peter, because he's—" In the nick of time she conquered the impulse to reveal his identity. "You just be careful!" she advised sternly. "And give him the slide rule at once!"

"Oh, *yes?*" Myles, gnawed by jealousy at her defense of the other man, almost barked it. "Believe me, I'll ask a lot of questions before I hand it over!"

"Peter will have the answers."

"He's certainly got you eating out of his hand!" Myles growled disgustedly.

"Any objections—and why?" she demanded, and that unanswerable question ended the dispute.

They rode in silence then, Myles gluing his eyes to the road while Ann looked anywhere but at his stern face. He smoldered with resentment at her championing of Bruce; she *must* be in love with the lawyer and Myles was helpless to plead his own cause so long as Sonia held him. That same engagement filled Ann with silent fury which swamped the relief at her escape and joy in the miraculous recovery of his arm.

A teen-age moon came glimmering through the parting clouds like a beacon above stormy seas, and the headlights flashed and glinted from the wet bare branches of the trees and bushes. But there was no beauty there for the two in the jouncing car; the moon was a sickly blotch of yellow drowning in somber clouds, the trees were glaring phosphorescent skeletons and the road seemed an inky river as black as the Styx which flowed to Inferno.

The Jerome house was ablaze with lights when they drew up at the front door and Sonia charged out onto the porch with a shout of welcome. Sarah panted after her, clapping her hands and tearfully imploring the Lord to bless them all. Sunny engulfed Ann in an hysterical hug and almost dragged her into the house. It did not please Myles, who had paused to get the slide rule, to see Peter Bruce leave the telephone in the hall and seize Ann's hands.

"Lord, am I glad to see you!" Peter exclaimed. "You're all right?"

"Perfectly, but I'd like to sit down." She sank into an armchair in the living room and while the others clustered around drew in a deep breath of satisfaction. Everything was as it always had been, the luster tea set glowing in the secretary, the gold-bordered mirror reflecting the brisk flames in the fireplace and the warm colors of the solid tiers of books beside it. Peace settled on her like a comforting blanket of down.

Bruce wiped his brow and blew out his breath.

"Whew, what a relief to see you all in one piece! I beat it over here as soon as I heard you'd been kidnaped and we've been crazy with suspense ever since!"

"Peter, I broke your code!" she exclaimed importantly. "We have the message you expected in—"

"Hold everything!" Myles interrupted so harshly that she stopped in surprise. He eyed Bruce. "So you heard that Ann was snatched? How come *you* got the news so fast?"

"From the police!" shrilled Sarah. "They phoned here and he called them, every other minute, and me praying between!"

"But," objected Myles softly, *"Mr.* Bruce has just said that he knew about it *before* he came over here!" He sat down on the couch, leaned back and folded his arms. "I'd like to know how!"

"I thought I'd better be here with Sonia," Bruce evaded, "until we had definite word, one way or another. I mean, whether Ann was alive or—"

"Don't say it!" Sunny cried. "It gives me the shakes! I'd have gone mad waiting here alone!"

Sarah fluttered around her, clucking like a mother hen. "Don't take on so!" she implored. "Don't give way, child!"

"Take it easy, everybody," Myles urged. "Ann's here safe and sound, so there's no sense in getting worked up at this late date. I'd still like to know how *Bruce* got in on this in the first place."

Peter stared at him thoughtfully for a moment.

"I'll explain about that later, Langdon. Ann says she found a message from Walter. Right now that is the important thing."

"I agree," Myles growled. "So important that we've had gunplay and kidnaping over it. But where—"

"What are you all talking about?" Sonia danced with impatient curiosity. "What code did Ann break? What message did she get? I don't understand."

"I'm with you there," Myles muttered. "Bruce, just

where do you fit into the picture, aside from *claiming* to be Walter's cousin? This doesn't seem to be a family matter."

"Myles!" Ann protested, bewildered by his chip-on-the-shoulder attitude. "Peter will tell you—" She caught herself and looked at the maid. "Sarah, be a dear. Make us some coffee? We need reviving."

"Won't take a minute!" Sarah scurried out with a muttered, "Glory be, the child is safe after all!"

"Now," said Ann, "you'll have to explain, Peter. Myles can be very stubborn."

Bruce smiled and shook his head.

"He isn't being stubborn, just cautious. More power to him." He took out his wallet, and with the gesture Ann remembered, flipped it open to present his gold badge to Myles's startled gaze. "As you say, Langdon, this isn't a family matter."

Sonia gave a suppressed yelp. *"A policeman!"* but no one paid attention to her.

"That answers all my questions," Myles admitted, nodding at the badge. "A federal agent is one thing I never expected." From his inner pocket he produced the leather case. "Walter's message—decoded by your assistant, Miss Jerome—said only, 'Note in my boss's leather slide rule.' I haven't examined this, too busy with other matters. You take it from here."

Grim-faced, Bruce snapped open the end of the case and withdrew the rule. He peered in, then stepped to the table and tapped the case hard. A wad of tightly folded paper flipped out to skid across the table. He opened it and leaned toward the lamp for better light.

"Is that the information you wanted?" Ann whispered.

"This is what we've been waiting for, the names of the New York men behind the gunrunning to Loma. Quite an extensive list, too; Walter did his usual thorough job." He folded the paper, put it carefully in his wallet, and returned the slide rule and its case to Myles. "I'll find time later to thank you properly for your help and—"

"Better thank Ann, not me," Myles advised shortly.

"Ann, too, of course. Operative 13 really came through for me!" The smile and look he exchanged with Ann were delighted triumph but to Myles it seemed the mutual admiration of two people very much in love.

"You're lucky she came through at all!" Myles complained. "If you're here on this South American case, how come you never checked up on this Prestes, a stranger who shows up from S.A.?"

"We did—and got a satisfactory report on him, everything okay. That, by the way, is something we'll have to look into. Evidently someone fell down on their job when they'll whitewash a man like him. Excuse me, now, I have to get busy on the phone."

Myles frowned. "Don't you want to hear what happened to Ann?"

"Dying to, and also how you got into the game, but not until after I've called our New York office and started them on a roundup of the men behind this operation." He laughed. "Reminds me of that song from *The Mikado,* 'I've got a little list—of people who never will be missed.'" He went out to the telephone, whistling the Gilbert and Sullivan tune.

"A cool customer," muttered Myles with a glance at Ann. "Maybe if he knew what you've been through he would show a little more interest!"

"Do you expect him to let some criminals escape," Ann protested, "while he listens to a playback of our adventures?"

"Tell *me!*" Sonia begged. "Only start from the beginning!"

"Count me out. Ann will tell you the story." Myles rose to his feet and turned to leave, feeling that he could stand no more loyal defense of Bruce by Ann. "I must get home and tell Aunt Pam and Uncle John that everything's under control. Although," he added bitterly, "they may know nothing about this—not having Mr. Bruce's inside connections with the police!"

Ann watched his abrupt departure with a worried frown, puzzled as much by what he had not said as by what he had. During all the conversation Myles had failed to mention the wonderful news about his arm, even after Peter had gone to the phone and left them alone. Surely his fiancée was entitled to be among the first to hear about it. Ann was bursting to spread the glad news, but hesitated lest he have some good reason for the delay.

She looked uncertainly at Sonia, perched on the arm of a chair.

"Did it strike you that Myles acted sore about something?" she demanded.

Sunny tossed her head.

"He sure made some sour cracks at Pete!"

"Could he be jealous? You two have been getting rather chummy of late, you know. And after your carrying on with Joe Snell this might seem too much of the same."

"Don't start picking on me again!" Sonia's sharp retort was accompanied by deepening color and she flounced out to the hall to see how Peter was progressing with his call.

"It *does* look like jealousy," Ann murmured, without the faintest suspicion that she was both right and wrong.

Myles had indeed taken a sudden leave, afraid that he might betray his true feelings if he watched what was going on between Ann and Bruce any longer, but even the short drive to the Leslie house cooled his irritation. That process was greatly assisted by the pleasure of driving with two hands. The more he used his left arm the more it returned to normal; it was hard to believe that such a numb, useless thing could come to life so suddenly.

It was lucky the cure had come when it did, he thought. Now he could get back in his chosen profession and leave this place and all its associations. Staying to watch Ann won by another would be torture; it had been bad enough to be around her when she was free and he was tied to her sister. He would get out of town—and stay out! Maybe he could still join Red Fallon on that new job.

The prospect cheered him out of his depression. If he went away again Sunny might tire of their senseless engagement and free him. For what? he wondered gloomily, if Ann were lost to him. He'd better forget that and tune in on another wave length; follow Aunt Pam's maxim— "Count your blessings." He flexed his arm, forced a gay whistled tune as he put the car in the garage, and walked to the house.

The whistle stopped short when a shadow moved away

from the back door and blocked his path. Conditioned by the day's events to expect the worst, he sidestepped and clenched his fists. The shadow chuckled gleefully.

"Nervous as a cat, ain't you, Myles?" Charley Duval taunted, moving forward into the moonlight. He was holding a slice of pie from which he took bites while he talked. "Heard the car; figured it was you. Had quite a time for yourself today, huh?"

"Quite a time, Charley. But I guessed right; Ann was being taken to Snell's cabin on the ridge."

"Heard all about it on the police station radio. They let me listen in on the reports from the prowl car," the old man boasted. "That Prestes guy come to after the cops got there—told you it would take him awhile—and I went along when they carted him off."

"You were a friend in need, Charley, and thanks! I want to go in and tell my family about it, so I'll see you tomorrow."

"They know. I come right along and give 'em the details." Duval chuckled, choked on pie and coughed. "You should have seen 'em, Myles, standing around the kitchen table to hear me while I was eating! Mabel gave me supper; that was all right, wasn't it? She sure can cook!"

"Of course it's all right; go back for more if you want— you earned it! If it hadn't been for you things could have turned out a whole lot differently—and much more unpleasant!"

"Sure." Duval needed no further encouragement to head for the kitchen. Over his shoulder he jeered, "Like I told you before, Myles, a gun in your hand is better than under your coat!"

"After what you did today, old timer, you can carry it in your teeth if you like."

To avoid running the gauntlet of Mabel's welcome, which he suspected would be hysterical, Myles entered by the front door, but his reception there was quite as hectic. All three members of his family quitted the dinner table with a rush to surround him, firing a barrage of questions in soprano, bass and Kathy's piercing treble.

Although they had already received Duval's report they clamored for a play-by-play retelling. From some of their questions Myles judged that Charley must have provided more exaggeration than accuracy and he tried to keep his own story matter-of-fact, minimizing the dangers when he could. Even so it was a hair-raising story and Kathy nearly burst with pride because Myles credited her with an important role in the triumph over the gunrunners.

"If my favorite niece hadn't dug that daybook out of the packing case," he explained with an affectionate tug at her pony-tail, "Ann wouldn't have seen the poem and decoded Walter Bruce's message in time. Then, sooner or later, Prestes would have got hold of the right slide rule case and destroyed the list of names. And the FBI would have had to start all over again.

"But you did it, *gatita,* bless your big black eyes! And now," he suggested with a grin, "how about letting me join you at your interrupted dinner? I seem to be starving!"

XXIV

The meal did not progress far before it was interrupted again but in a different way. Myles purposely had made no mention of his restored arm, waiting—as he had at the Jeromes'—for someone to notice it. Either Pamela Leslie's eyes were sharper than Sonia's, or her heart was more deeply involved with Myles, for she startled the others with a suppressed scream.

"Myles! You took that roll with your *left* hand!"

"Sure did," he laughed, tossing it up and catching it deftly. He enjoyed their amazement until he saw the tears on his aunt's cheeks and at once regretted the delay in telling her; he had been cruel, not humorous, to spring this on her without warning.

"I'm sorry, Aunt Pam, I should have told you at once. My arm seems perfectly all right." He patted her shoulder to prove it. "When I saw Ann in that car—slipping away from me—" He drew a shaky breath and shivered at the memory. "Well, I didn't *think*—I just knew I must use both hands to save her—I had to!"

"And that did it?" Mrs. Leslie stopped wiping her eyes and beamed. "I always said that *something* would bring it right, didn't I?"

"You did," Mr. Leslie chuckled, "although that's about as vague a prophecy as the old Delphic oracle used to deliver."

"Nevertheless," Myles insisted, "it came true. Prescription Pam scores again!"

"Thank God for it!" John Leslie reached to grip Myles's hand in congratulation, then leaned back in his chair, not completely dry-eyed himself. "You don't know how we've worried about you, boy—but everything is wonderful now!"

"Yes, sir." Myles hesitated, dreading to spoil his uncle's happiness but determined not to risk another emotional scene by postponement. "Wonderful for me, but not for you, I'm afraid. You see, if my arm is as good as ever—so am I; and I can have another try at my own line—engineering."

He had always admired John Leslie deeply, but never more than at this moment when the dream of years was shattered. The banker stared, gray eyes wide and appealing, slowly opened his mouth—then shut it with a snap. Folding his arms he nodded and smiled.

"Of course—more power to you, son! We—we'll miss you at the bank, you made a great start. But ever since you were a boy you aimed straight for one profession, so go to it!"

"You're going away again?" Aunt Pam's eyes filled anew at the prospect. "But not right off?"

"The sooner the better."

"Not back to that terrible jungle!" she begged.

Myles laughed. "Perish the thought. Not so far away as that this time, I hope. My old foreman, Mike Fallon, tried to sign me up for a bridge the Carrington Company is starting in upper New York. If they still want me, and they seemed to, last I heard, I'll give that a whirl."

"What's the rush?" Mr. Leslie rubbed his chin, glanced

at his wife and asked, "How about your fiancée? Have you consulted her on this?"

"No, but I doubt if Sonia will object to waiting until I've established myself," Myles answered gravely. "In fact, I'm sure she won't."

"But she might!" Aunt Pam suggested in so hopeful a tone that Myles eyed her sharply. She seemed intent on pouring a cup of coffee and murmured, "Have you told Ann? She worried herself sick over you in that dreadful place down there."

"I haven't told anyone," Myles admitted. "I made up my mind on the way here. And this job I'm thinking of isn't in a 'dreadful place'! The state of New York is as civilized as anything you have around this town; maybe more so!" he added irritably. "Anyway, Ann——" Almost he blurted out the bitter announcement that her heart and mind seemed thoroughly occupied with someone else, but he changed it to a blunt, "She won't worry this time."

He pushed back his chair.

"If you'll excuse me, Aunt Pam, I'll get a letter off to Carrington tonight. Have to look up the address of their New York office. I'm sure it's somewhere in my case of stuff."

"*Ooh!*" Kathy squealed. "Can I look in there again, Uncle Myles?"

"Sure can, *gatita*. Who knows what you'll find this time?"

The packing case was still in his room and Myles felt the thrill which had been missing these last weeks when he opened it. After the visit of the sneak thief Mabel had piled everything back just as it came, and he began rummaging through the conglomeration of blueprints and bundled papers. Kathy crowded close to him and demanded the identity of everything he unearthed.

"That bundle of letters tied up with string!" she exclaimed. "Could I look at the stamps?"

"*You* collect stamps?"

"Well—the pretty ones—birds and animals."

Myles laughed and handed over the packet.

"Sorry to disappoint you, but most of my mail was from the United States. Someone evidently tied these together when they packed up for me. There might be a few

South American stamps—I did get letters from a friend building a dam in Peru."

When she moved over to the lamp on the desk, to examine the envelopes, he resumed his search with more freedom.

"Uncle Myles!" Kathy exclaimed a minute later. "Here's one you never opened!"

"Probably an advertisement I couldn't be bothered with."

"It doesn't look like that with the pretty handwriting. And it has Spanish words printed on it—I guess they're Spanish."

Myles sat back on his heels.

"That doesn't sound familiar; chuck it over here." He caught the envelope she scaled across the room, stared at the unbroken flap and turned it over. "Why, it's from Sunny!"

Printed at one side in faint red ink was a post office notice and a scrawl of Spanish. He made out with difficulty that the letter had been mis-sent to some town with a name which he could not decipher. He could sympathize with the South American postal official; Sunny's flourishing address must have been quite as incomprehensible to him.

"Looks as if she were wildly excited when she wrote this," he chuckled. The date on the postmark was too blurred to read and he opened the envelope to see when Sunny had written the letter. "Good Lord, she sent it weeks before the bridge was blown up!" he cried.

Kathy, immersed in stamp-hunting, was paying no attention to him, so he sat down on the edge of the packing case to read.

Dear Myles.

Here he muttered a wryly amused comment. "I'd know this was one of her later efforts even without a date. She used to begin 'Myles dearest' or something equally intimate, but that toned down. After a while I began to expect one to start formally, 'My dear Mr. Langdon.'" He resumed the letter:

This is the hardest letter I ever tried to write and I feel like a heel about it but I guess the best way is to tell you the bad news right off and get it over with. Only maybe it won't be bad news for you; how do I know, it's been so long.

All his amusement vanished with the first words and he sat grimly scowling as he finished the letter and realized that Sonia was breaking their engagement. Although she had tried hard to convince him, and evidently herself, that the betrothal had been a mistake from the beginning and mentioned no names, Myles was not deceived. From the gradual cooling of her letters to Loma and what he had learned since his return it was easy to read between the lines and what he read was "Joe Snell."

He sat hunched on the box, the letter dangling from slack fingers, his mind in a whirl of emotions. He wondered if any other man had received such a message with the relief he felt. Relief—but fury, too. Not at his dismissal, but at the delay. This letter must have wandered around South America while he lay ill with fever, only arriving at Loma after his job had vanished in the roaring, billowing smoke of the explosion.

Someone had evidently tied it together with his other letters and slipped it into the box Walter had packed, never noticing that it was unopened. And it had been here in the case all these weeks while Sunny made her gallant gesture of standing by him because he had returned a cripple—while Ann fell in love with Peter Bruce.

He was jerked from his gloomy thoughts by Kathy's voice.

"What's the matter, Uncle Myles?" she asked hesitantly. "You look funny."

"I don't feel *funny* in the least!" he grumbled.

"Was that a bad letter? Are you sorry I found it?"

Myles pulled himself together at the near-to-tears question. If the child was so impressed he must look like the tragic Muse in person. There was no reason to take it out on her.

"I'm glad you found it, *gatita!* You're the luckiest finder I ever ran into." Stuffing the letter in his pocket, he went over and flipped her pony-tail in his customary gesture of affection. "If you don't find anything there that interests you, go through the rest of the box. I have to run over to the Jeromes' for a minute."

"Are you mad at them?" She stared at him anxiously. "You still look funny."

"Maybe—but I'm not mad at anyone, unless it's Fate."

"Who's he?"

"It's a *she*." He frowned. "Come to think of it, maybe you're right. Fate is the postmaster of some town in South America who takes so long to forward letters that all sorts of things happen. And more are going to happen right now!" he added grimly as he left the room.

Myles took the short cut to the Jerome garden and hurried toward the house. Against the golden flood of light from the long living room windows two figures were silhouetted where they sat on the glider. As he approached along the path, his feet making no sound on the grass, he heard the impatient, commanding voice of Peter Bruce.

"We are not letting things drift any longer! I have to go to Washington in the morning; I want to know where I stand!"

Myles felt a stab of heartache at the confident tone; the man must be very sure of Ann to issue that ultimatum. To his surprise it was Sonia who answered.

"But I can't do anything, Peter! You know I can't!"

There were tears of frustration in the protest, if Myles was any judge. Easy to guess the subject of their argument, too, because he himself had so often consulted one sister about some problem connected with the other. Bruce was trying to gain Sunny's support in convincing Ann that they should not wait any longer to announce their engagement.

"Then *I* will do something—" Bruce's angry assertion stopped short when Myles noisily mounted the brick steps to the terrace. Sonia gave a gasp of surprise, and she and Peter moved apart.

Myles did not notice that; he was too intent on his errand and annoyed that Bruce should be present.

"You all through gathering in the criminals?" he snapped.

"Why, yes." Peter stood up, struggling to adjust to this new subject so far removed from what was on his mind. "New York has reported all the men on that list arrested

and jailed, and we have operatives watching the various
caches of arms waiting shipment; they'll pick up any
others connected with the deal."

He smiled at the other engagingly.

"I talked to Lieutenant Lynch, who took your statement on Prestes when he relieved the prowl car at the
bridge. I've also weeded out a few cold facts from your
bank guard's boastings and heard Ann's story. I'd like to
congratulate you for having done a magnificent job for
all of us!"

Myles grunted, dragged a chair nearer, and sat down,
embarrassed by praise from someone he'd tried to dislike.
Grudgingly he made conversation, waiting for Bruce to
have the decency to leave him with his fiancée.

"This Prestes?" he asked. "Why should he come all the
way up from South America to get that list, when your
New York crooks must have a dozen sharpshooters they
could send?"

"They did send someone up here—the thug who ab-
ducted Ann. Maybe your fake telephone repair man and
the sneak thief in the bank, too, for all we know."

Peter sat down on the edge of the table and folded his
arms.

"Prestes came himself, in my opinion, because he had
something to do with Walter's getting the information. In-
directly, probably, because he isn't the type who'd blab;
he may have introduced Walter to the person who did let
out the secret. In that case he might feel bound to re-
deem his mistake. Those rebels are fanatics, you know,
and he was one of the leaders.

"He knew that if we received Walter's information the
revolution was licked, the shippers knew that it would
put them behind bars. Everyone involved realized that
they must stop at nothing to suppress it. Of course we
found out who Prestes was, too late. Our routine check
when he came here went no farther than a glowing testi-
monial in his behalf from a prominent New York ex-
porter—who now turns out to be one of the head men
in the gunrunning business. He's out of it now, for several
years, and the case is closed."

Bruce stood up and faced the other, determination in
every line of his figure.

"There's a matter I want to take up with you, Langdon," he said bluntly, "and this is as good a time as any, I think—"

Myles did not let him finish. If Bruce had any wild idea that as Sonia's fiancé Myles should be informed of his love for her sister he was completely off the beam.

"In case you are talking about a certain girl," he growled, "you should know that it is no concern of mine!"

"*Myles!*" gasped Sonia from the glider.

Peter waved her to silence without turning.

"I don't get you, Langdon! You and Sunny are engaged—"

"Oh, no, we're not!"

There was a moment of stunned silence. Myles walked to the doorway and snapped the switch of the terrace floodlights. While they all blinked at the sudden glare he came back, tossed Sunny's letter onto her lap and resumed his seat.

"We haven't been engaged since you wrote that letter, Sunny," he explained, "even if I never received it until tonight. That's the most definite brush-off a man could get, effective as of that date."

"You got it *tonight?*" she whispered.

He nodded. "It went to the wrong address, probably didn't get to Loma until I was in the hospital. I found it among the things the company shipped home for me."

"But, Langdon—!" Peter appeared dazed by the turn of events. "You two have been engaged all this time—"

"To borrow a hackneyed phrase," Myles scowled, "engaged—in name only. It had been announced before I went away, so when I came home crippled, Sunny insisted on standing by me even if she didn't love me—and never has!"

Bruce turned and looked down at Sonia.

"A girl with courage to match her beauty!"

The tremor of emotion in his voice caused Myles to study them with puzzled surprise. Such tenderness seemed odd, coming from a man in love with Ann, accepted by her. Uneasily he remembered her remark at the dance about fellows who deserted her when they met Sonia. But she had been joking, of course; that he should remember it at all showed how demoralized he was. He'd better cut the scene short and get away.

"I give Sunny the highest marks for gallantry," he admitted, "in spite of the complications she caused. But the masquerade is over."

"It is not!" Sonia muffled a sob. "I'm still standing by you, Myles—!"

"Forget it—there's been too much sacrifice already and there's no longer any need for more. See—?" He doubled his left fist and shook it dramatically above his head. When they exclaimed in unison he laughed. "Everything's okay again and I'm leaving for another bridge job right away—I hope. Good-by and good luck!"

As he turned toward the steps Sonia jumped to her feet.

"Have you told Ann?" she demanded breathlessly.

"About my arm? She knows. She was present when I discovered I could use it again."

"I meant, that you were going away. You can't just leave without a word to her!"

A parting with Ann was what he dreaded most.

"Say 'good-by' to her for me, will you, Sunny?" he muttered.

"Better do it yourself," Peter Bruce protested earnestly. "She might be disappointed if you didn't."

The well-meant advice irritated Myles. The victor being magnanimous toward the loser!

"Don't worry about Ann!" he snapped.

"You can't be so brutal!" Sonia wailed. "She'll be heartbroken if you duck out like this. She thought you were angry about something when you left tonight—now she'll be sure of it!"

Myles hesitated as his conscience pricked. He *had* walked out on them abruptly, and after several ill-tempered remarks. Reluctantly he surrendered to courtesy.

"All right," he grumbled, moving toward the house. Passing Bruce, he could not refrain from adding pointedly, "I won't be long, in case you're waiting to talk to her." He wondered at the other's look of bewilderment, but forgot it when he opened the French door and stepped into the living room.

XXV

Ann sat in a corner of the living room sofa and stared unseeingly at the crackling fire. Only the lamp near the French windows was on, leaving the rest of the room in shadow, but the flickering scarlet and orange flames gave light enough for her pensive mood.

Slowly she smoothed a hand across the faded rose brocade of the old sofa. It was such an ancient piece that women of many generations must have sat on it, some of them perhaps with thoughts as sad as hers, longings as vain as hers. Why should she love Myles Langdon so unbearably? Her throat ached and her lids burned as she considered the unfairness of it. She hadn't asked for it; why did she have to be hurt?

Sunny showed every symptom of being in love with Peter Bruce, although for once she had failed to take Ann into her confidence. Still, she had been just as involved with Joe Snell, and dropped him when Myles returned, as what girl with any sense would fail to do? Peter, for all his charm, might be only another passing fancy. Even if Sunny released Myles, could Ann win him? Once she would have thought so, but he had come back from the jungle indefinably changed. The old friendly comradeship was missing; often he seemed to avoid close contact with her, not only physical but mental.

For a while she was dimly aware of voices on the terrace where Sonia and Peter had gone after supper. It had required little urging to have him stay and share the delectable griddle-cakes and crisp tiny sausages which Sarah delivered in an inexhaustible stream, introducing each new platter with abject apologies for letting the roast lamb burn to a crisp during the excitement of Ann's return.

The meal had been interrupted by frequent telephone calls for Peter, but now the house was quiet. Ann was too absorbed in her own reflections to even notice when the terrace lights flashed on. Her first intimation that Myles was present came when he walked in and stood staring at her as though hypnotized.

"Hello, Ann," he said quietly.

"Hello."

After the turmoil of her thoughts the banality of their greeting made Ann smile. To her surprise he snapped his fingers loudly.

"That smile completes the picture!" He came to sit on the arm of the big chair opposite, looked from her around the room and shook his head with a reminiscent smile. "You can't imagine how often this was in my mind down there in the jungle; this soothing room and the comfortable old furniture, the book-lined walls. I even remembered that silver bowl on the mantel, always with flowers in it. And you sitting before the fire, Ann, just as you are now."

"And Sunny curled up in that chair," she prompted.

"Sunny, too, of course." He dropped his eyes from her face and stared at the fire, rubbing his hands on his knees. "It's a wonderful memory for a man to take away with him. I'm glad I'll have it where I'm going."

"You're leaving?" she whispered with sinking heart.

"Back to engineering now. Why not?" He lifted his two hands, opening and closing the fingers triumphantly.

"Oh, Myles, how marvelous!" Knowing that he could have his heart's desire lifted her spirits, banished some of her despair. "But it's no surprise; I knew you could do it someday!"

"You had more faith than I, then. And you helped, Ann; you are about the only one who didn't baby me, treat me as though I'd fall to pieces in a light breeze. Then I found you in that sliding car—" Emotion choked him and he stood up to lean against the mantel, abandoning the dangerous field of personalities.

"So I'm off to build another bridge. Just dropped in to say *adios* and tell you not to worry. No jungles this time."

The warm glint in the brown eyes looking down at her

sent Ann's pulse to a quick step. Desperately she murmured, "Sunny will be glad to hear that."

Myles grunted. "You think so?"

"Well, for heaven's sake, yes! She'll be going with you, won't she?"

"Of course not! Why didn't you tell me Snell was the reason she wrote to me in Loma, breaking our engagement?"

"Then you did get her letter!" Indignation sharpened Ann's tone. "How *could* you let her believe you never received it, allow her to waste these months—?"

He held up his hand to stop her.

"I didn't get it until *tonight!*" and he told how the long-overdue letter finally came to light.

Ann wondered that he could speak so calmly of what must have been a shattering experience.

"Didn't it upset you *at all?*"

"After these last weeks of trailing Sunny around as her fiancé in name only?" He drew down the corners of his mouth and leaned an elbow on the mantel. "It was anti-climax, believe me!"

"Suppose you had received it down there, how would you have felt?" Ann demanded.

Myles considered, rubbing a finger along the scar on his cheek.

"Well—mad, I guess—the normal male reaction. But not for very long. Worry about my bridge would have snapped me out of it."

"You weren't in love if you could let her go so easily!"

"I'd been letting her go for some time." His eyes were on the fire; he pushed back a smoldering ember which had fallen too far forward. "Plenty of time to think down there, at night in my shack," he said slowly. "To think, and look back, and know that our engagement was a mistake. Sunny's a wonderful girl, but not the one for me.

"A marriage," he murmured, remembering his talk with his aunt, "a real, till-death-do-us-part relationship—needs two people willing to work for its success, make adjustments—" He sighed. "For me, Sunny wasn't the answer. My feelings had changed."

An unwelcome imp of memory took Ann back to a

morning in the bank and Uncle John gloomily apprehensive about his beloved nephew in a rough country and among strangers.

"Myles, have you fallen—did you meet someone else for whom you cared a lot?" At his challenging look she bit her lip and apologized. "Sorry, I spoke out of turn! It's none of my business and I shouldn't have asked that question."

"The question's all right—it's the answer which would be out of turn now," he muttered, and struck his open palm with his fist. "Why did Sunny have to insist on holding me when I came home a cripple? I tried to break it off then, for her sake."

"Do you think a girl who loved you would turn you down because of a helpless arm?"

"I discovered that even a girl who *didn't* love me would stand by, as she called it—or hang on, as I call it! Merely because she was afraid of what people might say. And meanwhile, enter Peter Bruce, the hero of the FBI!"

"That's mean, and not like you, Myles!" Ann protested. "Peter doesn't act heroic in the least!" She looked up questioningly. "Are you and Sunny definitely finished?"

"Lord, yes! Without one dissenting vote."

"Then I hope she marries Peter! That will show you what I think of him."

Myles gripped the mantel to steady himself from the shock.

"Peter marry *Sunny?*"

"Certainly. I've never seen two people more in love— nor suffering more because the girl was engaged to someone else. Love at first sight, too," she sighed enviously. "You didn't see them meet that night at the Club dance— it was like an atomic explosion."

Myles bent to catch her arm and draw her up beside him. His hands gripped her shoulders until it hurt, his turbulent eyes, dancing with golden sparks, set her blood racing.

"I thought it was you and Bruce who were in love!" he accused. "He's been hanging around here—"

"To see Sunny," she whispered breathlessly.

"He got *you* to help him find Walter's message. *You* defended him every time I criticized—"

"Of course I did!" She tried to conceal her growing exultation with indignation. "You made some very nasty remarks, remember?"

"It was resentment—I was sure you'd fallen for him!" He drew her closer, stared down at her bent head, whispered, "Ann, I love you—I always have!"

She put her hands against his chest to push away and look up at him and felt how his heart pounded. Her own was shaking her whole body.

"You certainly concealed the fact!" she jeered. "Since you came home you've hardly noticed me."

"Because of Sunny! Do you think I enjoyed tagging around after her when all the time I wanted to be with you? This is nothing new, sweetheart. Down there in Loma, as her face grew dim it was *your face* which kept intruding between me and my work. It was *you* I thought of constantly—there, and in the hospital, and flying home. The morning I arrived, when you came racing across the garden to meet me I thought, Here comes my girl—*for always!* How about it, darling?"

Ann gulped back a sob of happiness. "You wouldn't be proposing marriage to me, would you?" It was hopeless to attempt the light touch, her unsteady voice betrayed her.

"That's the general idea—but remember, it means following me to a construction camp—for a while, anyway. So what's your answer?"

"Answer? Oh, Myles, what do I care where we go— together?"

He rested his cheek against her satin soft hair as her arms crept around him.

"Seems to me this is where I came in—only that morning in the garden you cried, 'Myles—*darling,* welcome home!' " he huskily reminded her.

"Myles—darling—"

His passionate lips smothered the rest.

BRING ROMANCE INTO YOUR LIFE

With these bestsellers from your favorite Bantam authors

Barbara Cartland

☐ 11372	LOVE AND THE LOATHSOME LEOPARD	$1.50
☐ 10712	LOVE LOCKED IN	$1.50
☐ 11270	THE LOVE PIRATE	$1.50
☐ 11271	THE TEMPTATION OF TORILLA	$1.50

Catherine Cookson

☐ 10355	THE DWELLING PLACE	$1.50
☐ 10358	THE GLASS VIRGIN	$1.50
☐ 10516	THE TIDE OF LIFE	$1.75

Georgette Heyer

☐ 02263	THE BLACK MOTH	$1.50
☐ 10322	BLACK SHEEP	$1.50
☐ 02210	FARO'S DAUGHTER	$1.50

Emilie Loring

☐ 02382	FORSAKING ALL OTHERS	$1.25
☐ 02237	LOVE WITH HONOR	$1.25
☐ 11228	IN TIMES LIKE THESE	$1.50
☐ 10846	STARS IN YOUR EYES	$1.50

Eugenia Price

☐ 12712	BELOVED INVADER	$1.95
☐ 12717	LIGHTHOUSE	$1.95
☐ 11189	NEW MOON RISING	$1.75

Buy them at your local bookstore or use this handy coupon for ordering:

Bantam Books, Inc., Dept. RO, 414 East Golf Road, Des Plaines, Ill. 60016

Please send me the books I have checked above. I am enclosing $_____
(please add 75¢ to cover postage and handling). Send check or money order
—no cash or C.O.D.'s please.

Mr/Mrs/Miss_____

Address_____

City_____State/Zip_____

RO—12/78

Please allow four weeks for delivery. This offer expires 6/79.

EMILIE LORING

Women of all ages are falling under the enchanting spell Emilie Loring weaves in her beautiful novels. Once you have finished one book by her, you will surely want to read them all.

☐	2287	FAIR TOMORROW	$1.25
☐	2294	WITH THIS RING	$1.25
☐	2320	WE RIDE THE GALE	$1.25
☐	2390	HOW CAN THE HEART FORGET	$1.25
☐	6619	KEEPERS OF THE FAITH	$1.25
☐	10846	STARS IN YOUR EYES	$1.50
☐	10551	SPRING ALWAYS COMES	$1.25
☐	11228	IN TIMES LIKE THESE	$1.50
☐	10272	GAY COURAGE	$1.25
☐	10821	AS LONG AS I LIVE	$1.50
☐	10819	UNCHARTED SEAS	$1.50

Bantam Book Catalog

Here's your up-to-the-minute listing of over 1,400 titles by your favorite authors.

This illustrated, large format catalog gives a description of each title. For your convenience, it is divided into categories in fiction and non-fiction—gothics, science fiction, westerns, mysteries, cookbooks, mysticism and occult, biographies, history, family living, health, psychology, art.

So don't delay—take advantage of this special opportunity to increase your reading pleasure.

Just send us your name and address and 50¢ (to help defray postage and handling costs).

BANTAM BOOKS, INC.
Dept. FC, 414 East Golf Road, Des Plaines, Ill. 60016

Mr./Mrs./Miss_____
(please print)

Address_____

City_____State_____Zip_____

Do you know someone who enjoys books? Just give us their names and addresses and we'll send them a catalog too!

_____

Mr./Mrs./Miss_____

Address_____

City_____State_____Zip_____

Mr./Mrs./Miss_____

Address_____

City_____State_____Zip_____

FC—9/78